The Chain of Lies
A Paradise Valley Mystery: Book Three

DEBRA BURROUGHS

Copyright © 2013 Debra Burroughs

All rights reserved.

ISBN: 1482345765
ISBN-13: 978- 1482345766

All rights reserved as permitted under the U.S. Copyright Act of 1976, no part of this publication may be reproduced, distributed, or transmitted in any form or by any means, or stored in a database or retrieval system, without the prior permission of the publisher.

This is a work of fiction. Names, characters, places and incidents either are the product of the author's imagination or are used fictitiously. Any resemblance to actual persons, living, dead (or in any other form), business establishments, events, or locales is entirely coincidental.

Lake House Books
Boise, Idaho

First eBook Edition: 2013
First Paperback Edition: 2013

THE CHAIN OF LIES by Debra Burroughs, 1st. ed. p.cm.

Visit My Blog: www.DebraBurroughsBooks.com

Contact Me: Debra@DebraBurroughsBooks.com

DEDICATION

This book is dedicated to my amazing husband, Tim, who loves me and encourages me every day to do what I love – writing.

*I also dedicate this book to my awesome
Beta Readers,
Buffy Drewett, Cathy Tomlinson, and Janet Lewis, who inspire me and help me with their words of encouragement and critique.*

Finally, this book would not be what it is today without my amazing editor, Lisa Dawn Martínez, The Finicky Editor.

THE CHAIN OF LIES

TABLE OF CONTENTS

	Prologue	Page 1
1	Saying Good-Bye	Page 3
2	The Hidden Files	Page 21
3	Friendly Suspicions	Page 27
4	The New Man in Town	Page 47
5	The Peeping Tom	Page 55
6	Jethro's Questions	Page 65
7	Dinner at Isabel's	Page 77
8	The Girl in the Bathroom	Page 85
9	Lunch at Goodwood	Page 95
10	Welcome Home, Colin	Page 105
11	Body in the River	Page 117
12	The Football Party	Page 131
13	Mr. Osterman's Discovery	Page 143
14	Meeting at the Morgue	Page 155
15	What Happened to Molly?	Page 165
16	The Jade Thai Spa	Page 183
17	Peter's Performance	Page 195

18	The Hotel Sting	Page 207
19	The Hidden Room	Page 221
20	The Hospital Visit	Page 231
21	Daughter Delia	Page 241
22	Jethro's Interview	Page 253
23	Killer Trapped	Page 269
24	Colin's Surprise	Page 287
	Excerpt – The Scent of Lies	Page 303
	Excerpt – The Heart of Lies	Page 325
	Excerpt – The Pursuit of Lies	Page 343
	Author Biography	Page 361

"Oh, what a tangled web we weave when first we practice to deceive."

~ *Sir Walter Scott*

PROLOGUE

Undeniably, the first lie is the easiest to tell. After that, one finds himself having to tell the next and the next in a desperate attempt to cover the first, until he finds he has told a chain of lies and is praying none of the links pull apart under the pressure.

~*~

At twilight, a young redheaded woman stood pensively on the bank of the flowing Boise River, pulling her black jacket tighter around her chest against the crisp autumn air. Maybe she should cut her losses and get out, before it was too late. She looked to the water, wishing for a sign. Something caught her eye and she began to scream wildly, her arms flailing about.

From the walking path, her lover dashed to her side. "What's wrong?"

She continued to shriek, pointing frenetically toward something large and dark bobbing in the river, caught in the thick branches of a low-hanging tree.

"It's probably nothing, someone ignoring the no-dumping sign, just a black trash bag. Stay here." The man zipped his leather jacket shut and cautiously crept toward it, gingerly nearing the river's edge to discover what it was.

The woman's clenched hand was pressed hard against her lips, fighting to stifle her cries, watching him with rapt attention as he inched closer, closer.

Once he was near enough to identify the floating mass, all composure was lost. His feet stumbled and slipped in the mud as he desperately scrambled to back away—this was not mere rubbish caught in the brush. It was a woman's lifeless, half-naked body.

"What is it?"

"A body," he huffed, straining to catch his breath.

"I'll call the police," she said, frantically digging her phone out of her jeans pocket.

"No, let me," he argued, reaching for his own cell phone. "I'll stay and wait for the cops."

"Then I'll wait with you."

"No! You have to go," he snapped, dialing nine one one. "No one can see us together."

"Afraid your wife will find out?"

CHAPTER 1
Saying Good-Bye

"EVAN, NO!" Emily Parker shot up straight in her bed, her eyes clamped tight.

"No!" she screamed, both arms outstretched, hysterically reaching for him. Her eyes flew open and she sat frozen in the dark for a moment, her arms still extended in desperation.

She dropped them. It was all a bad dream—the same horrifying dream she had been having night after night. The anniversary of her husband's murder was right around the corner, and the nightmares were plaguing her more often, and with growing intensity.

She buried her face in her hands as she sat sobbing, drenched in perspiration. Her damp nightgown clung to her slender body and her honey-blonde curls stuck to her sweaty neck and forehead.

Having convinced herself that she was finally recovering from her loss, she had begun to date again, but these terrifying visions were evidence she was not as over Evan's death as she had tried to believe.

It was nearly a year ago now since Emily's husband had been shot, close range, in the back of the head. He was found dead, in a pool of blood, lying next to the steel file cabinet in the corner of his office. The police detective that had investigated postulated that Evan had gone to retrieve something from the cabinet.

Something vital enough to be killed over.

Evan Parker had been a private investigator in the small, affluent town of Paradise Valley, not far from the state capitol of Boise. He'd had a great track record for unraveling mysteries—ironically his own case was never solved.

In her recurring nightmare, Emily is standing in the corner, observing Evan's interaction with a vague, shadowy figure, but she can never make out who the person is, not even their gender. She can see her husband sitting at his desk speaking amiably with someone dressed in dark clothing, seated across the desk from him.

Evan is smiling his engaging, crooked smile, running his hand through his sandy-blonde hair as he leans back in his chair, casual, as if the person across from him is someone he knows—or perhaps a new client he is getting acquainted with.

In the dream, Emily watches helplessly as Evan rises from his chair and steps to the file cabinet. She sees the muzzle of the gun rising as he turns away from his visitor and reaches for the drawer handle. She is screaming, warning him, but he never hears her, never turns around—never survives.

The crack of gunfire, a blinding flash, and Evan drops to the floor, hard. Blood begins to stream from the back of her husband's head.

"Evan! No!"

And Emily wakes up, drenched in sweat and shaking. Every time. When she does, it doesn't matter how hard she tries to discern who was in the office with him, the shooter remains a dark nebulous mirage.

The nightmares in themselves were bad enough, but add to that, six months after Evan's murder Emily learned that her late husband had kept a whole tapestry of secrets from her—including his real identity.

Now, over the past few months, she had unraveled some of the secrets, but there were so many more yet to uncover.

Emily peeked over at the digital clock glowing on the nightstand. Two thirteen a.m. She expelled a long sigh of frustration then dragged herself out of her sweat-soaked bed. Emily stumbled to the dry bed in the guest room to try for a few more hours of sleep before the sun came up, hoping the nightmares would not return.

As the sun began to peek through the bedroom window, Emily pulled her hand up to shade her eyes from the glaring light. Disoriented, she glanced around the room and realized she was in her guest room. She didn't remember getting up and coming in here through the night.

She reclined in the bed with one arm draped across her eyes, trying to remember the night before. She recalled the going-away party she'd attended at her friends Alex and Isabel's house. The party had given her boyfriend Colin a festive send off back to San Francisco for a time.

"Colin," she muttered softly, her eyes still closed, seeing a vision of his strong and handsome image in her mind—his thick, deep brown hair, his smoky hazel eyes with a fringe of dark lashes, his strong angular jaw.

Her heart fluttered as she recalled the promise he had made to her the night before, vowing that he would move heaven and earth to come back to her after he'd scooped her off her feet into his well-muscled arms. Emily relished the profoundly romantic gesture.

The mere thought of him caused a gentle heat to spread over her body and she shivered at the light ripple of goose bumps that followed closely behind. She softly touched her finger to her mouth as she laid there and reminisced about his soft warm lips on hers.

Then she bolted upright.

What time is it?

There was no clock in the guest room, so she tore the covers back and dashed to her bedroom. Halting at the door, she noticed the clock on her nightstand read seven sixteen a.m.

"Shoot!" Colin was coming to pick her up at seven thirty to take her to breakfast before heading out on the road back to San Francisco. The oversized t-shirt she had slept in went flying over her head and onto the floor as she ran to the bathroom and hopped in the shower.

~*~

A sharp rap at the front door brought Emily running from the bathroom, still tugging her deep purple t-shirt over her head. She fluffed her honey-blonde curls before opening the door and greeting Colin with a bright smile.

"Looks like someone had a good night's sleep," Colin said as he stepped into her bungalow. He swept her into his arms and kissed her softly.

Pushing the door shut with her bare foot, she laced her arms around his torso. She knew they only had a little time left together and he would be gone again for who knows how long. She laid her head against his chest and clung to him, enjoying the nearness of his body.

"No." She closed her eyes, inhaling his masculine scent of fresh soap and a mild aftershave. "I woke up in the night, thinking of you, wishing you didn't have to leave again."

He had declared his love for her the night before, at the party, saying those three little words she'd longed to hear, and she had returned his sentiments.

"I'll be back before you know it, Emily." He kissed her temple as he held her tight.

"You'd better be, or I'll have to come looking for you," she teased in an attempt to cover her sadness.

She and Colin had dated for a few short months before he was unexpectedly called back to San Francisco, where he had moved from not long before they'd met. It was there that he had been dealing with an extended family emergency for the past couple of months, but he had recently been able to steal away from his obligations for a few days.

He had surprised Emily early one morning, showing up on her doorstep with her favorite mocha cappuccino and slices of lemon poppy seed bread. But inevitably, now the time had come for him to return to California and it was breaking her heart.

"I'll be back, I promise. Now let's go and get some breakfast before I have to hit the road. I'm starved."

"All right." She reluctantly let go of him. "Just let me grab my shoes."

~*~

They claimed a booth at The Griddle—it was upholstered in cheery yellow and had a great view of the river. They placed their orders with a friendly middle-aged waitress.

After she left them, Colin reached across the dark wood table and gently took Emily's hand.

"I wish you didn't have to leave," Emily said for the umpteenth time. "I was just getting used to having you back." She forced a weak smile, holding back her tears. That wasn't how she wanted him to remember her while he was in California, but the thought of his leaving again made her heart heavy, knowing she'd have to fight the loneliness once more.

"I know and I'm sorry." He tightened his hold on her hand.

Emily recognized his departure was painful for him, too—she could see it in his misty eyes. She drew in a calming breath and offered him a genuine smile this time, not wanting to make his leaving any more difficult.

His eyes brightened in response. "You know, it's kind of funny when I look back to when we first met," he said with a slight grin. "I never thought we'd wind up together."

"Me either."

There had been fireworks, all right, but not the good kind.

Emily shook her head at the thought. "I was more than a little irritated at Isabel for trying to set us up."

Isabel Martínez, one of Emily's tight-knit circle of friends, along with her husband Alex, had thrown a barbecue at their upscale home about six months before. They'd deliberately invited Colin so Emily could meet the handsome new police detective in Paradise Valley.

Though Emily's husband had died over six months before that, she'd had a hard time letting go of the grief and moving on. She and Evan had been deliriously happy, or so she'd thought. He had been her knight in shining armor, handsome and strong, decisive and fearless, yet he had loved her with such tenderness and passion that she trembled with longing at his memory.

Over time, her closest friends encouraged her to think about dating again, to get on with her life, but she didn't know how she could. So, she would respond to their promptings by putting up her defenses and maintaining that she wasn't ready.

Isabel's husband was a trial lawyer and he had met the new detective at a weekly basketball game he played with his buddies at the local Y. Alex had immediately told his wife about the young man.

Another of Emily's best friends, Maggie, was teaching an aerobics class at the Y, and the new man in town did not escape her notice either.

So between Isabel, Maggie, and their friend Camille, Emily didn't have a chance if she wanted to avoid meeting Detective Colin Andrews.

Camille was a caterer and event planner, and she had planned the whole get-together at the Martínez home, along with Isabel's and Maggie's help. However, all of the elaborate planning, staged introductions, and purposely seating them together could not guarantee smooth sailing. Almost from the start there were sparks and conflict.

"You really didn't like me, did you?" Colin asked.

"Well, I couldn't help but notice how good-looking you were, I mean I'm not blind, but after we chatted for a while about my career choices, well...you were so condescending. I just couldn't stand it."

"You have to admit, though, going from selling real estate to becoming a private investigator is a bit of a leap. Who could blame me for questioning it?"

"I could. But don't worry, I've already forgiven you for being so irritating that day." She smirked at him. He couldn't have known at the time that it wasn't *that* big of a leap, that she had helped her husband on a few of his cases.

"Thanks," he replied sarcastically.

"But even though we had kind of a rocky start, I'm glad you didn't give up and you asked me out anyway." She cast him a playful smile, grateful she had not chased him off back then by her stubbornness and sass.

"You certainly made me work for it, though, but I guess part of the fun is in the chase." The corner of Colin's lips turned up into a mischievous grin.

"Yeah, the chase was definitely fun."

"Here we are," the waitress said as she set their plates down on the table. "Is there anything else I can get for you?"

"We're good." Colin looked over at Emily and she nodded her agreement.

"Okie dokie." The waitress grabbed a nearby glass coffee pot, refilled Colin's coffee cup, and moved on to another table.

"I still can't believe that Delia McCall hired you with practically no experience." Colin took another drink of his black coffee. "What was she thinking?"

"Oh, come on now, it wasn't that big of a stretch." She buttered her french toast and licked her finger. "I wasn't a complete newbie, I did have some experience. Evan just didn't like it known around town, for my own protection."

"Okay, okay," he surrendered, briefly raising both his hands slightly. "You're right, but I didn't know that then."

Emily picked up the small metal pitcher to drench her french toast in maple syrup.

"I probably shouldn't tell you this and give you a big head, but I was really impressed with how you handled Delia's murder case."

"You were?" Emily arched an eyebrow, wondering what he meant by her getting a big head.

"I was. But I have to say, what totally hooked me was that thing you did in New York City."

"What thing was that?"

"When I flew to New York City to interrogate that suspect in Delia's case—you know, that Russian mobster—and you showed up there, too, going all Charlie's Angels on me."

Charlie's Angels? Emily wasn't quite sure what he

meant by that either. The title conjured up visions of beautiful women with kick-ass moves and guns blazing. "That hooked you? Why?" As she recalled, he'd looked none too pleased with her at the time.

"Well, I wasn't very happy with you at first, because I specifically told you to stay in Paradise Valley," he replied, then took another gulp of coffee, "but you didn't listen."

"Get to the good part."

"Well, that day you showed me you were the kind of woman who wouldn't take no for an answer, you wouldn't give up, and I kinda liked that."

"You did?" She was surprised, yet pleased, at his comments. She smiled to herself as she stuck another bite of french toast in her mouth.

"It was actually pretty hot the way you marched into the detective's area at the station, with your wild mane of blonde hair and your tight jeans, demanding to be in on the questioning."

"I didn't realize I came across that way." She grimaced. "My hair's not usually wild. It must have been from sleeping on the plane." She ran her fingers through her hair as she visualized what she must have looked like. "Is that why your New York detective friend dubbed me the smokin' hot lady PI?"

Colin laughed at the description. "Could be, but I had to agree with him." He grinned and nodded at her as he cut into his omelet and took a bite. "You did look pretty hot."

Emily looked down and blushed, taking a sip of her water. She hadn't realized she appeared in such a brash way. When she looked up, she caught Colin still grinning at her.

They dug into their breakfasts and reminisced about the cases they had worked together and how their relationship had grown. Before long, their food was nearly gone and it was almost time for him to shove off.

"So, tell me, when did you realize you were in love with me?" Emily swirled the last little piece of french toast around in the pool of syrup on her plate.

"The night Ricardo Vega's murderer almost shot you. I knew I couldn't live without you."

Emily thought back to that night and how Colin had been so terrified of losing her. She recalled him describing how he had lost his fiancée a couple of years before, shot in the line of duty, and how he had tried to fight against his feelings for Emily because of her dangerous job as a private eye.

"Now it's your turn," he said. "When did you realize you were in love with me?"

She looked down at her watch. "Oh, my gosh, look at the time. You'd better take me home now so you can get on the road. You have a long drive ahead of you."

"No fair." Colin cast her a quizzical frown.

Emily considered telling him it was from their first kiss, when her knees went weak and his touch sent tingles shooting throughout her body, but that was lust more than love.

But then there had been the multitude of suspicions and questions flying around in her head as she investigated her husband's murder. With mistrust running rampant, a dark cloud settled over her desire to completely allow herself to trust him.

As she uncovered more facts about her late

husband, Emily questioned her own judgment. If Evan was not who he had led her to believe he was, how could she know for certain that Colin was who he claimed to be?

She had wanted to trust Colin fully, give him her whole heart, but she was not convinced until the previous night, at his going-away party, that he was who he claimed to be. Her conversation with Ernie, the Paradise Valley police officer who had known Colin his whole life, had put her suspicions to rest and set her free to love Colin without reservation.

As he sat across the table from her, Colin's questioning stare was unrelenting. She had to tell him something.

"I knew early on that I was falling for you, but I suppose it wasn't until you first left to go back to San Francisco that I felt this enormous, gaping hole in my heart—and in my life. I knew then that I didn't want to live without you."

A satisfied smile spread across his face and he reached over and laid his hand on hers. "I'm sorry this visit has been so short and that I need to get back, but you have to know I feel the same way. It's agony being away from you."

"That's a good word for it—agony." Emily smiled weakly, willing back the tears again.

He waved at the waitress to bring their bill.

~*~

Colin drove her back to her home in the charming older part of town and walked her up to her front porch to say their reluctant good-byes. He gathered her up in his arms and held her close, studying her striking turquoise eyes and her rosy lips, not knowing when he would see them again.

"Don't cry, Emily. I'll be back before you know it." He wiped a tear from her cheek and pushed a golden curl back from her face.

"Promise?" Her watery eyes looked into his. "San Francisco is such a long way away."

"But I didn't leave my heart in San Francisco, Emily, like the song says. My heart is in Paradise Valley, with you." He kissed her deeply and fervently, as if it might be their last.

They were both very aware that life can be fragile and no one is promised tomorrow.

~*~

Before leaving, Colin agreed to phone her while he was on the road and also to let her know when he arrived at his folks' house. "And please, Emily, keep your doors and windows locked."

"I will," she assured him.

"And remember that black sedan that's been tailing you—keep your eyes open. We still have no idea who it could be."

"I will, I promise."

"Call Ernie, or my friend Decker at the Boise PD, if you need anything."

"Yes, yes, I will."

"Call me if—"

"Please, don't worry about me, Colin. I'll be fine.

I'm a big girl—I can take care of myself. Remember? I'm a pistol-packing—"

"Smokin' hot lady PI. I know. I know. But I can't help but worry about you, Babe." Being protective was in his blood. Colin had once been a marine and then he had been a policeman in San Francisco, rising to lead police detective for five years before moving to Paradise Valley. Taking over as their new police detective had been a fresh start for him, and an opportunity to heal from the loss of his fiancée.

"I know. I'll call you if anything happens," she promised. "You need to get going."

"All right, but make sure you call me."

She waved as he drove away in his red Jeep, doing her best to keep a brave smile spread across her lips. Once he had gone, she wiped a couple of tears from her cheek.

During their last morning together, she hadn't wanted to remind Colin about the suspicious black sedan or that someone had broken into her house a couple of times searching for something. She knew it would only cause him to worry. Still, with no mention of it from her, he didn't seem to be able to leave without warning her again.

Emily wished she knew what her stalker was after. All she could do was speculate that it had something to do with Evan and the surprising things she had recently uncovered about him, particularly the suspicious handgun, a Beretta pistol, she had found hidden in his secret safe deposit box.

Sadly, she watched as Colin drove out of sight. She missed him already. As she stood on her sunny porch thinking about him, Emily wondered when he would be able to return for good. Saying good-bye for the second time was excruciating. She wiped another tear that trickled down her cheek and then took a long, deep breath.

With resignation, she lumbered across the porch and stuck her key in the lock. As she unlocked her front door, she glanced up and down her street to be certain she and Colin hadn't been followed back to her house.

Seeing no one out of the ordinary, she slipped into her house and kicked off her shoes by the door. She pulled her handgun out of her purse and carefully crept back to the kitchen, peeking around corners, with her weapon poised to shoot. Emily was determined not to be a victim, and she silently reminded herself of that fact.

I know how to handle a gun—I teach self-defense classes—I can take care of myself.

By the time she reached the kitchen, she was reasonably certain she was safe and alone. Setting her purse and gun down on her breakfast bar, she noticed an opened envelope lying on top of a stack of mail. It had come the day before, but she had set it aside because she was headed out to the going-away party.

Perching herself on a barstool, she pulled the folded paper out of the envelope. Addressed to Evan Parker, it was a letter from a storage facility alerting her late husband that his next year's rent on the unit was due. She hadn't been aware Evan had a storage unit.

Her thoughts flew to the unidentified brass key she had found in his safe deposit box a couple of months before. She still hadn't figured out what it opened. But now, with this letter coming from the storage facility, she wondered if it would open a padlock on that unit—Evan's unit.

Having seen Colin off, her day was wide open, and rather than spend it missing Colin, she hopped in her car and headed to the storage facility to check it out. It was only mid-morning—she'd have plenty of time to search through whatever Evan had hidden there.

Making sure she wasn't being followed, she kept a sharp eye on her rearview mirrors as she made a series of three right turns in the center of town. Since no car appeared to be tailing her, particularly not a black one, she drove to the storage company on the edge of town.

While she was driving, her phone began to ring, and she dug it out of her oversized leather handbag that lay on the passenger seat, noticing it was one of her friends. "Hey, Maggie."

"Just checkin' in," Maggie said. "Don't forget to pick Molly and me up at noon at Camille's place."

Emily had promised to take Maggie and Molly, Camille's teenage daughter, to the airport to catch a flight for their trip to Hawaii. Maggie had invited Emily to go with her, but Emily was not ready to leave her home exposed to additional break-ins and searches, especially when she was uncovering more and more clues to her late husband's true identity. So instead, Maggie invited seventeen-year-old Molly, the only other single female she was close to, as an early graduation gift.

What a pair they would make on the beaches of Hawaii, Emily thought. Maggie was a beauty—a southern-belle fitness queen, lightly tanned with flowing blonde waves and dazzling blue eyes. Even in her mid-thirties, she would do her bikini justice. Molly, on the other hand, was a pretty girl, tall and slender with fair skin, long red hair, and shockingly deep emerald-green eyes. The red hair had come from her mother and the green eyes courtesy of her father, but the I-take-no-crap-from-anyone attitude was all her own.

"I didn't forget. I'll be there at noon."

"Did y'all get Colin off to California this mornin'?" Maggie asked.

"I did. We went out for breakfast first, then I sent him on his way."

Emily wasn't sure she wanted to spill the beans about the storage unit yet. There was plenty of time to do that later if it came to anything.

"And did he say those three little words y'all've been waitin' for?"

Emily could hear the curiosity in Maggie's voice and knew her well enough to know it was killing her to find out. "As a matter of fact, he did."

"Yay!" Maggie squealed. "I'm so happy for y'all, Em. I just knew it. I told Camille he'd say those little gems before he left."

"Actually, he told me last night at the going-away party. He promised he'd move heaven and earth to come back to me."

"Oh, how romantic," Maggie gushed. "Words like that make my heart melt. No one deserves to be happy more than y'all, after all y'all have been through."

Emily swore she could hear a quiver of sadness in Maggie's voice. As sweet and lovely as Maggie was, she had terrible luck with men—one loser after another. Emily hoped Maggie's luck would change soon—for the better. "So do you, Maggs."

"I'd better let y'all off the phone and finish packin', or I won't be nearly ready when it's time to come and pick us up."

CHAPTER 2
The Hidden Files

"LET'S SEE...FOUR-FIFTEEN, four sixteen, four seventeen," Emily muttered as she read the numbers on the door to each of the outdoor storage lockers. "Here it is, four eighteen."

Nervously anticipating what might be behind it, she stood for a moment, staring at the door. Then with a held breath, she shoved the brass key into the padlock and exhaled loudly when it fit perfectly.

She twisted the key and the lock slipped a bit as it released. A wave of excitement poured through her as she unhooked the lock from the metal loop and swung the door open.

Exposed before her was a small storage area, maybe five feet wide and twelve feet deep. She had brought a six-inch pocket flashlight, suspecting there may be no lights. It proved useful toward the back of the unit, because the bright sunshine only illuminated the space closest to the entrance.

Emily stepped in and flashed the narrow beam around. Along one wall were several steel shelving units, three shelves high, each one holding white cardboard banker boxes. She stared at the boxes. What could Evan possibly have been hiding in them?

Several months ago, when she discovered the first clue that he was not who he said he was, she had been devastated. They had been married for five years and she'd thought they were blissfully happy. But months after his death, she began to uncover evidence that he was someone else entirely. Rather than a private investigator, she had eventually learned that he was a CIA operative with a vast array of secrets.

After many tears, and sleepless nights, she had finally gotten control of her emotions and accepted that his lies were to protect her. With Colin's help, and the aid of her close friends, she was able to move on from her grief, but the mystery of who killed her husband still hung over her. Emily would never be able to completely close the door on that chapter of her life, and fully commit herself to a new relationship, until the mystery of Evan's murder was solved.

With the flashlight poised in one hand, she pulled the snugly fitting lid off one of the boxes with the other, causing a faint cloud of dust to waft up. She batted at the air to clear the dust and peeked into the box.

Fingering through the old files and papers, she hoped she wouldn't have to rummage through every single document in each and every box before she would discover anything of value—fortunately, there were only seven of them.

Emily wasn't sure what she'd expected to find in this storage place, but a bunch of boring-looking file boxes was definitely not it. Unlike Evan's secret safe deposit box that was filled with fake passports and bundles of cash, along with a suspicious gun, these boxes only seemed to contain files, papers, and old photos.

No matter what lay in the boxes, though, they had to contain something Evan didn't want anyone else to see. So, for the next two hours, she searched through the boxes, folder by folder, page by page.

Most of the documents looked like photocopies, as if Evan had copied them to keep a set of his own files on his CIA assignments. She wondered why he felt he needed protection—or was he searching for proof of something? Documentation to back up his actions, maybe?

Along with the copied documents, there were photos of locations and people, as if he had snapped the candid shots as his target was meeting with someone, or clandestine pictures showing what his mark was up to.

Emily searched for more photos of the mysterious brunette—the one standing with Evan in the single snapshot kept hidden in his safe deposit box—but she found none. Her identity had plagued Emily since the first time she'd discovered the picture of this woman snuggled in Evan's arms.

Digging for another picture of her husband with the dark-haired beauty was now more out of curiosity than anything else. After reading the hidden note she had found from Evan, she knew the woman had been a girlfriend, accidentally killed in the crossfire during a shootout in which Evan was involved.

But why did he keep only that photo—the photo of the two of them—hidden in the safe deposit box? Why not here with the others?

After spending a couple of hours methodically pouring over the contents of a few of the boxes, she realized it was time to take Maggie and Molly to the airport. As she was sticking some files back into one of the boxes, a small, black-leather notebook slipped out from between a couple of the folders and smacked onto the cement floor.

"How did I miss that?"

Emily crouched down and picked it up. She flipped through it, recognizing the handwriting as Evan's. It was an address book with cryptic names and numbers written in it.

She read a few of the names, but then her gaze landed on an entry that said, *Handler, Izzy*, with a phone number. Was Handler someone's name or was it someone's position?

Izzy.

Suddenly, she recalled Evan referring to Isabel as *Izzy*. Was Isabel's maiden name Handler? Or was Evan noting that Izzy was his CIA handler, writing that information in the book as if that was the person's full name—Izzy Handler—to throw anyone who got possession of this book off the track. Or was it an alias? Or code?

Maybe she should take the boxes back to her house? Then Emily's breath caught in her throat. The person in the black sedan, possibly a BMW, could very likely be the one who had broken into her home, and maybe they were looking for something in these boxes, like this book.

Giving her head a shake for being temporarily oblivious to the mysterious stalker, Emily peeked out of the storage unit to see if anyone was watching her now. She glanced around but saw no one.

She didn't have any more time to look through the black book at the moment. Maggie and Molly would be waiting for her. So she tucked the book, and the flashlight, in her purse for later. She'd have to give the *Izzy* question some more thought.

THE CHAIN OF LIES

CHAPTER 3
Friendly Suspicions

WHILE MAGGIE AND MOLLY were winging their way to Hawaii, Emily returned to the storage unit, keeping an eye out for any tail. Page by page, she again foraged through each box, reading about her late husband's exploits as a secret agent at the CIA. Though some of the comments were abbreviated, she found she could decipher most of the text, but she wondered when she kept seeing orders for him to handle someone with extreme prejudice. What exactly did that mean?

He appeared to have been in some very dangerous situations. She didn't know he could be so bold and cunning, so physically aggressive. The Evan on those pages was not the man she had fallen in love with.

She had grieved for him, mourned the loss of their love and life together, for more than six months when the series of accidental discoveries led her to realize the man she had married was *not* who he said he was. So she really shouldn't be surprised now. She was grateful, though, that she hadn't uncovered these things earlier on. It would have been more than she could handle, piled on top of the shock and sorrow of his death.

These discoveries, as painful as they were, forced her to dig down deep and become a stronger woman, which presented her with the opportunity to follow in his footsteps as a private investigator. The things she had learned as she had covertly helped Evan on various cases had given her the skills.

Her thoughts drifted back again to the note he had left for her, folded and concealed in the center of one of the bundles of cash he had secreted away in the safe deposit box. He had to have known she would eventually find his hidden stash, because the note was addressed to her. In it, he explained who he really was and why he did what he did.

Studying the case files, reading about the operations, Evan's face came to her mind—his sandy blonde hair, his piercing blue eyes, that sexy off-centered smile that she loved so much. Even though that note said his real name was David Gerard, she knew she would always think of him as Evan Parker.

Some of the descriptions of the dangerous secret operations read like something out of a bestselling spy novel. She thought for a split second that maybe she would turn these gripping scenarios into a novel one day, but that made her laugh. She was no writer. If there truly were *grammar police* she surely would be given a citation or two. Better to just continue to solve mysteries rather than write about it.

Poring over the files, minutes quickly turned into

hours. Before she knew it, several had passed and she realized it was time to head home. Even though Maggie was gone, the rest of the girls were getting together for their weekly Thursday night girls-only potluck supper, and it was Emily's turn to host again.

The theme this week was end-of-summer barbecue. Isabel promised to provide barbecued chicken, enlisting Alex and his superior grilling skills—at least that's what she had told him to get him to help her. Camille, with her culinary flair, offered to bring scrumptious twice-baked potatoes and a luscious lemon crème cake.

Not being known for great cooking, Emily offered to provide a crisp green salad and a fresh loaf of sourdough bread from the local bakery, which happened to be the same contributions she had made to last month's Italian-themed potluck.

She raced home to her little bungalow, stopping first by the bakery around the corner to buy the bread. Rushing around, setting the table, making a big pitcher of sweet tea, doing a bit of last-minute picking up, she thought of Colin and wondered how far he'd made it by now.

The phone began to jangle in her purse as it sat on the breakfast bar. She raced to grab it and saw it was Colin calling.

"I was just thinking about you."

"That's always good to hear."

His warm and comforting voice brought a smile to her lips.

"Where are you now?" Emily slid onto a bar stool and crossed her legs.

"I just drove through Reno, so I've got a few more

hours to go. Enough about me, how was your day?"

"I got Maggie and Molly to the airport. They should be landing soon in Hawaii."

"Lucky dogs."

She was glad he called, happy to tell him about her day. She *needed* to tell someone. "Oh, by the way, I wanted to let you know that I figured out what that mysterious brass key goes to.

"From the safe deposit box?"

"Good memory." Emily remembered standing in her walk-in closet the day the whole mystery about Evan came to light. She'd been contemplating packing his clothes away, hoping it might help her move on with her life. As she began taking his folded t-shirts off a shelf, a long silver key fell out from between the shirts and bounced on the floor. Once she'd figured out it was to a safe deposit box, well, her entire history with Evan came into question then.

"How did you find out what the key went to?"

"Funny thing, I sorted through yesterday's mail and there was a letter from a storage facility. It said Evan's annual prepaid renewal was coming due again the first of next month, so I assumed there must be a padlock on the unit."

"There usually is. Did you know he had a storage unit?"

"No, I didn't. Just one more thing he hid from me. I thought maybe the key would fit the lock, so I went by and checked it out today."

"Did the key fit?"

"Yeah, but all there was in the place were some banker boxes with files in them."

"I would have expected weapons, maybe, or some spy equipment—that sort of thing."

"Me, too, but no—just files. I went through almost half of them today. It was pretty interesting reading."

"I'll bet. You'd better not tell anyone else about it, though. I doubt the CIA would want anyone knowing that intel is floating around out there."

"You're probably right. I have enough drama in my life right now. I don't need the CIA giving me grief too."

"Maybe you should think about moving those boxes somewhere more protected," Colin suggested. "What about Isabel's place? Don't they live in a gated community? I imagine they have an alarm on their house."

"Yes, but..."

How could she tell him she had suspicions about Isabel? That she wasn't sure if she could trust her anymore? They had been best friends for the last five years, but lately she was starting to suspect Isabel wasn't who she seemed, either.

"I don't understand. What's the hesitation?"

"You're probably going to think I'm crazy, but—"

"But what?"

"What if Isabel is the one who's been searching for something in my house? What if she's not who she says she is?"

"Wow. What on earth would make you say that?"

Emily went silent. She thought of the note again that Evan had left her. In it he had told her that if she was reading the note it meant he was dead and she was to trust no one. Those words still echoed in her mind. She had learned enough about Colin Andrews to feel confident she could trust him, but Isabel was another story.

Isabel Martínez worked for the FBI as a financial analyst, but Emily was beginning to suspect she was actually more than that. The two had met over five years ago at a cooking class that Camille was teaching, shortly after Isabel moved to Paradise Valley from back east, or at least that's the story she told. Isabel had met Alex in Paradise Valley and married him soon after.

The cooking class was where they met Maggie too, and the four of them had become fast friends. But since finding Evan's note, warning her to trust no one, she wondered if Isabel had intentionally signed up for that class to meet Emily and insinuate herself into her and Evan's lives.

As Emily had unraveled the truth about her late husband, she'd learned of his past involvement in the CIA, and more about his murder. She had recently discovered that his shooting might have been carried out because someone wanted to exact revenge on him as payback for a young woman's death.

She wondered how much of her suspicions she should divulge to Colin. He'd probably just think her paranoid. Colin didn't know all that Emily had uncovered. She hadn't told him about the ominous note she'd found in the safe deposit box, or the totality of the box's contents.

"Emily?" Colin waited for her answer. "What's going on?"

She didn't want to go into all of it right then and there, but she knew she had to say something in response to his question. "Let's just say with all that's been happening lately, the black car, the break-ins, and with Isabel's FBI friend Jethro poking around, I'm feeling a bit suspicious and uneasy."

"That's understandable. But suspicious of Isabel or of Jethro?"

"Both. You probably think it's silly."

"No, I wouldn't say it was silly. As a cop, I know you have to sometimes trust your gut when nothing else makes sense. If you don't want to leave the boxes with Isabel at this point, then you'd probably better leave them where they are while you hunt for a better place to hide them."

"I appreciate the support." Emily slid off the stool and went to the refrigerator to start her salad. "Still, I feel uneasy."

"You're watching for a tail, aren't you?"

"I am, don't worry."

She pulled the lettuce, tomatoes, and cucumbers out of the vegetable drawer.

"What's all the noise?" he asked.

"The girls are coming over for our weekly potluck and I'm making the salad. I was just pulling the fixings out of the fridge."

"Say hello for me."

"Speaking of the girls, I did find something in one of Evan's boxes that I think might have to do with Isabel." Emily tugged a salad bowl out of the cupboard and cradled the phone against her shoulder so she could rinse the vegetables off and begin chopping them on the cutting board.

"What was it?"

"A little leather address book. It had the name Izzy

Handler in it, with a phone number."

"Izzy Handler? Who's that?"

"I think Izzy Handler might be Isabel." Emily chopped the first tomato and tossed the pieces in the salad bowl on top of the torn lettuce.

"You think Izzy is a nickname for Isabel?" he questioned. "It does make sense."

"Emily! Hello!" came a female voice wandering through the house.

"Hi, Isabel. It's good to see you." Emily wiped her hands on a towel and uncradled the phone. "I'm on the telephone," she whispered, giving Isabel a quick one-arm hug, the phone still in her hand.

Isabel was holding a tray of barbecued chicken pieces covered with foil. Although Emily couldn't actually see the chicken, the savory, barbecued aroma was unmistakable.

"Colin, Isabel's here and I'm sure Camille is not far behind. Call me when you get home, okay?"

"All right. I know when I'm not wanted." He laughed. "I love you, Emily."

"I love you, too." She clicked her phone off and tossed it in her purse.

"So that's where we are, is it?" Isabel said, setting her platter down on the counter. "He finally said those three little words."

"Yes, he did." Emily beamed as she picked up the utensils to toss the salad.

"I assumed he would take the leap before leaving for Cali. He was acting like a smitten teenager last night at the party. I'm happy for you, girl."

"Isabel, there's something I need to talk to you

about." Emily's cheerful voice grew serious. "Do you think you could stay awhile after Camille leaves tonight?"

"She's not here now. What's on your mind?"

"Not now, she'll be here any minute."

"Emily! Isabel! Can someone help me?" a high-pitched voice rang out from the direction of the front door.

"See." Emily's head cocked slightly as she flashed Isabel her *I-told-you-so* look, and then they both dashed to Camille's aid.

Camille had a pan of twice-baked potatoes in one hand and a large clear-plastic covered cake plate with a tall lemon crème cake in the other. "Can you guys help me out? I can't hold onto both of these much longer. If Isabel hadn't left the door ajar, I wouldn't have been able to get it opened."

"I didn't leave the door open," Isabel replied.

Emily took the cake, casting a puzzled glance at Isabel.

If Isabel didn't do it, who did? And where is that person now? Did they overhear her conversation with Colin?

"Was the door open when you arrived, Isabel?"

"No, but it was unlocked." Isabel leaned over to Emily and spoke in a low voice so as not to rattle Camille. "You want me to take a quick look around?"

"Please." An uncomfortable chill rippled over Emily as she and Camille meandered back to the cozy kitchen. After setting the cake down, she hurried back and locked the door, trying to convince herself it was probably nothing.

"My goodness, Camille, how many people did you think were coming tonight?" Isabel chuckled as she noticed the pan loaded with potatoes on the breakfast bar.

"Sorry, I got carried away."

"All's clear," Isabel whispered in Emily's ear.

Emily nodded.

"Now that we're all here, let's eat. I'm hungry." Isabel grabbed one of the plates from the table and the other girls followed her lead.

Each one filled their plate and took a seat at the kitchen table.

"Hey, did I tell you my brother is coming to visit," Camille mentioned, spreading her napkin on her lap.

"No, you never said," Isabel replied, enjoying her barbecued chicken leg.

"Which brother?" Emily asked. She knew Camille had several spread around the country.

"Peter, the youngest one. He's thirty-five. He was a TV news reporter in Buffalo, but he's been hired by one of the stations in Seattle. Peter's taking a month off between jobs, so he's stopping by to see me for a while. He grew up here, you know."

"Just him?" Isabel asked. "No wife or kids?"

"No, he's single." Camille took a forkful of potatoes and wagged it at Isabel as she spoke. "Hasn't found the right woman, he says."

"When will he be here?" Emily asked, cutting into her chicken.

Camille swallowed her mouthful of potatoes. "Tomorrow." She took a sip of her sweet tea. "I'd like to do a brunch at my house on Saturday to introduce you all to him. Can you come?" She looked from Emily to Isabel.

They both nodded at her, their mouths too full to speak.

"It's too bad Maggie and Molly won't be here. The last time Peter saw Molly she was in grade school." Camille took another long drink of her sweet tea. Her phone began to buzz in her pocket. She pulled it out and read a text. "Molly says they just landed in Hawaii."

"I hope they have a great time. I bet Maggie will be sorry she missed your brother though," Isabel added.

"I'm not sure how long he's staying. Maybe I can convince him to wait until they get back," Camille supposed. "I know Molly will be disappointed if she doesn't get to see her uncle."

"You'll have to get him to stay at least that long," Emily said. "Maggie will be heartbroken she didn't get to meet him."

"Don't you think it's a little too soon to be looking for another man for Maggie?" Isabel asked.

"I didn't mean it that way, Is." Emily frowned. "I just meant she'll feel like she missed out on something we all shared. You know how she is."

"That cake looks heavenly, Camille." Isabel glanced at the lemon cake on the counter, an obvious attempt to change the subject. "I'll have to make sure and leave room for it."

The subject of Maggie's love life did not come up again the rest of the evening. After her last disastrous relationship, it was probably best.

Camille cut the cake and brought a slice for each of them back to the table.

"Mmm, looks delicious," Isabel said with a grin as Camille set the dessert plates down on the table and took her seat.

"Any new events you're planning, Camille?" Emily inquired, cutting into her cake.

"Why, yes, there is," she replied, fluffing her short, spiky red hair as she sat back in her chair. "I'm planning, as well as catering I might add, an important event next weekend at the Hilton Hotel for the Zigon Corporation."

"Sounds like a sizeable job." Emily refilled her glass with the pitcher of iced tea on the table. "Aren't they that huge computer chip maker south of Boise?"

"They are, and it is a big job. As a matter of fact…" Camille drew out the words as she flashed a sheepish grin at Emily and then at Isabel. "I'm having a hard time finding enough servers for the event. I was wondering if you might be able to help me out that night."

"Now I know you're not talking to me," Isabel said, dipping her chin as she raised her eyebrows at Camille, flipping her long, dark waves over her shoulder.

"Emily?" Camille turned to her and pleaded, batting blue doe-eyes. "I've already wrangled Molly into helping me, but I'm still short handed."

"What day next weekend?" Emily pulled out her phone to check her schedule.

"Saturday. I'd need you from late afternoon until the end of the evening. Please say yes."

"Looks like I'm free."

Camille leaned over and patted Emily's forearm. "I'll owe you, Em."

"Big time, I'd say," Isabel added.

"I'm happy to do it. With Colin gone, my Saturday

nights will be pretty much free again. It'll give me something to do."

"No investigations waiting for you?" Isabel put another forkful of luscious cake in her mouth.

"After winding up the Lucas Wakefield case, I've only had a few small cases, but I'm sure more work will come. It always does." Emily smiled weakly then took a drink of her tea. She hoped more work would come. At least the break in cases gave her time to dig deeper into Evan's murder.

Once dessert was finished and conversation exhausted, Camille said it was time for her to head home. "Don't forget brunch on Saturday—eleven o'clock." She packed up her belongings, hugged Emily and Isabel, and went home.

Isabel lingered behind, as Emily had asked her to, and helped clear the dinner table and load the dishwasher. "Now that we're alone, what did you want to talk to me about?"

Emily poured dishwasher detergent in the cup in the door, snapped the lid shut, and started the machine. She decided there was no point in beating around the bush, so she faced Isabel and dove right in. "Did you know Evan when he worked in Washington, DC?"

Isabel dried her hands on the kitchen towel, seemingly unruffled by the question. But then again, that was Isabel, level-headed and unflappable. "That question seemed to come out of nowhere, Em. Why do you ask?"

She wondered why Isabel didn't just reply yes or no. It was a simple question. Was she trying to evade the question or find out why Emily wanted to know before answering?

Emily leaned a hip against the counter and crossed her arms, staring directly at her. She could answer her, but she didn't want to show her hand too early. "Just answer the question, Is."

Isabel's eyebrows furrowed a bit and her dark eyes locked on Emily's. She crossed her arms, too, in a defensive manner. "What's with this change in attitude? One minute we're the best of friends, the next you're the interrogator. What gives?"

"Answer the question."

"I don't know what this is about, but—"

"Answer the question—*Izzy*." Emily used the nickname to see what response she'd get from Isabel. No one in their group called her that, except Evan.

Isabel's intense stare softened at the name. She dropped her arms and took a step back, her eyes widening a bit, as if she realized Emily had discovered something.

"Did you know my husband in DC?" Emily's voice rose with irritation.

Isabel's eyes lowered momentarily. "Yes."

"So you were in on the whole chain of lies?" Emily's eyes moistened and her voice cracked as she snapped her accusation at Isabel.

"You don't understand. I—"

Isabel stepped toward Emily, reaching out to touch her arm.

Emily shook it off. "I understand you have lied to me for the last five-plus years!" She turned away, a couple of tears escaping, and she stepped to the table. She pulled a chair out and dropped down onto it.

"Please, let me explain." Isabel dragged a chair next

to Emily's and sat beside her.

Emily did not respond. She stuck her elbows on the table and buried her face in her hands.

"I did know Evan in DC—I was CIA, too. Although, when I knew him back then his name was David. He was a field operative, but I worked in the office at Langley, monitoring his operations." Isabel had never told Emily this, not in all the conversations they'd had in the last few months about Evan's CIA involvement.

Isabel rested a hand gently on Emily's shoulder, but she shrugged it off again.

"We worked together for a few years and we had become friends."

"Did you sleep with him?" Emily muttered through her hands.

"No, Emily, we were just friends. I remember the day he told me he had met someone special, unlike any woman he had ever known, he said. Then he told me he may even leave the agency for her, if he could get her to agree to marry him."

Emily sat up straight and wiped her tears away with her hands. Taking a deep breath, she leaned her head back and ran her fingers through her loose curls. "He was talking about me?" She looked at Isabel with a sideways glance.

"He was."

"How do I know I can believe you?"

"I may not have always told you the truth, but I've always watched out for you, I've always been your true friend."

Emily took another calming breath and relaxed her

shoulders. She turned toward Isabel, ready to hear the rest of the story.

"A few weeks later, he came into the office and had a meeting with the head of our department. After the meeting, Evan told me he was leaving the agency, going back into private life. He had asked you to marry him and you said yes. He wanted to start fresh, he said, so he was moving the two of you across the country to begin a new life in a small town."

"Paradise Valley."

"Yes. Because of the dangerous nature of Evan's assignments, my supervisor wanted him to have a lifeline, a safety net, in case anyone came after him. My boss had contacts in the FBI and he got me a job with them and a transfer to the Boise office. That way I could be here for David—I mean Evan—and have contacts in both the CIA and the FBI."

"I'm sure Evan appreciated having you here." There was no way she could know for sure, but if Isabel was telling the truth, Emily assumed Evan would have been grateful for her presence.

"How did you know I knew him in DC?"

"I didn't know for sure."

"Something must have made you suspect?"

"I found an address book that belonged to Evan. One of the entries in it was *Handler* comma *Izzy*. I remembered Evan used to call you Izzy, but no one else did."

"I see. Where is this address book?"

"It's safe."

"Em, if that book were to get into the wrong hands, it could cost agents their lives."

"I realize that, but forget about the book for now. What about Jethro?"

"What do you mean?"

"You brought him to my house under the auspices of trying to find out who Evan really was—when you knew the whole time exactly who he was."

"I wanted you to find out about the real Evan, I just didn't want you to find out about me. Evan's gone, but I'm still here and I value our friendship. I was afraid I'd lose it if you knew my secrets. A true friend like you doesn't come along very often, Em, especially for someone in my line of work."

Emily nodded that she understood.

"Now, where is the address book?"

"I'm not ready to give it up yet, but I will. Give me a few days." Emily wasn't finished studying it, there may be more for her to learn from it.

"You never said where you found it."

"Funny thing. I discovered what that brass key from the safe deposit box was for."

Emily explained getting the letter from the storage facility and how she had dropped by there that morning. She had suspected the key might fit the padlock on the storage unit after reading the letter and she was right.

"What was in the unit?" Isabel asked.

Emily considered for a moment if she should say or not. Remembering how her husband had scribbled *Handler, Izzy* in the address book, she wondered if that was enough proof that Evan trusted her. After mulling it over, Emily decided to trust her too. She hoped she wasn't making a huge mistake.

She wished Evan hadn't said *trust no one* in the

note he had left her. He should have written *trust no one, except Isabel*. Perhaps he wrote the note before Isabel came to Paradise Valley, which would mean he put the note in the safe deposit box as soon as they'd moved to town.

It was possible, she thought, that Isabel honestly didn't know anything about Evan's safe deposit box, or its contents, until she told her.

"The storage unit just had some boxes of old files. That's where I found the book."

"What kind of files?"

Emily could lie and say they were from Evan's private investigation cases, but hadn't there been enough lies already? She yearned to trust her closest friend again, and she hated the suspicion that stood between them. With trepidation, she hoped she was doing the right thing.

"They were copies of CIA files. They looked like they were documents from Evan's old assignments."

"Are you kidding me?" Isabel's eyes widened and her voice rose. "He's not supposed to keep those documents."

"It's kind of a moot point now, isn't it?"

"I guess, but I'd like to get a look at them."

"What was that?" Emily's head snapped toward the direction of her front door. She had heard the sound of the wooden floors creak in her 1920's bungalow, followed by the faint sound of a door clicking shut.

Isabel reached into her purse for her gun and Emily followed her closely down the hall and to the front of the house. Emily had tucked her weapon in the nightstand next to her bed before the girls came over and was glad

Isabel's was close by.

The front door was unlocked. Emily had recalled locking it after the girls arrived, but Camille could have left it unlocked when she went home. Camille had said the door was ajar when she arrived, but Isabel insisted she hadn't left it open.

Could someone have been hiding in her house while she and her friends had dinner? Staying to listen to their conversations? Isabel had done a quick search through the house and gave her an all clear, but maybe the person was clever enough to avoid being found.

"You don't think…?" Emily wondered if someone heard her talking with Isabel? Emily shivered at the creepy feeling that spread over her body.

"Think what?" Isabel put the safety on her firearm.

"That someone was here and overheard our discussion about Evan."

THE CHAIN OF LIES

CHAPTER 4
The New Man in Town

SATURDAY MORNING, Emily woke up thinking about the address book. She had lain in bed the previous evening, scouring it, looking for anything else that might make sense to her. Nothing did. It seemed to be a jumble of cryptic names and phone numbers, sometimes followed by other numbers that made no sense at all. She assumed it must have been some kind of code that Evan would have understood, but likely no one else.

For safekeeping, she had tucked it under her pillow, sleeping with her phone and gun on the night table and her purse nearby. Someone had been searching for something in her house, likely the gun from the safe deposit box, and they weren't going to stop until they found it. If someone had been in her house Thursday night while she talked with Isabel about the book and the boxes in the storage unit, it was possible they'd be after that information, as well.

Emily had half expected an intruder on Friday, keeping her guard up throughout the day, but it had been a quiet day. She'd spoken with Colin on the phone a couple of times, received a few texts with photos attached from Maggie and Molly, and got a call from Isabel asking when she could get a peak at the contents of the storage unit.

After hitting the shooting range in the afternoon, a kickboxing class in the early evening, and receiving a reminder call from Camille about the brunch for her brother Peter, she'd stuck a frozen meal in the microwave and watched a romantic comedy on the television before heading to bed. Nestled under the covers, she stayed up late studying the black book.

The bright morning sunlight streaming in her bedroom window told Emily she'd better drag herself out of bed and get ready for Camille's brunch or she'd be late and have to make her apologies. She hated making apologies.

A quick shower, a dollop of hair mousse, a few blasts of hot air on her loosely tousled curls, and a dab of make-up was all she would need and she'd almost be ready to head out the door. She chose a deep turquoise top, which her friends all said played up her blue-green eyes and dark blonde hair, and her black jeans which she knew hugged her tush and legs in just the right places.

Was she trying to impress the guest of honor? No. Looking good simply boosted her self-confidence and lifted her spirits, although making a good impression in front of Peter would make Camille happy.

She thought of Colin and smiled, wishing he was going to the brunch with her. Catching her reflection in the full-length mirror, she stopped and did a once over, thinking how pleased Colin would be with what he saw.

Autumn was just around the corner, making the morning air crisp and cool. Emily pulled on her short black-leather boots, with just enough spiked heel to make her legs look longer. She stuck her gun, her phone, and the little black book in her large leather purse, slung it over her shoulder, and she was out the door.

~*~

"Knock, knock," Emily called out as she walked through Camille and Jonathan's front door. She could hear music and conversation coming from the open kitchen and family room at the rear of the house.

"We're back here!" she heard Camille holler.

Isabel and Alex had already arrived. Isabel hugged her as she entered the open great room area. Alex and Jonathan were sitting on the couches, deep in conversation with Peter. Camille fluttered about the kitchen, putting the last minute touches on the delicious spread she had prepared.

After Isabel greeted her, Emily walked over to Camille at the stove, gave her a sideways hug, and asked if there was anything she could do to help.

"Oh, you haven't met my brother yet. Here, let me introduce you, then you can help me cut up the fruit and take the muffins out when the buzzer goes off." She grabbed Emily by the hand and led her over to where the men were seated.

"Peter MacKenzie," Camille said, which caused her brother to rise to his feet, "this is my friend, Emily."

"It's nice to meet you, Peter MacKenzie." Emily stuck out her hand, expecting to shake his. Rather, he took her hand, lifted it to his lips and gave it a light kiss. She wanted to draw it back, but for fear she would offend him, she let him hold it a moment until he released it.

"The pleasure is all mine," he said in a deep voice, perfect for television.

Peter looked down at her with his brilliant blue eyes—just like his sister's. He even had red hair, like Camille did, but his was more of a deep auburn. He was tall and lean, six three or four, she guessed, with sparkling white teeth that filled out a perfect smile. "Would you like to sit with us?" he asked, gesturing toward the couch he had been sitting on.

"Thanks, but no, I promised Camille I'd help her in the kitchen."

"Well, let's talk later. My sister tells me you're a private investigator, and I find that fascinating."

The timer on the oven beeped loudly, alerting Camille the muffins were ready to come out.

"We'd better get back and tend to the food so we can eat." Camille hooked her arm through Emily's and walked her back to the kitchen area.

Within minutes Camille announced the food was ready. Spread across the long breakfast bar there were platters of two kinds of quiche, a sausage frittata, cinnamon-swirl french toast, thick slices of bacon, crispy hash browns, blueberry muffins, and fruit compote with strawberry whip. Stacked at the end were the plates, napkins, and silverware.

"Grab a plate and serve yourself, guys," Camille

instructed. "Nobody's waiting on you in this house."

The six of them sat around the dining table and enjoyed all Camille's hard work and talent. Peter took a seat next to Emily and they shared friendly conversation and enjoyed the food. She found him interesting and easy to talk to with stories about his work, the places he'd traveled to, and his plans for the future at his new job in Seattle.

Though he shared quite a bit about himself, he often peppered his conversation with questions about her life and her work, which gave their exchange a nice balance. He told her about some of the stories he'd covered and she told him about some of the cases she had worked. He made her laugh a few times, but he also shocked her when he described a story he had covered recently on the trafficking of sex slaves in the United States. Occasionally, the other guests joined in on their conversation, but mostly it was just between the two of them.

When the food was consumed and the conversation died down, Emily took her plate and Peter's to the kitchen and laid them in the sink. While the others enjoyed their coffee around the table, Peter picked up the remaining plates and silverware and brought them to the kitchen and offered to help Emily stick them in the dishwasher.

"There's no need to do that, Peter." Emily smiled at his helpfulness.

"Like Camille said, nobody's waiting on me in this house. We all pitch in."

"All right, then. If you insist," she teased.

~*~

On her drive home, Emily's phone began to ring and she saw it was Camille.

"Hello," she answered cheerfully.

"Hello, there, Emily. This is Peter."

Emily was startled a bit at the man's deep voice. "Oh, I was expecting Camille."

"She lent me her phone—you know, roaming charges. Anyway, I was wondering if you'd like to have dinner tonight."

"Dinner? Tonight? You mean with you and Camille and Jonathan?"

"No, I mean with me. Nothing fancy, just somewhere casual."

For a moment she thought she'd say yes, it would be fun. Certainly better than sitting home alone on a Saturday night, but then she remembered Colin. How would she feel if he took another woman out to dinner, even a casual and friendly one?

"I'd better not."

"I don't understand. I thought we had a connection today. Or was I the only one who felt it?"

She didn't want to hurt his feelings, he seemed like a great guy, not to mention the fact he was her dear friend's brother, but she had to be honest with him. "I like you, Peter. I had fun talking with you today. But...well, it's just that I'm seeing someone."

"Oh, I see. I didn't realize. Camille didn't say anything. I would have thought she would have invited him over this morning, too."

"He's out of town for a little while, but he should be

back soon." Or at least she hoped he would be. "I think you guys would really hit it off."

"Well, you can't blame a guy for trying."

Emily peeked up at her rearview mirror and noticed a black sedan four cars back. She made a sharp right turn at the next corner to see if the car stayed with her. "I appreciate the offer, but I think I'd better say no. Sorry."

She looked again in her mirror and the car was still there. She hung another sharp right and checked again. This time the car was gone. *Coincidence?* There were a lot of black cars on the road—still, until the mystery was solved, she'd have to stay vigilant.

THE CHAIN OF LIES

CHAPTER 5
The Peeping Tom

SATURDAY EVENING PROVED BORING and uneventful. Emily almost wished she'd accepted Peter's dinner invitation so she'd have something to fill the lonely evening, but no, she decided, that was a bad idea. At least she was grateful that the nightmares about Evan's murder hadn't come back to haunt her the last few nights.

The bright spot in the evening was a phone call from Colin. She had been sitting on her bed, already in her pajamas, perusing the address book once more.

"I'm so lonely for you, Colin." Her heart ached for him.

"Maybe this will cheer you up." His voice was deep and warm. "I spoke to the police chief about getting my old job back—that is, when I'm ready to come back to Paradise Valley."

"Did he agree?" she asked, lying back against the

pillows.

"He did, said ol' Ernie is itching to get back to his old position as a patrolman."

"Yes, Ernie mentioned that several times to me during the Wakefield case—that he wasn't cut out for being a detective."

"He *mentioned*? That doesn't sound like Ernie." Colin chuckled.

"Well, more like complained—I was trying to be nice. I can't wait for you to come back, Colin, I miss you." Emily twisted a strand of hair around her finger.

"I know. I miss you, too. It won't be much longer, Babe, I promise. Dad's doing a lot better."

"That's good to hear." She sat up straight and crossed her legs Indian-style on the bed. "Oh, did I tell you that Camille's brother is in town?"

"No. Just visiting or moving there?"

"Just visiting. His name's Peter MacKenzie. He's a TV reporter. He starts a new job in Seattle soon, and he's here to see Camille and her family before it begins. I think he's planning to stick around until after Molly gets back from Hawaii so he can see her."

"What's he like?"

"Handsome, interesting, funny." How could she tease poor Colin so?

His voice became serious. "Hmmm, should I be jealous?"

"Well, he did ask me out."

"What!" Colin shrieked. "What did you tell him?" Suddenly his voice was high and intense.

"What do you think? I told him no, that I was seeing someone, of course." She probably shouldn't have baited him that way, but it felt kind of nice to hear a sizzle of jealousy in Colin's voice, standing up for his woman. It made her want him all the more. "I told you I'd wait for you."

"I guess I'd better be moving my butt back there sooner rather than later."

"I guess you'd better." She laughed. "Not to change the subject, but I had a heart-to-heart with Isabel the other night and it turns out she *was* Izzy Handler from Evan's address book."

"No kidding."

Emily explained to him what Isabel had shared about her relationship with Evan, and how she had moved to Paradise Valley to help him. However, the part where someone was possibly hiding in her house while the girls were there and may have overheard her conversation with Isabel, well, she thought she'd keep that to herself. It would only upset Colin and there was nothing he could do from seven hundred miles away.

"I'd better let you go, Emily. It's getting late. I'll call you again tomorrow."

"That'd be nice," she replied, reclining against the pillows once more.

"I love you."

"I love you, too."

~*~

With nothing on the agenda for Sunday, Emily hadn't bothered to set the alarm, hoping to get some extra sleep. She'd had too many exhausting nights with little sleep because of Evan, so sleeping in would be a treat.

At nine o'clock, there was a loud knock at her front door. She was still in bed, hovering in that dream-like space between sleep and waking. She was dreaming Colin had come back to Paradise Valley and was knocking at her door. Then another loud knock interrupted her dream and she realized someone really was at her front door.

"Coming!" she hollered as she grabbed her robe, not knowing for sure if the visitor could hear her or not. As she rushed to the entry, she could see the top of a police officer's hat through the windows across the top of the door. "What on earth?"

She cinched the belt on her robe and opened the door part way, peeking around it. "Good morning, can I help you?"

"Emily Parker?" the officer asked.

"Yes. Is something wrong?"

"Do you mind if I step inside?"

She knew most of the officers in Paradise Valley, but this one didn't look familiar to her. She looked past him and saw his cruiser parked in front of her house, then she looked for the familiar police badge on his uniform before agreeing.

These days she was suspicious of just about everyone. She backed up, opening the door all the way for him and he stepped inside the entry.

"What is this about?" Emily pulled her robe a little tighter around her chest.

"We got a call a little while ago from one of your neighbors who said he saw a man peeking in your windows. We just wanted to make sure you knew about it and that you were okay. Are you all right?"

"I'm fine. I was sleeping." She wondered if the peeping Tom could have been the same person who'd been breaking in. "What neighbor called it in?"

"The report said anonymous, but the dispatcher said it sounded like an elderly man."

"Mr. Cooke, next door." She motioned toward his house with her thumb. "That was kind of him to look out for me." She thought for a second about reporting the other break-ins, but then she would have to explain the entire story of Evan and his mysterious past. She decided she'd rather leave that investigation to the Feds. "Did the man see Mr. Cooke?"

"I believe he did. The report said the man ran off when he saw he'd been spotted."

She wondered if Mr. Cooke would be in danger now. Emily decided to pay him a visit, see if he could describe the man.

"I'll go have a talk with Mr. Cooke. I appreciate you stopping by, Officer, but as you can see, I'm fine."

"You should make sure your doors and windows are locked when you go to bed, ma'am, just to be safe. You might also think about investing in an alarm system or at least a big dog."

"I appreciate your suggestions," she said, opening the door for him to leave. "I'll give them some thought."

As soon as the officer was gone, she went to her bedroom and threw on jeans and a red pullover sweater. She ran her hands through her hair and fingered it into place. After shoving her phone in her pocket, she stuck her gun in the back of her waistband and pulled her sweater down over it. She stepped into her flats and headed out the door to see her neighbor.

Knocking briskly on the front door, Emily could hear Mr. Cooke's German Shepherd bark ferociously in response. She listened to the elderly man holler at the dog to be quiet right before he opened the door.

"Hello, Emily," the short and stocky old man said with a grin. His eyes twinkled behind his glasses and the sunlight reflected off his shiny bald head. "Are you okay?"

"Yes, I'm fine. The police stopped by my place and told me you'd reported a peeping Tom at my house."

"I never gave them my name. How'd they know it was me?"

"They didn't. I figured it out. Do you mind if we talk for a minute?"

"Oh, sure, sure." He shuffled a couple of steps back and opened the door wide. "Come on in."

The dog growled and Emily hesitated to go inside.

"Rocky!" the man yelled.

The dog quieted and Emily stepped in.

"Here, let me move those newspapers. Have a seat." He gestured toward the sofa and picked up the papers before he dropped down onto his leather recliner.

"I appreciate your looking out for me, Mr. Cooke. Could you tell me what happened exactly?"

"Well, I was coming back from taking Rocky here for a walk. I saw the man looking into a window on the side of your house and I hollered at him, 'Hey, what are you doing there?' The man took off, jumped in his car, and drove off."

"What kind of car was it?"

"It was black. One of those foreign jobs."

"Could you describe him?"

"Older white guy, or maybe Latino, full head of gray hair. Not as old as me, though."

"Is there any way he would know you lived next door?"

"What do you mean?"

"I just want to make sure you're safe, in case he's the type to pay someone back for being a witness to him trying to break in."

"You think he'd have the gall to show his face around here again? Old Rocky would tear his leg off." The dog sat watch next to the old man, as if confirming.

She had to put a hand over her lips to stifle a giggle and cleared her throat. "Maybe, if he thought you could identify him—"

"No, no, I don't think so." The old man shook his head. "I was standing on the sidewalk with Rocky when he drove off. I can't see how he'd know where I lived."

"That's a relief."

"You really think I'm in danger?"

"I don't want to scare you, Mr. Cooke. I simply want you to be safe."

"I have Rocky here." He patted the dog's head. "I think I'm safe enough."

"Did you happen to get his license plate number?" She could only hope.

"I'd like to tell you I did, but my eyesight ain't what it used to be, even with these dang spectacles." He pulled off his large wire-rimmed glasses and held them out to her briefly, then stuck them back on his face. "But I can tell you the color of the plate."

"You mean it wasn't local?"

"Naw, it was different." His gaze lifted to the right as he apparently worked to remember. "It was white, no light blue maybe. I recall the letters were dark blue and there was a red bird in the left corner. I think there might have been flowers around it."

"Around the license plate?"

"No, around the bird."

Virginia! Emily had lived in Virginia before she married Evan and moved west, and she immediately recognized the description. She wondered if it had been someone from DC, someone from the CIA or the FBI.

"That's quite a memory you've got, Mr. Cooke." She didn't want to give away anything she was thinking, so she decided she'd better head back home. Rising to her feet, she thanked him for his time. "I should be going. If you ever see that man or the car again, please let me know. I'd sure like to know who it was."

"Sounds like you don't think it was just a random burglar."

"Oh, it probably was." Emily shrugged as casually as she could, hoping to conceal her suspicions. "Thanks again," she said, backing toward the door.

As she left her neighbor's house, she thought about phoning Colin, but there was nothing he could do for her from California. So, she decided to call Isabel instead.

"Hey, Em, what's up?" Isabel asked.

"I just had a visit from the police. Seems someone was peeking into my windows this morning while I slept, and one of my neighbors called the cops."

"Do the police know who it was?"

"No, not at all. I went and talked to my neighbor to see if he could tell me anything, but no, he doesn't have a clue either. Although, he did give me a pretty good description of the perp, older guy, white or Latino, gray hair, and that his license plate was from Virginia."

"Gray hair? Virginia? I wonder…"

"What?"

"No, it wouldn't be."

"Wouldn't be who?" Emily had to know.

"Jethro."

THE CHAIN OF LIES

CHAPTER 6
Jethro's Questions

EMILY ASKED ISABEL if she was free around noon on that Sunday afternoon and perhaps would like to take a peek into the boxes in the storage unit. Isabel jumped at the chance. Emily promised to swing by and pick her up.

After Emily made sure all her doors and windows were secure and her laptop hidden, she drove to Isabel's, keeping an eye out for anyone following her.

Am I going to have to be checking my rearview mirrors forever?

As she drove, her mind wandered to the unsettling events she was dealing with, namely the tail and the repeated break-ins. More and more it seemed it was probably the same person. It wasn't like they were trashing the place, but things had been moved and she could tell they were searching for something. Evan had been dead for a year, so why was someone searching for something in her home now?

Jethro.

Was he the missing link? It seemed to fit.

The tail and the break-ins started after Isabel connected her with Jethro. As a favor, when Emily had become desperate to find out Evan's real identity, Isabel had introduced her to Jethro, someone she had known for years in the FBI. He had recently retired and was now living nearby in Boise.

Isabel had brought Jethro to Emily's home one evening to talk about Evan. Emily had shown him the photo from the safe deposit box, and had asked him to help her find out who Evan really was—and who the mysterious brunette cuddled up to her husband was. That was the night she had mentioned a *hypothetical* gun to him, although everyone, including Jethro, knew it wasn't as hypothetical as she had intended it to be.

Suspicions were all she had. How could she prove he was the culprit? And why?

Emily pulled into Isabel's driveway and honked a couple of times.

"Hey, Em," Isabel greeted as she climbed in the car. "Thanks for inviting me. You can't imagine how curious I've been since you mentioned the storage locker."

"Hopefully we can find something useful, something giving us a lead in Evan's murder." Emily backed out of the driveway.

"I'm all for that." Isabel fastened her seatbelt.

"Were you serious about suspecting Jethro as my stalker?" Emily drove down the wide winding streets of the upscale neighborhood.

"The description fits."

"Yes, but it could describe a number of guys. Even your husband is Latino with graying hair."

"True, but Alex and I don't have Virginia plates."

"That's a good point."

"If it is him, though, I wonder why he'd be tracking you."

"The gun we told him about?" Emily wished she'd kept the gun a secret if she'd known it would cause her this much trouble, but she couldn't get away from the fact that Evan had hidden it in the safe deposit box for a reason.

"Maybe."

"Let's hope something in the files will tell us." Emily peeked one more time into the mirrors but saw nothing suspicious.

Arriving at the outdoor storage facility, Emily unlocked the padlock and pulled open the door. Armed with flashlights, Emily began with the boxes she hadn't yet scoured, and Isabel agreed to recheck the ones she had.

Isabel grabbed a hair band out of her jeans pocket and pulled her long, dark hair back into a ponytail. File by file, document by document, with flashlights in hand, the two spent the next couple of hours reading through every piece of paper they found.

"Hey, I think I found something." Emily held up a few sheets of paper stapled together.

Isabel stepped in for a closer look. "What is it?"

"It looks like a background check on Delia. Funny, it wasn't in a file, just loose between a couple of folders."

"I wonder if Delia knew Evan had checked up on

her," Isabel remarked.

Emily shone her flashlight on the document and read through it, flipping the pages as she went on to the next one. Isabel read with her, over her shoulder. "It says her full name is Delia Banderas McCall. Banderas...why does that sound familiar?" Emily looked to Isabel, but she did not reply. "Banderas must be her maiden name, don't you think?"

"Yes." Isabel replied slowly. Her eyes seemed to be looking blankly off into the distance, lost in thought.

"What's wrong, Isabel? You're so quiet."

"Jethro."

"I don't get it."

"Remember I told you we would call my friend *Jethro*, because I couldn't tell you his real name?"

"Yeah."

"You have to promise to keep this between us—"

"All right, already. Spit it out." Emily's impatience was showing.

"His real name is Jerry Banderas. Which would mean—"

"He's related to Delia somehow."

Suddenly Emily remembered why the name sounded familiar—Evan's note. He had said the woman in the photo was Natalia Banderas, and he had blamed himself for her death. That would mean Delia could be somehow related to Natalia, as well.

The note also warned Emily to trust no one. Could she trust Isabel enough to tell her about it?

It was likely already too late to be asking that question. After all, Isabel was here, going through Evan's things with her. Since Emily had learned Isabel had been Evan's handler, and that she had moved to Paradise Valley to help him, she contemplated if she should take another leap of faith, even if it was just a small one.

Emily took the leap. "You said you've known Jethro, or Jerry, for a long time."

Isabel nodded.

"Did he have a daughter named Natalia?"

Isabel's eyes widened. "Yes. As a matter of fact, he used to talk about her all the time. In fact, he had two daughters. How did you know?"

"Two daughters?" Emily's mind raced ahead of Isabel's, not stopping to answer her question. "Maybe the other one is Delia."

"She could be. I don't recall him mentioning her by name. She was older than Natalia. But how did you know that?" Isabel's eyebrows wrinkled in curiosity.

"Evan told me."

"When?"

"In a note I found in his safe deposit box."

"When were you planning to tell me about that?"

Emily stared her friend in the eyes. "I'm not sure I was."

"What does that mean?"

"In the note, Evan warned me to trust no one."

"Not even me? I'm your best friend." Isabel put her hand on Emily's arm.

"Yes, my friend who's been lying to me for the past five years." Emily pulled away.

"I wasn't keeping my identity secret to hurt you. I was trying to protect you."

"And now you've brought Jethro into the mix and

all hell is breaking loose!" Her arm waved around for dramatic emphasis, the papers flapping in her hand.

"If you recall," Isabel lowered her voice and spoke in a calm, serious tone, "I asked you if you wouldn't be happier to simply remember the great marriage you had, let this investigation drop, and get on with your life. You insisted you absolutely had to know. That's why I brought my friend into it—as a favor to you. I had no idea he might be involved."

Emily crossed her arms and shifted her weight, taking a moment to absorb Isabel's words. "I guess you've got me there. This whole mystery has me so wound up. I'm sorry. You're right—it was me who pushed it."

"I'm not your enemy, Em. I'm here to help you, if you'll let me."

Emily looked at Isabel, then down at the papers in her hand, pausing to consider her options. She could continue to keep things from Isabel, continue to have her suspicions about her, or she could lay it all out there.

"Okay, no more secrets." She pulled the note out of her purse and handed it to her friend.

Isabel moved to the sunlight at the opening of the unit. She unfolded the paper and took her time reading the message aloud, softly.

"Dearest Emily,

If you've found this note, it means I'm dead. I hope you'll forgive me for keeping things from you. You may have figured out Evan Parker was not my real name. My name is David Gerard. Again, I'm sorry.

"*The gun belongs to someone who tried to kill me*

once, after moving to Paradise Valley. I wrestled it away from him before he got away, but I don't know who it was. He must have succeeded on a second attempt or you wouldn't be reading this note. I hid the gun because I had hoped to track him by it. Sorry I never told you, I didn't want to worry you.

"The woman in the photo was a girlfriend when I worked for the Agency. Her name was Natalia Banderas. She was a natural history student at the Sorbonne that I met at a café in Paris. She was killed in France when a case I was working on went south and she was caught in the crossfire.

"I blame myself for her death. I should have known better than to get involved with a civilian. That's why I left the Agency when I fell for you, Emily.

"I figure the gun could belong to someone seeking revenge for her death or it could be related to another case—it's hard to say. I don't know how they found me, but if you're reading this note, it means they did. Keep these things hidden. Trust no one. I love you, Emily.

Evan, aka David Gerard."

When Isabel was finished reading, she slowly refolded the paper and handed it back to Emily. "That explains a lot."

~*~

Emily dropped Isabel off at home and agreed to come back for dinner that evening. Isabel wanted to talk more about what to do regarding Jethro and how to find out what he was really up to.

Pulling into her own driveway, Emily glanced up and down the sunny tree-lined street for anything suspicious before heading inside. Everything looked normal. She stepped onto her porch and took a second look before unlocking her door and going in.

Once inside, she clicked the lock into place, kicked off her shoes and headed for the bathroom. She paused at the bathroom door and decided to take a quick look around her house and make sure the back door was locked, as well. With her pistol held low, she skulked from room to room, making sure it was all clear.

A long, hot soak in a tub full of bubbles was all she wanted right now—something to relax her and help her worries float away, at least for a while. As she turned the water on and poured in the liquid bubbles, her phone beeped, alerting her to a new text.

The message was from Maggie, telling her what a great time they were having, and she had attached a photo she must have had someone else take. It was a picture of Maggie and Molly on the beach, in their bikinis, lying on colorful towels with big smiles on their faces.

Emily felt a little jab of envy at the sight of them, wishing she could go somewhere and totally relax without a care in the world. Someday, she promised herself, she would take a vacation too—when Evan's murder was solved.

As the claw-foot tub filled, she slipped out of her clothes and set her towel on the vanity chair, laying her phone on top. She climbed into the tub and immersed herself, still feeling a little unnerved and exposed.

Leaning back, she closed her eyes and tried to rest,

but the thought that someone might be right outside her window kept her on edge.

As the warm water finally began to relax her, Emily mulled over the pieces of her puzzle.

Natalia was Jethro's daughter. Was Delia also his daughter? Evan had said in the note he felt guilty for getting Natalia killed. Jethro had said when he was showing Evan's photo around to his colleagues, that someone had mentioned something about revenge for her death.

Isabel had explained that Jethro had moved to Boise from Virginia recently, after retiring from the FBI. Had Delia given him her late husband's black BMW after his death, maybe before Jethro's move to Boise? Is that why it still had Virginia plates?

Did Delia know Evan was involved in Natalia's death? If so, why would she have hired him to investigate her husband? And where did the file go, the photos and reports of the work he had done for her? Did his murderer take the file? Why wasn't the background check in that file?

Emily had chosen to take a bubble bath hoping for relaxation, but as her mind began to unwind, the questions flew at her in rapid success, one after the other. There was no rest in it whatsoever, only more questions. She dragged herself out of the tub and wrapped the towel around her breasts, tucking it in beneath her arm.

She threw on her jeans and a knit top and decided to make herself a cup of Chamomile tea, hoping that would help. While she waited for the tea kettle to whistle, she sat at the breakfast bar and opened her laptop to cruise the Amazon.com site for a while, hoping to occupy her mind with something else.

Colin phoned. Emily smiled as his photo popped up on the screen of her cell phone.

"Hello, Colin."

"Hey, Babe, how's your day going?"

"I took Isabel out to the storage unit."

"How'd that go? Did you girls find anything useful?"

"Actually, yes. We found a printout of a background check Evan had done on Delia McCall."

"Why is that important?"

"Delia *Banderas* McCall."

"Is that supposed to mean something to me?"

"I didn't tell you about the note I found, did I?" she asked sheepishly.

"Note? What note?"

"I found a note Evan had left me in the safe deposit box. I hadn't seen it before when I first checked the box."

"When exactly did you find this note?" The suspicious tone of his voice told her he wasn't pleased she had kept this from him.

"Right before you left. Are you sure I didn't mention it to you?" She tried to shift the onus on him. After all, she hadn't been sure she could trust him until she had spoken to his old friend, Ernie, the night of the party at Isabel's, which put her suspicions about Colin to rest. Then later that same night, Colin had professed his love for her. That wouldn't have been the time to tell him about the note. Then he was leaving for San Francisco early the next morning. She knew she was making excuses, but she hoped he'd let it go.

"No, I'd remember something like that." His voice was flat and almost accusatory. "Tell me now."

"Please don't be cross with me. I'm sorry. It must have slipped my mind. I have had a few other things jostling for front position lately." She waited for his response, which took a painful few seconds for him to formulate.

"All right. I'll give you the benefit of the doubt. I'd hate to think you were keeping something from me on purpose."

"I promise, from now on I'll be totally upfront with you, whenever I can."

Colin choked out a sarcastic snicker. "What do you mean *whenever you can?*"

"Look, Colin. I want to be honest with you about everything. But in my line of work, as in yours, there will always be things we can't divulge." She hoped he would understand. She also hoped he wouldn't notice that the note had nothing to do with her work.

"Keeping something confidential is one thing. Hiding something is another entirely. I need to know I can trust you, Emily."

It felt peculiar having the trust-table turned on her. "Okay then. You can't see me, but I'm raising my right hand to take an oath. I promise from here on out, not to hide anything from you. I want you to trust me, to be confident that I love you and I have our best interest as a couple at heart."

"I can live with that."

"I want to hear you say it too. Raise your right hand."

Colin repeated her promise, word for word, in his deep, rich voice, and she enjoyed hearing every syllable of it. As for the hand, well, he didn't say.

"Now tell me about the note," he insisted.

CHAPTER 7
Dinner at Isabel's

WHEN EMILY ARRIVED Isabel's, she was mixing together a big green salad. Alex was out on the patio trying a new recipe for grilled pizza.

"Grilled pizza?" Emily was a little dubious. She peeked out the window at him standing before the hot grill. "Has he ever grilled pizza before?"

"No. It was a recipe he found in a magazine and wanted to try it." Isabel brought the large glass salad bowl from the kitchen island to the table. "I got a text from Maggie and Molly this afternoon."

"Me too, with a photo. They looked like they were having fun."

"It's good to see Maggie smiling again, what with her son having been arrested and all." Isabel opened the refrigerator and hunted for something.

"Not to mention the scumbag she was engaged to," Emily added, noticing four glasses on the table. "Why are there four glasses?"

"Alex didn't know you were coming. He invited Peter." Isabel grabbed a few bottles of dressing from the refrigerator door. "I guess Camille and Jonathan had some function to go to."

"I see." Emily hadn't told Isabel about Peter having asked her out.

"Is that a problem?" Isabel grabbed a stack of dinner plates from the cabinet.

"No, why should it be?"

"Just the way you said, *I see.*"

"No problem, but—"

"But what?" Isabel stopped what she was doing and focused on Emily's reply.

"He asked me out to dinner. Of course I said no, that I was already seeing someone. It was a little awkward, if you know what I mean."

"I see." Isabel chuckled as she said Emily's words back to her.

"Say, while Alex is outside," Emily glanced around, "before Peter gets here, why don't I let you in on an idea I had about Jethro, or should I call him Jerry?"

"Let's just call him Jethro, in case anyone else overhears. What's your idea?"

"What do you think of inviting him to meet you for lunch tomorrow? I'll find his car in the parking lot after he's gone into the restaurant and put a tracking device on it. We can track his movements and see what he's up to."

"You mean see if he's the one following you?"

"Yup."

"I think that's an excellent idea, Em, but we can't."

"Why not?"

"He called me this afternoon, said he's heading out of town for a few days to do some consulting work in DC. He asked about the gun again." Isabel paused and dipped her chin toward Emily. "He suggested taking it to DC with him in his checked luggage to have it tested at a government lab there."

"What did you say?" Emily asked.

"I told him I didn't know if there really was a gun, which is kind of true—I've never seen the gun for myself. I told him that as far as I knew it was a hypothetical question you had asked him."

"You think he bought that?" Emily filled the glasses with iced tea.

"Probably not, but what was he going to say? Accuse me of lying?"

"I guess I'll have to wait 'til he gets back to bug his car."

"Bug whose car?" Alex asked as he walked through the door carrying a beautifully grilled pizza with a vaguely rectangular artisan crust.

The doorbell rang and the girls were saved. "Our guest is here, honey, right on time. Why don't you go and let him in," Isabel suggested as she took the pizza from him.

He glowered at them, then proceeded to the front door.

~*~

After a delicious dinner and lively conversation, the men went to the family room to watch Sunday Night Football on Alex's seventy-inch flat screen.

Isabel and Emily puttered around the kitchen, cleaning up after dinner, giving them a chance to talk in private.

"Working on any interesting cases, Em?" Isabel put plastic wrap over the leftover salad and stuck it in the crowded refrigerator.

"Just another wife having me dig up evidence on her cheating husband."

"Any luck?"

"I followed the guy down to a massage parlor on Overland Road, over in Boise."

Isabel cut the peach pie she had made into wedges and scooped them onto small plates. "Oh, yeah? What's it called?"

"The Jade Thai Spa. Why?" Emily laid a dessert fork on each plate.

"I think the Feds have been watching a few of those places." Isabel shook the aerosol can of whipped cream.

"Really? Can you find out if that particular one is on their watch list?"

"Sure, if it'll help." Isabel spritzed a mound of whipped cream on each piece of pie.

"It might." Emily moved to the sink, looking over the breakfast bar to the family room, watching the guys hollering at the screen.

"Emily?" Isabel prompted. "Emily? I asked you a question."

"Yes, Peter is really a nice guy, I agree."

"That's not what I asked you. I asked if you had any other ideas about Jeth—Emily?" Isabel snapped her fingers. "Em...does Colin have something to worry about?"

"No." She broke her stare and turned back to Isabel. "I was thinking about Maggie."

"Don't you think it's a little soon to be looking for another man for Maggie? She just got out of a serious relationship, almost married the creep."

"I know, I know. It's just that she's had such poor luck with men. I'd love to see Maggie with a great guy like Peter, you know, when she's ready."

"But Peter will only be here a little while longer, then he's off to Seattle."

"I know." Emily turned back to her task and began scraping the dinner plates into the garbage disposal. "It was just a thought." She looked up from the sink and peeked over at him once more.

Peter must have sensed her looking at him because he turned his head and met her gaze, flashing her a quick smile before returning to the football game.

Her cheeks flushed red as her stare was discovered. She didn't want him getting the wrong idea.

~*~

Before Emily went to bed that night, Colin phoned again.

"Did you do anything fun today?"

"Isabel invited me over for dinner so I wouldn't have to spend another lonely night microwaving a frozen dinner by myself."

"That's good. Just you?"

Why did he have to ask that? Now she'd have to tell him about Peter. "No, I wasn't the only one. Alex didn't know Isabel had invited me, so he invited Peter who was going to be stuck at home alone too."

"So it was Isabel and Alex, you and Peter—how cozy."

She was sure she detected a hint of jealousy in his voice again. Who could blame him? Peter was a great guy, handsome, too. But Colin had to trust her or what hope was there for the two of them? Their relationship wasn't that flimsy, was it? "Don't be jealous, Colin. I love you and no one else."

"I know that deep inside, but it's nice to hear it from your lips."

"Speaking of lips, I'm missing yours." She cringed, wondering if that sounded too cheesy, but it was the truth.

"Well, you won't be missing them for long."

"What?" she shrieked with excitement. "What are you saying?"

"Looks like I'll be back in Paradise Valley, back to my old job before long."

"Oh, Colin, that's the best news I've heard in a long time! I can't wait." She wanted to laugh and cry at the same time. Her hand flew to her throat as her heart fluttered in her chest, tears of joy brimming in her eyes.

"Neither can I, Babe."

~*~

A few days later, Maggie and Molly returned from Hawaii. Camille, Jonathan, and Peter drove to the airport to pick them up.

The three sat in the waiting area, expecting the arriving passengers to come through the automatic glass doors before long. Watching through the glass, Camille noticed Peter catch sight of his niece approaching the threshold, then she saw him notice Maggie. He jumped to his feet at the sight of the stunning blonde, clad in white shorts that exposed long, tanned legs.

Camille and Jonathan hopped up and followed.

The massive automatic doors glided open and Molly saw her Uncle Peter, grinning at her with arms open wide. With a big smile, she rushed to him and gave him a warm hug. Peter returned the embrace, but his gaze turned toward Maggie.

"Uncle Peter, I didn't know you'd be here," Molly said excitedly, after releasing her hold on him.

"Your mom wanted it to be a surprise," he replied.

"Surprise!" Camille shouted, glancing from Molly to Maggie.

Maggie hugged Camille.

"Who is this?" Peter asked, displaying his sparkling white smile.

"Uncle Peter, this is Maggie Sullivan."

He stuck out his hand and she offered hers.

"I'm Peter MacKenzie, Camille's brother. It's very nice to meet you, Maggie." He held her hand until he was finished speaking, looking directly into her dazzling blue eyes.

The gesture may have escaped Jonathan's notice, but it did not escape Camille's or Molly's. They glanced at each other and grinned.

"Let's get to the baggage carousel before the crowd," Jonathan suggested.

If Maggie noticed Peter's delight at meeting her, she didn't let on. She had gone to Hawaii to get some much-needed rest and to get away from the horrendous events that put an end to her most recent disastrous relationship. The last thing she wanted right now was to take up with another man.

"Tell me all about your trip," Peter said to his niece as she linked her hand around his arm and walked with him to baggage claim.

"Maggie and I had an awesome time, Uncle Peter. Didn't we, Maggie?"

Maggie walked with Camille and Jonathan, just a few steps behind Peter and Molly.

Peter turned and glanced over his niece's head, in Maggie's direction, as they walked toward the baggage carousel. "What did you girls do?"

"Oh, we laid out on the beach at Waikiki," Molly explained. "We hiked up on Diamond Head, we took a helicopter tour of the island, we went to Pearl Harbor, we ate tons of pineapple—oh, lots of things."

"Sounds like a blast," he commented.

"It totally rocked!" Molly exclaimed, looking up at her uncle with a huge grin.

He smiled back at her.

"Did it rock, Maggie?" Peter asked, turning his head again toward her.

"Totally." Maggie broke out in a smile.

CHAPTER 8
The Girl in the Bathroom

SATURDAY ROLLED AROUND and it was time for Emily to fulfill her promise to Camille. She and Molly filled in as servers at the Zigon Corporation's Gala at the Hilton Hotel. After hours on her feet, Emily was ready for the evening to be over.

Once most of the guests had left, she and Molly headed to the ladies room to freshen up. As they entered the restroom, they heard the sound of someone weeping in one of the three stalls. They glanced suspiciously at each other. Before either could utter a word, a beautiful young Asian woman in a sexy, short black dress and strappy high-heeled shoes opened the door to one of the stalls. She stepped out, carefully dabbing her eyes with a piece of toilet paper, as if she was trying not to ruin her considerable eye makeup.

"Are you okay?" Emily stepped close and asked her in a calm, sympathetic tone.

Her eyes were lowered and she seemed reluctant to meet Emily's gaze. Before the young woman could respond, another Asian woman, this one middle-aged and wearing a khaki pantsuit and an angry expression, shouted something curt to the younger female in their native language. The young lady nodded her head, as if she was agreeing to the woman's harsh words. The older woman grabbed the girl by the arm and practically dragged her out of the bathroom, continuing the tongue-lashing.

"What on earth was that about?" a wide-eyed Molly questioned.

"I have no idea." Emily shrugged.

"Looks like that girl was in trouble with her mother."

"Could be," Emily muttered, looking toward the door before turning to the sink to wash her hands. "I remember one time my mom caught me dressed like that. I had snuck out on a date with an older boy that my folks didn't approve of." Emily grabbed a couple of paper towels and dried her hands. "My mom marched right out onto the dance floor and grabbed me by the arm. Then she dragged me out to the car. She and my dad grounded me for a month."

"How old were you?" Molly asked.

"Fifteen."

"Well, that girl was a lot older than that," Molly commented. "She looked at least eighteen or nineteen to me."

"I don't think so. She was wobbling on those heels like she wasn't used to wearing them. And that sexy dress and all that make up could make any teenage girl look older."

"I'd hate to be the guy she was with if my mom had caught me doing that."

"You're right," Emily laughed. "Camille would rip him a new one, not to mention what your dad would do to him."

~*~

A few days later, Molly phoned Emily and asked if she'd go shopping with her. Camille's birthday was coming up and Molly wanted help to find a gift for her mom.

"Why don't I pick you up tomorrow after you get home from school, say four o'clock, and we'll head for the mall," Emily suggested. "We can get something to eat at the food court—my treat."

"Sounds cool. See you at four."

As promised, Emily stopped by to collect Molly for their shopping date. Rather than Emily driving, Molly insisted they take her new car. Her dad had just bought her a small, economical late-model compact to drive to school. She no longer had to take the bus for her senior year, and she was happy to show it off.

"Okay, okay. Let's take your car." Emily gave in, remembering what it had been like to be seventeen and the thrill of freedom she experienced at having her own vehicle.

As they drove through the neighborhood, an older silver Mercedes began backing down its driveway and into the street.

"Watch out for the car backing out," Emily warned,

instinctively putting her hand out.

"Don't worry, I see it." Molly slowed down, almost to a stop, and the other car drove past them in the opposite direction.

"Did you see that?" Molly snapped.

"See what?" Emily looked around.

"The car that backed out."

"It was a family in it, wasn't it?"

"I mean the girl in the backseat. Did you see the girl in the backseat? The one closest to the window—she had these sad, dark eyes." Molly's words came with growing intensity. "I think I know her."

"I'm not surprised, she's your neighbor."

"No, Emily, I think it was the girl from the restroom at the hotel—the one that was crying."

"Are you sure?" Emily twisted in her seat and looked for the car, but it was too far away, so she turned back forward. "She probably goes to your school, don't you think?"

"I haven't seen her there, but I'm sure she's the girl from the hotel. Oh, Em, she looked so sad."

"Maybe her parents grounded her for life because of her little stunt. I'd be sad, too."

"Or worse. What if they beat her?"

"There's no reason to think that, Molly."

"What if they're not her parents? What if they kidnapped her and are holding her against her will?"

"Where are you getting those outlandish thoughts? You're letting your imagination run wild."

Molly peered in her rearview mirror. "I guess you're right."

"I can't imagine why you would even think such

crazy things, Mol."

"Probably because of the assembly today."

"What assembly?"

"We had an assembly at school with a special speaker from the A-twenty-one Project. She spoke on human trafficking and how it's everywhere now. Some of the things that lady said were pretty shocking. I guess it's still on my mind and it made me wonder about that girl."

"Oh, that's what this is about. I think that sort of thing mostly happens in big cities, not in quiet small towns like Paradise Valley."

"Not according to the speaker today."

"Really? I'm surprised to hear that."

"Did you see there were three girls in the backseat?" Molly looked over at Emily as they came to a stop sign.

"No, sorry, I didn't. You had a better vantage point than I did."

"Like you said, it's probably nothing."

"Yeah. They're probably just her sisters."

~*~

A few days later, Emily dropped by Camille's for a short visit, wondering if Molly had mentioned the Asian girls to her. Camille said she did mention them, but she tried to tell her daughter that Emily was likely right, it was just parents trying to raise teenage daughters who wanted to be with boys their parents didn't approve of. Molly seemed to accept it, Camille said.

"Can you imagine anyone thinking we have sex

slaves here in Paradise Valley?" Camille shook her head and sipped her iced tea.

"It does sound pretty far-fetched." Emily ripped open a packet of sweetener and stirred it into her tea.

"What sounds far-fetched?" Peter asked as he entered the kitchen.

"Oh, hello, Peter." Emily smiled to hide the rush of warmth she felt, a little surprised by his presence.

"Emily and I were talking about the possibility of human trafficking in our area." Camille took another sip of tea. "The idea of sex slaves in Paradise Valley, I think it's highly unlikely."

"After the investigative reporting I did back east, I believe it could be anywhere." Peter pulled out a chair and sank down onto it. "I think most people would be surprised to learn it might be in their own backyards."

"Oh, pish-posh." Camille eyed her brother.

Emily giggled at Camille's odd reply.

Peter rolled his eyes. "Our mom used to say that when she thought something was a bunch of bologna."

"That's right," Camille agreed, wagging her spoon at her brother, "a bunch of bologna."

Emily pushed her chair out and stood to leave. "I'd better get going. I have some errands to run. Thanks for the tea, Cam."

"Was it something I said?" Peter grinned. "I didn't mean to chase you off."

"No, really, I have to be going."

"Don't forget, Saturday is the season opener for Boise State football. Everyone's invited over to watch the game here," Camille said. "I have some amazing food planned—pulled pork, nachos supreme, chicken and bacon sliders, hot parmesan artichoke dip."

"I'm getting hungry just hearing about it." Peter's eyes lit up as he commented.

"What can I bring?" Emily offered.

"Don't worry about it." Camille waved her freshly manicured hand as she stood up. "It's all taken care of."

"I know I'm not the cook you are, Cam, but I can certainly stop by the store and pick something up."

"Why don't you bring drinks, then?" Camille relented.

Emily smiled and gave Camille a light hug. "See you both later." She turned to leave but stopped and spun back around. "I almost forgot to tell you, I'll be bringing Colin, too."

"Colin? That's wonderful, Em." Camille rushed at her and gave her a hard squeeze. "I knew he'd eventually come back, but you never said a word."

Camille released her firm hold on Emily and she caught her breath. "Until I knew for certain, I didn't want to say anything. You'd all be asking me about it, driving me crazy."

"So I finally get to meet this mystery man who holds your heart." Peter looked into Emily's eyes, locking on her gaze.

Was that envy she saw? "Yes, you'll finally get to meet him. I think you guys will hit it off." She hoped they would, anyway.

"I look forward to it." He slowly broke his gaze from her and turned his attention to his sister. "Is Maggie coming, by chance?"

"Why yes, I believe she is." Camille glanced at Emily and raised her eyebrows as if to say *Is he interested in her?*

Emily hoped so. She remembered her conversation with Isabel about this very thing. The best way to get over one love is to find another, they had agreed.

~*~

As Emily pulled away from Camille's house, it was about four o'clock in the afternoon. She encountered the same older Mercedes backing out of the driveway and slowed for it. Hoping to be inconspicuous, she casually glanced over at the car to check out its occupants, trying not to stare. A stocky Asian gentleman was behind the wheel, and the older woman from the hotel ladies room was in the front seat.

As they pulled by Emily, she glanced in the backseat and saw the girl from the restroom seated behind the driver, with two other young women in the back. The girl was staring back at her with hauntingly sad eyes—just as Molly had described her.

After her recent conversations with Molly and then with Peter, her interest was piqued about this family. She decided she would follow the car and see where it was headed. She turned around in a neighbor's driveway and followed the sedan at a safe distance.

The car headed out of Paradise Valley, toward Boise, about fifteen minutes away. Emily watched as the car pulled into a driveway on Overland Road and parked on the side of the small, single-story building.

It was one of a row of small older homes that had been converted into businesses. Emily pulled her car to the curb, across the street from the enterprise, to watch.

The man opened the car door and the three girls climbed out of the backseat and went into the rear of the building with the woman.

This location felt familiar to Emily. She shielded the sun from her eyes as it glinted off the marquis sign—it was the Jade Thai Spa.

That's it! She realized this place was familiar because she had followed a client's husband to this establishment late one night. It promoted itself as a massage parlor, but the husband, when confronted by his wife and the credit card bills, admitted he went there for sex. Thinking of the young girls she just observed being escorted inside, Emily's stomach lurched.

She recalled that Isabel had confided in her that the Feds might be watching the place. Emily decided she'd do a little reconnaissance of her own. She dashed across the busy street and tried to open the front door but found it locked. Knocking casually on the door, she hoped one of the girls would open it and she could get a better look around.

No one came. She knocked harder. Still no answer. She slinked to the window to try to get a peek inside, but the blinds were drawn shut. There was a sliver of a gap between the blinds and the window frame where she could see movement, noticing a woman pass by the window.

Emily stepped back and went to the door again. She raised her fist to knock once more, but the door opened a bit and the older woman stuck her head out.

"Not open yet," she snapped with a heavy Asian accent.

"When will you be open?" Emily tried to ask as

sweetly as she could.

"Open one hour. What you want?"

"You do massages, right?"

"Yeah." The woman sounded suspicious of Emily.

"I'd like to buy a gift certificate for a one-hour massage. I have this friend—"

Emily stuck her foot in the door and tried to get a peek beyond the woman, but she would only open the door wide enough to poke her head out.

"We no do gift certificates," the woman cut her off, then pushed Emily's shoe back with her own and shut the door.

Emily walked away and sprinted across the street, back to her car. *That's no way to treat a potential customer, unless their primary income stream is not massages. Was there some secret knock I should have used?*

The mystery surrounding the girl from the hotel was growing more suspicious by the minute.

CHAPTER 9
Lunch at Goodwood

ON HER DRIVE BACK to Paradise Valley, Emily decided to phone Isabel and bring her up to speed on what she'd found. It was going on five o'clock and Isabel would likely still be at the office.

"Hey, girl. What's up?" Isabel could be heard shutting the drawer of a metal file cabinet, and Emily assumed she was getting ready to call it a day.

"Just wanted to check in and let you know what I've discovered."

"About Evan?" Isabel's voice became low and serious.

"No, nothing new on that front. I was talking about the massage parlors. Remember, you were going to check and see if the Jade Thai Spa was on the Fed's watch list."

"That's right. I've just been so slammed here at work I almost forgot. I did send an email out to someone

I know and asked about that. Give me a sec and I'll check my email, see if I got a response."

Emily could imagine that Isabel was running her finger down the screen.

"No, I don't see anything yet. Let me write myself a note to check on it again tomorrow."

Emily heard the sound of a drawer opening and what she thought sounded like Isabel rummaging through it.

"I can't find a pad of sticky notes to save my life," Isabel declared. "Oh, there it is. So, tell me, why is this massage parlor so important to you?"

"I think they're running under-aged girls as prostitutes out of that place."

"That's probably why they're being watched," Isabel said.

"But why the Feds? I could understand the local cops, but the Feds?"

"I'm not free to say, Em."

"They suspect a sex slave ring, don't they?"

"What makes you say that?"

"Something I saw," Emily replied. "Why don't the Feds go in there and rescue those girls?"

"I'm really not at liberty to talk about it," Isabel hedged. "But, hypothetically, let's say that was what's going on there, my guess is the FBI is gathering the evidence they need to make an arrest. They can't simply go busting in there on a hunch."

"I get it." Emily hoped for those girls' sake the Feds moved quickly. If not, maybe she could help move things along.

"Oh, by the way, Em," Isabel said, breaking into

Emily's thoughts, "Jethro's back in town. He called me today just to check in, he said."

"What do you say we try what I suggested before?" Emily looked in her rearview mirrors. Just the mention of Jethro's name prompted her to do it. "You invite him to lunch and I'll stick a tracking device on his car."

"I'm already a step ahead of you. I invited him to lunch tomorrow at Goodwood at twelve thirty. All you have to do is text me when you've done it, so I know when to let him leave."

"You got it." Emily figured it should be easy enough to find his black BMW in the parking lot, especially with Virginia plates.

"I better get going. Traffic's going to be murder."

"I'll see you at Camille's on Saturday for the game?"

"We'll be there. I hear you're bringing a special guest."

"Boy, news travels fast." Emily laughed.

"Only when it's told to Camille." Isabel laughed, too.

Emily said her good-byes and clicked off her call with Isabel. She peered into her rearview mirrors again, almost expecting to see the black sedan following her. She blinked—could it be? Three cars behind her was a black car.

She quickly pulled to the curb and stopped, watching the next few cars go by. As the black BMW whizzed past, she caught a quick glimpse. She could have sworn it was Delia McCall with her long brunette hair brushing her shoulders and her large dark sunglasses. *Was Delia following me? Or were we only going in similar directions?*

Seeing her again gave Emily an idea. She decided she'd call Delia and invite her to lunch—at Goodwood—and see what sparks might fly. She punched in Delia's phone number and waited while it rang.

"Hello," came Delia's low sultry voice. "Emily?"

Emily knew she must have seen her name come up on her caller ID. "Yes, Delia. It's Emily."

"How are you, dear? It's been ages since we've talked."

"I know it has, and I'm sorry for that. I saw someone this afternoon that reminded me of you, and it gave me the idea that I should call and invite you to lunch. Are you busy tomorrow?"

"I'll have to check my calendar when I get back to the office, but I think I'm free. Where would you like to meet?"

"So you're driving?"

"Yes, I had a business meeting this morning, but I'm headed back to my office. I'll check my schedule when I get there. What time were you thinking?"

"How about one o'clock at Goodwood?"

"That sounds lovely, Emily. I'd love to chat and catch up."

She sounds pleasant enough. Let's tighten the screws, put a little pressure on her, and see how she reacts when she sees Jethro, or should I say dear old Dad.

"Sorry, Delia, I have another call coming in that I have to take. It looks like it's Colin."

"I'll let you run, then. Give my love to him, won't

you?"

"Sure thing." Emily hung up from one call and picked up the other. "Hey, Colin."

"Hello, gorgeous."

His voice was deep and sensual, and she enjoyed it every time she heard it. "Have you left San Francisco yet?"

"Tomorrow, first light. Then I'm on the road home."

"I can't wait to have you back, Colin." The thought of him returning to Paradise Valley for good made her heart beat a little faster and a soft heat radiated over her body.

"I should be there by dinnertime."

"Let's go out." Emily imagined a romantic candlelit dinner at a fancy restaurant to celebrate Colin's return to Paradise Valley.

"No, I'd rather stay in. I'll be on the road all day. I'd like to have a nice quiet dinner at your place and just be alone with you."

"You know I'm not a very good cook." She was good at a lot of things, but there was no denying that cooking wasn't one of them.

"Oh, honey, that's what take-out is for."

Emily couldn't help but laugh out loud. "Well, I'm not *that* bad."

She told him about the football party Camille and Jonathan were planning at their place on Saturday and that all their friends would be there. She filled him in on what she had learned about Jethro's possible connection to Delia McCall and how the mysterious dark-haired woman in the photo with Evan was likely Jethro's daughter. Wracking her brain for any other news, she was intent on not hiding anything else from Colin.

"Oh, and another thing…" she started to say.

"What's that?"

"There's something I'm investigating where I will need to enlist your help."

"Sounds intriguing. What's going on?" Colin asked.

"There's a possibility of a prostitution ring operating around here, and it may have ties to Camille's neighborhood."

"Prostitution ring? Boy, that really surprises me. I've had some experience dealing with that in San Francisco, but I didn't think I'd have to deal with it in a quiet place like Paradise Valley."

"Looks like you may have to." Emily went on and described her and Molly's experiences with the suspicious Asians and what she had discovered about their business.

"I don't understand why you're involved, though," he said.

"I'm a concerned citizen, doing what I can. If human trafficking is happening right under our noses, how can I sit and do nothing, knowing what those girls are being put through night after night?"

"Shouldn't you report what you know and let law enforcement handle it?"

"Without concrete evidence, they'd just laugh at me."

"You're probably right, but—"

"Colin, what if someone had taken a girl you knew, let's say your sister, and forced her into a life of prostitution? I know you'd be the first to jump in to rescue her. Well, those girls aren't commodities, they're somebody's daughters."

"I get it, Emily. I'll help in any way I can, just don't do anything dangerous before I get there."

~*~

The next day Emily showed up at the Goodwood restaurant at twelve forty-five. She drove around the parking lot, scanning each vehicle until she spotted the black BMW with Virginia plates. She swung her white Volvo into a space a respectable distance away and sauntered over to the BMW, doing her best to inconspicuously slink by it as she stuck a magnetic GPS device to the car's frame.

Emily casually waltzed back to her car and texted Isabel that the deed was done. Now she needed to sit and wait for Delia to show up. She hoped her little ploy would prove useful.

Right on time, Delia entered the lot and parked her dark BMW. Emily jumped out of her car and headed to the restaurant, reaching the door at the same time as Delia.

"Hello, Delia." Emily greeted her with a quick hug and pulled the heavy glass door open.

"Oh, Emily. It's so good to see you." Delia's dark eyes twinkled with apparent sincerity.

Delia was a stunning woman in her early forties, dressed in a handsomely tailored business suit in fine tan wool with a fitted pencil skirt. Her dark waves danced around her shoulders as she teetered to the door in her brown-leather designer high heels.

Emily felt a bit underdressed in her black jeans and cropped black-leather jacket over a scoop-necked white sweater. She politely smiled as she held the door open and followed Delia to the hostess station, glancing nonchalantly around the crowded restaurant. She spotted Isabel sitting opposite Jethro, along the window side of the room, with his back to them. *Perfect.*

"Table for two?" the hostess asked.

"Yes, along the windows, please," Emily requested.

"Right this way." The hostess grabbed a couple of menus from her station and led the women to their table, just beyond Isabel and Jethro. Emily filed in right behind the hostess with Delia trailing close by.

Isabel looked up as they approached the table and her eyes widened momentarily as she appeared to try to hide her astonishment.

"Isabel," Emily said as they walked past, pausing at her table. "What a nice surprise."

"Isn't it, though," Isabel remarked.

"Delia, you remember Isabel, don't you?" Emily watched Delia's eyes for any signs of discomfort at being in Jethro's presence.

"Yes, of course. How nice to see you again, Isabel."

"And this is my friend. We call him Jethro." Isabel looked at him, then her gaze went to Delia. "Jethro, this is Delia McCall."

Emily picked up on Isabel doing the same thing she was, watching for any signs of recognition in Jetho's expression. Emily noticed a slight flash of recognition in Delia's dark eyes, but when she glanced at Jethro, he was controlled and unflinching.

Delia put her hand out and he shook it. "It's a

pleasure to meet you, Jethro."

"The pleasure is mine, Ms. McCall."

If there was surprise in his eyes, Emily missed it. It could be simply a coincidence they both had the name Banderas. Not every person who has the same last name is related to one another, Emily had to admit. However, if they did turn out to be father and daughter, or related in some way as suspected, there had to be a reason why they worked at keeping their relationship secret. She was anxious to get Isabel's read on their interaction.

"It was nice to see you too, Emily," Jethro uttered as the women walked away. Emily chose not to reply, acting as if she hadn't heard him. The very sight of him brought visions of the man peeking into her windows, and likely being the person who had been breaking in, so it was all she could do to bite her tongue and not tear into him over it. When she had hatched the plan to invite Delia to lunch to monitor her response to him, she hadn't counted on her own intense reaction.

"You know that man, too?" Delia leaned forward and whispered, taking her seat at the next table, facing toward Jethro.

Emily nodded casually, back to back with Isabel. She picked up her menu and began reading it, not wanting to give away her true feelings. Her cheeks grew hot and the blood pounded in her head sitting this close to her possible stalker. She hoped the heat had not turned her cheeks red. "Let's see what's on the menu. I'm starved."

THE CHAIN OF LIES

CHAPTER 10
Welcome Home, Colin

EMILY UNDID THE PLASTIC WRAP on the baby back ribs she had brought home from Goodwood for her welcome-home dinner for Colin. She figured she could do an adequate job of baking the potatoes and making a green salad herself, but she knew that man loved his ribs. She rewrapped them tightly in foil and set them in the oven at a low temperature to stay warm.

She had borrowed a box overflowing with strings of white twinkle lights from Camille and strung them around the deck and the garden. This was the first time she had invited anyone out into her backyard since Evan's death. Until now, she couldn't bear to be out there in the garden they had designed together, planted together, and lovingly tended together. A beautiful white gazebo sat at the end of the garden, the gazebo that Evan had built for her as a wedding anniversary gift one year.

When Evan was killed, she could not bring herself

to spend time out there anymore. It brought back too many painful memories. She had hired out the care and maintenance of the lawn and the flowering bushes and trees. For the past year, it had been meticulously maintained by The Green Thumb, but no one except the landscaper ever took the opportunity to enjoy it.

A couple of hours earlier, Colin had phoned to let her know when he thought he'd be there. After stopping by his apartment for a quick shower, he promised to rush over to her house. He wanted nothing more than to be with her, he had said.

As she dashed around her house, finalizing last-minute preparations before dressing for dinner, Emily daydreamed about her man walking through the door and sweeping her up in his arms. Thoughts of everything else going on in her life would have to be put on hold. She wanted this evening to be perfect.

She pushed open the kitchen window over the sink to let the cool fresh air into the bungalow before assembling the salad and storing it in the refrigerator. She had already scrubbed a couple of plump baking potatoes, rubbed them with olive oil and sprinkled coarse salt on the outside before setting them on a cookie sheet, planning to pop them in the oven as soon as Colin arrived. Already sitting in the refrigerator was a decadent chocolate torte Camille had prepared for them, as a surprise, garnished with a swirl of whipped cream and a handful of fresh raspberries. Camille had presented it to Emily when she stopped by to nab the twinkle lights.

She set the round patio table with a crisp white-linen table cloth and her best dishes. In the center was an array of tapered candles of various lengths, which were seated in a mixture of different styles of crystal candle holders set among fresh greenery, waiting until the last minute to be lit. The sky on that early September evening was clear with a few wispy pink and gold clouds, compliments of the warm glow of the setting sun.

"Perfect," she sighed.

She kicked off her flip flops by the back door and padded down the hall to her bedroom to change. A shiver of excitement feathered up her back.

On her shopping trip with Molly the other day, Emily had picked up a new dress to wear for this evening—a short, off-one-shoulder number in a beautiful shade of aubergine. Molly had told her she looked fabulous in it and she had to agree as she studied her reflection in the full-length mirror. She pulled her soft golden curls up into a twist, held it in place with a pearl-studded comb, stuck her dangly silver earrings in her ears, and took a moment to admire her handiwork.

The sun was going down and the house was beginning to get dark. Emily flipped the front porch light on, then turned on lamps in the living room, which cast a warm glow out to the wide front porch. She peeked out the big living room window to see if Colin was coming yet and noticed a black BMW across the street pull away from the curb as soon as she spotted it.

Though it was close to dusk, the street lights had not come on yet. The dim lighting made it difficult to make out the driver of the car, but Emily had a good idea who it was.

Jethro's back in town. She thought about checking the GPS monitor, but decided it could wait until later, being pretty certain she already knew what it would read. Emily traipsed through the house and out the back door to the deck to plug in the twinkle lights and light the candles. She was not going to let that man ruin her perfect evening with Colin.

She ambled back inside and stuck the potatoes in the oven to start baking. She turned her favorite instrumental music on low to fill the house with a romantic ambience, and she lit the sandalwood candle in the entry. The mood was set. Now all she needed was her man.

A light rap on the front door sent her heart racing. She flung the door open and there stood Colin smiling with a thick bouquet of chocolate roses in one hand. Pure joy spread across her face as he stepped in and drew her into his arms. In an instant, his soft warm lips covered hers in a long, slow kiss. She floated off to heaven. His arms held her passionately against him and she melted into his embrace. She pushed the door shut with her foot and let his kisses close the emotional distance between them.

"I love you, Emily Parker," he whispered in her ear as he let her take a breath. He tenderly kissed the curve of her neck as it flowed down to her bare shoulder. She was sure his lips could feel the fine layer of prickles that shimmered across her skin, responding to his words and his touch.

"I love you, too," she answered. What more was there to say? They held each other for the longest time, or at least that's how it felt. He kissed her again, then released his embrace.

"These are for you." Colin held out the bouquet of

chocolate roses he had brought for her. "I could have gotten red ones, but these will last a lot longer." There were three dozen of them.

Emily grinned with delight at his thoughtful gift. He knew of her fondness for anything chocolate. She would smile and think of him each time she stuck one in her mouth and thoroughly enjoyed it. She took the bouquet from his hand and pushed up on her tiptoes to give him a quick kiss of gratitude, but as soon as her lips touched his, his arms enveloped her once more.

When he let go of her, she drew in a deep breath to steady herself. "As much as I would enjoy kissing you all night, there's something I want to show you." She stepped out of his hold and took him by the hand. She led him through the kitchen, laying the roses on the table as they passed by, and took him out the back door to the deck and the garden.

"Is that ribs I smell?" Colin asked, craning his neck as he glanced back toward the kitchen, while she pulled him out the door.

"Yes, but that's not the best part."

Holding her hand, he stood still, in quiet awe, gazing across the garden. "Oh, Emily, this is beautiful." He slowly looked around at all she had done. The table was set for dining, with candles lit, and the garden sparkled with twinkling lights. "You've never brought me out here before."

"You're right, I haven't. I couldn't before. But now, well, I thought it was time."

"You even put some lights on the gazebo." He gazed down at her with a glint of recognition in his eyes, and she was certain he understood what she meant by that gesture.

"I see you decided to get a man instead of a dog to protect you, Emily." Mr. Cooke, her neighbor, was peeking over the fence at them. "That'll keep those peeping Toms away."

"What peeping Toms?" Colin asked, glancing from Mr. Cooke to Emily.

"Thank you, Mr. Cooke, for watching out for me. Now, go and have a good evening."

"It is going to be a pleasant night tonight," the elderly man replied, glancing up at the sky.

"No, really, go."

"Emily," Colin lightly scolded.

"I can take a hint, young lady." The neighbor chuckled. The sound of the door closing told them he went back inside his house.

"What did he mean about the peeping Tom?"

"You know how someone has gotten into my house a couple of times, looking for something related to Evan's death? At least that's what I believe it is."

"Yes." Colin crossed his arms as he stared into Emily's face, apparently waiting for the rest of the story.

"My neighbor saw some guy peeking into my windows one morning and he yelled at him and scared him off. That's all."

"That's all? You say it like it's nothing."

"It's not nothing, but I didn't want you turning it into a big deal, especially since there wasn't a thing you could do but worry from so far away."

He gathered her in his arms. "Well, I'm not in California now." He kissed her neck and leaned his cheek against her temple. "We're going to figure out who this character is and put a stop to him."

"Mr. Cooke saw the guy get away in a black car with Virginia plates, which Isabel and I think must belong to our mysterious FBI guy, Jethro." Emily told Colin about Isabel's lunch with Jethro that day and how she was able to stick a tracking device on his car while they were in the restaurant.

"Have you been tracking his movements since this afternoon?"

"Yes, but he went straight home." Emily leaned her head on his shoulder, but pulled it away as she remembered having seen Jethro after that. "Well, that is, until right before you got here. I did see a black BMW on the street when I peeked out the front window, looking for you. I'm pretty sure it was him."

"But you didn't see if the tracker showed it was him?"

"No. I've been so busy getting everything ready for this evening, then you showed up. You know, this didn't all happen on its own." She gestured toward the deck and garden with a sweep of her hand.

"It looks wonderful, Emily, and I appreciate it, but we will have to check that tracker."

She nodded her agreement. "Later."

His lips turned up in a mischievous smile as he snaked a hand around her waist and planted another kiss on her lips. "By the way, did I tell you how stunning you look tonight?"

"No." She dipped her chin and looked up at him through her lashes.

"Well, you do. I can't take my eyes off of you, Babe, or my hands." He pulled her into another passionate embrace, standing in the faint glow of the tiny lights and the sun setting at twilight. He kissed her so deeply her knees went weak.

A loud blast emanated from the kitchen, sounding like a small bomb going off.

"What on earth?" Mr. Cooke's voice could be heard from over the fence.

Emily and Colin shot each other a look of surprise, dropped their hold on one another, and ran into the house.

"What do you think that was?" she asked, her gaze bouncing around the kitchen as they walked through it, making their way through the rest of the house. She ran to her bedroom and checked the nightstand for her gun. It was there, undisturbed.

Colin checked the living room, then the front porch.

Emily looked in the guest room, then met him back in the entry. "I can't imagine what that was."

"A car backfiring, maybe?" Colin shrugged his shoulders.

"It sounded like it came from inside the house."

"I don't know what to tell you." Colin planted his hands on his hips. "We've checked everywhere."

"Well, before they burn, I'd better check on the ribs and the potatoes. Maybe having dinner will calm us down. Why don't you pour a couple of glasses of wine? The food should be ready in a minute." Emily meandered back to the kitchen to see about the food, with Colin close behind.

She opened the oven to take the ribs out. "I found it!" she exclaimed.

"Found what?" Colin peeked over her shoulder.

"The source of the explosion."

A deep belly laugh roared out of Colin. Emily had forgotten to pierce the baking potatoes and they'd exploded all over the inside of her oven.

Emily grimaced. "I guess we'll be having ribs and salad tonight." She began to laugh too, but her laughter soon turned to tears. She had wanted the evening to be perfect and she'd messed it up.

"Emily," Colin said tenderly as he put his hand gently under her chin and lifted her face, kissing her cheek where a tear had trickled down. "I can have potatoes anywhere, any time. The only thing I want tonight is you." He encircled her with his strong arms and held her close.

They stood in each other's arms for a prolonged moment.

"Sorry to be such a cry baby." She leaned her head against his chest and listened to the beat of his heart, feeling safe in his arms. "I'm so glad to have you back."

"There's nowhere else I'd rather be." He lightly kissed the tip of her nose and let her go.

Colin poured two goblets of red wine and took them out to the deck. Emily plated the dinner and carried the dishes to the patio table.

"Mmm, the ribs look amazing. I didn't know you knew how to barbecue ribs."

"I don't. Remember your suggestion for take-out?"

Colin laughed. "Either way, they look delicious." He licked his lips and grinned at her.

"Maybe later we can have dessert."

Colin's eyes perked up.

"Down boy. I meant Camille's chocolate torte."

~*~

After dinner, they went inside and settled on the sofa. He stretched his arm across the back of the couch and she curled into the curve of his arm. They talked about his starting his job again as the detective for the Paradise Valley Police Department, about some of the cases she had been working on, and what they hoped for the future.

She reminded him of the story she had previously shared about the Asian girl she and Molly had found crying in the restroom of the hotel and the suspicions they had that maybe the girl wasn't just a rebellious teenager, but something far worse.

"Let's not talk about prostitution rings my first night back." Colin kissed the side of Emily's temple. "This evening is about us."

"Yes, you're right. No more shop talk tonight." She smiled and looked up into his eyes and put her hand gently on his cheek.

He dipped his head down and kissed her softly. "I'm so glad to be back."

Before she could respond, he moved in for another kiss, this time more forceful, more urgent than the last. His arm came off the back of the sofa and drew her closer to him, pressing her body against his.

Colin's cell phone began to ring. Emily started to pull away so he could answer it. "Leave it," he said. "They can leave a message if it's important." He kissed her again.

After five rings it stopped, but only momentarily.

Again it began to ring, but he did not try to answer it, instead letting it go to voicemail. However, the third time the ringing started, Colin looked at Emily and shrugged apologetically. He dug the phone out of his pocket.

"Hello, Colin Andrews."

"Colin, this is Ernie."

"Hey, Ernie." He looked at Emily, with one arm still around her, as she listened to his side of the conversation. "This isn't a good time to talk."

Ernie was an older officer that had temporarily taken over as detective while Colin was on his leave of absence. He had been a friend of the Andrews family for a long time and had helped Colin secure the job in Paradise Valley in the first place.

"I'm not calling just to chat, boy, I need your help. I know you're not officially starting back as police detective until tomorrow, but we have a situation."

Colin disengaged his arm from Emily and stood up. "What is it?"

"A guy walking along the green belt by the river found a dead body."

"Tonight?"

"Yeah, about an hour ago. A young Asian woman, maybe fifteen to twenty years old, beaten pretty badly."

Colin's gaze shot to Emily and she stood up and listened.

"Where's the guy that found her?"

"In the back of my vehicle. I thought you'd want in on this."

"You're at the scene?"

"Yeah."

"And the body?"

"The medical examiner and the CSI team just arrived. They're going over the area where the body was found. We have the place cordoned off."

"Don't let them touch the body until I get there."

"The doc doesn't always listen to me, but I'll do my best."

"We're on our way."

"We?"

"I'm at Emily's."

"You sure you want to bring her down here? It's pretty grizzly."

"As if you think I could stop her."

Ernie snickered. "Guess you're right about that, boss."

CHAPTER 11
Body in the River

"WHAT BODY?" Emily pleaded.

Colin hung up his phone and stuffed it in his pocket. "Grab your shoes, we have to go."

"What's going on?" she asked, slipping into her flats by the front door and grabbing a jacket from the hall closet.

"The body of a young female was found by the river—Asian, Ernie said. I'll fill you in on the drive over." He held the door open for her.

"Oh, Colin, no." Emily gasped as she crossed the threshold. She felt her chest constricting as she envisioned the scene in her mind, wondering if it could be the girl from the hotel restroom.

As they drove, Colin relayed what Ernie had told him on the phone. "Now, I know what you're thinking, but let's not jump to conclusions."

"How do you know what I'm thinking?" Emily

questioned, crossing her arms as she frowned at him.

"The prostitution ring?"

"You say *prostitution ring* like those girls have any choice in the matter. Call it what it is—a sex slave ring."

"Maybe, but we need to check the facts first. This could be totally unrelated."

Emily crossed her arms tighter and sat silently, her eyes staring straight ahead. Her thoughts went back to the night she and Molly happened upon the girl, crying in the restroom. She hoped the dead female was not the one from the hotel. If she had known then what she knew now, or what she thought she knew, perhaps there was something more she could have done to rescue her.

But how could she have known? It looked like a spat between mother and daughter, much like the ones she'd had with her own mother. And, in fact, that might still be the case.

Emily could see emergency lights flashing up ahead. Colin turned onto a road that led to a small parking lot near the entrance to the green belt that ran for miles along the Boise River. Several police cars, a body retrieval vehicle, and the CSI van crowded the area. Yellow crime scene tape was strung between trees and benches to cordon off the area from curious bystanders.

Abruptly parking his Jeep, Colin and Emily jumped out and rushed to the scene. He ducked under the tape and held it up for Emily to squeeze under, and they headed directly to the body, still in the water.

Dr. Walters was standing on the bank, bending over, trying to get a better look at the body bobbing in the river.

"Hey, Doc. What do we have?" Colin asked as he

came to stand next to him.

The white-haired medical examiner straightened and glanced over at him. "Hello, Colin. I heard you were coming back."

"Just in time, I see."

Emily walked up and stood next to Colin.

"Hello, Ms. Parker. You helping with this case?"

"Possibly," Emily responded, glancing over at Colin.

"What can you tell me, Doc?" Colin asked.

"The body appears to be that of a young woman, maybe late teens. She looks like she's been beaten. Other than that, I can't tell you too much until we get her out of the water."

"Ernie!" Colin turned and shouted, getting the officer's attention. "Can you and the boys pull the body out of the water?"

Ernie waved his acknowledgement and stepped off to gather his guys. Several officers had to wade waist deep in the water in order to pull the body out. With Ernie's seniority, he managed to stay on the riverbank and he looked quite relieved to be doing so. They carried the dead girl a few yards and hoisted her up onto an awaiting gurney, readied by the CSIs with an opened black-vinyl body bag.

Emily followed the men and the body as they wrestled it into the open bag. When the officers backed away, she stepped in and studied the girl's face, relieved that even with the bruising she could tell it was not the girl from the hotel.

Colin and the doc stood across the gurney from Emily.

"Just like I thought," Dr. Walters confirmed as he did a cursory exam, "beaten pretty badly, but I won't know cause of death until I get her back to the morgue for autopsy. She does have signs of drug use, so I'll have to run a tox screen, get her blood work, see what comes back."

"Is rape a possibility, Doc?" Emily piped in.

"I can't say just yet, Ms. Parker, but I'll do that exam when I get her back to my lab. As soon as I'm done, I'll get the results to Colin. I can tell you one thing, though."

"What's that?" Colin asked.

"My CSI, Jackson, says it doesn't look like she was killed here—no signs of struggle. Looks like the body was dumped in the river and she caught on some thick branches in the water. That's where the guy found her, bobbing in the river where the officers pulled her out."

"That's good to know," Colin replied.

Dr. Walters zipped the dark plastic body bag shut over the young woman and motioned to the body retrieval team to take her away.

"I'll let you know as soon as I come up with something." Dr. Walters picked up his medical bag and turned to walk away. "Glad to have you back, Andrews," he called out over his shoulder.

"Thanks, Doc," Colin replied before turning his attention to Emily. "I'm going to have one of the officers take you home."

"I want to stay," she argued.

"I'm going to be here for a while, interviewing the man who found the body, talking to the CSIs and stuff. There's no need for you to be here. I'll call you in the morning."

"But I want to stay."

"Not this time, Emily, please."

She wanted to make her case to stay, but she could see there was no point in arguing about it. Colin had a job to do and it needed his full attention. "Okay, okay, you win. As much as I hate to, I'll go home."

"Thank you." He looked in her eyes, then leaned down and gave her a quick peck on the cheek before he turned to call for a ride. "Hey, Ernie," he shouted to his man, who came running, "can you get one of the guys to give Emily a ride home?"

"Sure thing, boss."

~*~

Emily went home, did a sweep of her little house, and checked the locks on her doors and windows. Feeling safe and alone, she made herself a cup of tea and crawled into bed to read a mystery novel.

She'd hoped the book would take her mind off Colin and the dead girl, but she couldn't get the ghastly image of the girl's pale, beaten, and lifeless body out of her mind. She read the same page over and over again, finding her mind drifting away from what she was reading, wondering what happened to that girl—and the one from the hotel restroom. Could they be connected?

Unable to sleep, she decided to check the GSP tracker to see what Jethro was up to. She checked the history of his movements since she attached the tracking device that afternoon. It showed him going back to his condo, making a stop along the way, probably at a store, then later taking a route down her street.

Then that must have been him out there before Colin arrived.

Emily checked his movements after leaving her street and saw he had gone back to his place. The vehicle had not moved since.

Exhausted, she climbed back in bed and decided to try to get some sleep. Her cell phone buzzed on the nightstand, and she saw she'd gotten a text from Camille reminding her of the football party the following afternoon.

She turned off the light and snuggled down under the covers. The phone buzzed again. She picked it up and read another text. This time it was from Colin. *Sweet dreams. I love you.*

She texted back, *I love you more.*

~*~

Early the following morning, Colin phoned Emily as promised. He filled her in on all the details of the night before—as much as he legally could. The interview with the man who found the body basically stated that he was walking by and spotted it in the water. Colin's conversation with the CSIs gave him little more than possible tire tracks and squishy footprints in the mud, for which they agreed to cast molds. They would have to wait for Dr. Walters' autopsy and blood test results to know more.

As his first official day back, Colin explained he needed to head into the office early and meet with the Chief of Police. Even though it was Saturday, he was back on the job and wanted to get his office set up.

He chuckled. "I hope Ernie hasn't changed it around too much since I left." Then he promised to pick her up in time to take her to Camille and Jonathan's football party.

After seeing Jethro at lunch the day before, Emily had been thinking about the gun Evan had hidden in the safe deposit box. She remembered their first meeting, along with Isabel, when Emily had asked Jethro a *hypothetical* question about what she should do if she found a gun. He suggested she give it to him to have the Feds run it through ballistics to see if it matched any open cases they had. If not, then they would turn it over to the local police.

Even though Emily and Isabel insisted they were only speaking hypothetically, they could tell Jethro wasn't buying their story. He had asked Isabel several times after that if he could see the gun, and she had told Emily she could tell that excuse was wearing thin.

Her bank was open on Saturday mornings, so Emily decided to go and retrieve the not-so-hypothetical gun from the safe deposit box. It was time to turn the weapon over to Isabel, and only Isabel, to have it tested.

Emily had realized from the first day she'd found the Beretta pistol in the metal box, that Evan had hidden the gun away for a reason. After finding his note a few months ago, saying he had wrestled the weapon away from someone who had attacked him and tried to kill him, she understood why.

She wondered if Jethro's repeated requests to get a look at the gun, under the auspices of having it tested, revealed his desire to take the piece off Emily's hands—

and out of circulation. But why?

If she gave it to him for testing, she feared it could easily disappear and no one would ever see it again. But if she gave it directly to Isabel, it had a better chance of actually reaching the lab.

The old photo she had found in the safe deposit box the first day she'd opened it—the one of Evan with his arm around the young dark-haired beauty—had haunted her as she'd wondered who the woman could be. Now, thanks to Evan's note, she knew. The picture of someone seeking revenge for Natalia's death was coming dangerously into view.

Emily phoned Isabel to be certain she would be home to receive the pistol.

"Yes, I'll be here. Do you want me to come to the bank with you?" Isabel asked.

"No, I don't want to draw any more attention to it than I have to. After I pick it up, I'll head straight to your house."

"Just watch to make sure you're not being followed," Isabel warned.

"I'll have the GPS monitor with me. That way I can make sure that at least Jethro isn't following me."

"He may not be the only one, so keep an eye out."

"I will." Emily said her good-byes and hung up, periodically glancing into her rearview mirror and at the monitor. She made it to the bank without incident.

"Hello, Mr. Johnson." Emily greeted the bank manager as she skirted past the teller stations. "I'd like to get into my safe deposit box, please."

"Certainly, Mrs. Parker. It's nice to see you again." He escorted her to the secure door, punched a few numbers into the keypad, and the door unlocked. He moved to the wall of safe deposit boxes and held his hand out for her key. He stuck his key and hers into the little door and turned them simultaneously. "I'll give you some privacy, ma'am."

"Thank you, Mr. Johnson." She pulled the box out of its space and laid it on the table in the middle of the room. Opening the lid, her gaze ran over all the items in the box—the passports, a few thick wads of cash, and some Euros. Moving the other items aside, she partially uncovered the gun. She glanced around the perimeter of the ceiling, searching for video cameras as inconspicuously as possible. There were two, in opposite corners.

She placed her sizeable leather handbag on its side, over the metal box, and surreptitiously slid the gun into it, ever mindful of the cameras. The rest of the contents, she decided, would keep for another day. She closed the lid, stuck the box back in its hole and closed the door on it.

Once she was in her car, she locked her doors and gingerly slipped the gun into a cloth bag and tied off the drawstring. She checked the GPS monitor that was wedged on her console, but she saw no movement of the tracking device. Either Jethro was still at his condo, or at least his car was, or he had found the device and stashed it somewhere in the parking garage. Before pulling out of the bank's lot, she glanced around and checked her mirrors again.

Feeling fairly assured she was not being followed, she headed to Isabel and Alex's house. Within minutes, she pulled into their high-end neighborhood with its expansive, neatly trimmed lawns and wide meandering streets. As Emily rounded a curve, the Martínez's spacious two-story brick and stucco home came into view. She pulled into the long driveway, catching a glimpse of Isabel bounding down the brick steps.

"Emily!" Isabel called out as her friend climbed out of her car.

Emily slung her heavy leather handbag over her shoulder as Isabel approached.

"Do you have the gun?" Isabel kept her voice low.

Emily nodded and patted her purse. "Right here."

Isabel linked her hand through Emily's arm and walked her to the house, glancing over her shoulder, up and down the street. "Let's get inside." As they went in the house, Isabel turned again and looked toward the street.

"Is Alex here?" Emily asked as they moved from the entry to the kitchen at the back of the house.

"No, he had a basketball game at the Y with some of his lawyer buddies this morning."

"He'll be back by kickoff time, won't he?" Emily asked, setting her purse down with a *thunk* on the round, glass-top dinette table.

"Of course. He wouldn't miss Boise State's first game. Maggie will be there, too, she told me." Isabel opened a package of Nutter Butter cookies and laid a couple handfuls of them on a plate. "I hope she brings some photos to share."

"I haven't seen her since she and Molly got back from Hawaii. I'm glad she's coming. I know she hates football, but she does love a good party."

"Yes, she does." Isabel set the plate of cookies on

the table. "Will Colin be there?"

"That's the plan."

"You don't sound so sure." Isabel turned and went back to the kitchen.

"Today is his first day back on the job and he's already been handed a case."

"Are you talking about the body they found in the river last night?"

Emily pulled out a chair and sank down onto it. "How did you know?"

"Heard it on the news this morning."

Emily heard Isabel open a cupboard, then the clinking sound of her pulling a couple of mugs out.

"They said she was a young Asian woman, late teens or early twenties—you want a cup of coffee, Em?"

"That'd be great, thanks. On the news this morning, huh? That was fast. But yes, that's the case." Emily pulled the fabric bag out of her purse and laid it gently on the glass table, next to the plate of Nutter Butters.

"Poor woman. I wonder what happened."

"I have my suspicions." Emily picked up a cookie and took a bite.

"You do? How are you involved in this?" Isabel carried two cups of steaming coffee to the table.

"Colin was at my house when he got the call last night about someone finding the body. We both went to the scene."

Isabel took a seat at the table and poured cream into her mug. "That must have put a damper on your romantic evening."

"That's for sure. So did my nosey next-door neighbor and the exploding potatoes." Emily grimaced before sticking the rest of the cookie in her mouth.

Isabel laughed, sending a spray of coffee across the table. Her hand flew up to her mouth. "Sorry about that," she quickly apologized, grabbing a napkin out of the holder in the center of the table.

"It wasn't that funny." Emily covered her lips with her fingers to contain a giggle. "At least at the time it wasn't." She tore a packet of sugar open and dumped it in her coffee.

"You'll have to tell me about that some time. Sounds like a scream." Isabel grabbed a couple of cookies from the plate. "But back to the dead woman—what are your suspicions?"

"Well…" Emily stirred her coffee, "I was planning on talking to you about this later anyway, so I guess now's as good a time as any. Remember I asked you about the Jade Thai Spa and you were going to check to see if it was one the Feds were watching?"

"Yeah, but I haven't gotten a response back yet."

"I think the young dead woman may have something to do with that."

"You mean the prostitution ring?"

"Yes."

"What makes you say that?"

"Call it a gut feeling."

Emily didn't have any actual evidence pointing to it, but there was something about the dead woman that made her think of the Asian girl in the hotel restroom. "I was hoping we could all put our heads together this afternoon and come up with a way to find out."

"Like a sting or something?"

"Exactly," Emily replied, wagging a Nutter Butter

at Isabel. "Camille's brother said he'd done an investigative report on human trafficking, perhaps he can give us some ideas."

"Maybe, but if the Feds are watching that place, they'll want to be alerted to anything you're planning to do so it doesn't blow up their case."

"You can be our liaison, Is." Emily dipped one end of her cookie in her coffee. "You know, a go-between."

"Let's not get ahead of ourselves, Em. We don't even know if the dead girl had anything to do with the Jade Thai Spa."

"Not yet, but soon I hope. Then we need to jump on it quick."

"I couldn't agree more." Isabel popped another cookie in her mouth.

"Oh, by the way," Emily softly patted the gun through the fabric, "where should we hide this baby?"

THE CHAIN OF LIES

CHAPTER 12
The Football Party

"HEY, Y'ALL!" MAGGIE CALLED out as she waltzed through the doorway of Camille's family room, holding a couple of loaded plastic grocery bags in each hand. "Sorry I'm late. Has the game started?"

"Maggie!" Camille squealed, running to her from the kitchen, giving her a big hug. Emily and Isabel weren't far behind.

"What's in the bags?" Isabel asked.

"I've got four different kinds of chips, that yummy granola from Costco, and I brought my famous chocolate pecan pie—my mama's recipe."

"That's not like you to bring so many carbs, Maggs," Emily commented, taking a couple of bags off her hands.

"I didn't say *I* was gonna eat 'em. They're for all y'all."

Peter stepped in and reached for the remaining

bags. "Here, let me help you with those," he offered, taking them from her and marching them into the kitchen.

"Maggie, you remember my brother, Peter?"

"Yes, from the airport." Maggie leaned on the breakfast bar.

"That was nice of you to think of us, Maggie," Isabel said as she followed Peter into the open kitchen area. "I'd love to sample your mom's chocolate pecan pie."

"Go right ahead," Maggie replied to Isabel, but her eyes were on Peter. "How long are y'all in town for, Peter?"

"Only another week or two, then I'm headed to Seattle to start a new job. I'll be a news anchor at one of the television stations there."

"I adore Seattle. It's such a great city—so clean, and all those trees."

"It's all that rain, I hear. If you're ever up that way, look me up and I'll take you out sightseeing."

"Sounds nice."

Emily watched Maggie, obviously working to be her usual upbeat self. Not long ago, she had suffered the heartbreaking loss of a relationship with a man she loved. The trip to Hawaii was intended to lift her spirits and help her on the road to recovery. Maybe Peter wasn't the right man for her, especially with him off to another city soon, but Emily hoped Maggie's budding friendship with Peter could at least give her a glimpse of a happier future.

A loud cheer roared from the family room where the men were huddled around the big-screen television watching the second quarter of the game. Emily figured BSU must have made a touchdown or some equally exciting play. Within minutes, every man was off the sofa, and like a herd, headed to the dining table which was now covered with Camille's delectable feast.

"What's happening?" Maggie asked.

"Halftime," Colin replied.

"We're ahead fourteen to nothing," Jonathan added as he picked up a plate and began loading it with a pulled pork sandwich and chips. "Hey, Red, where's the coleslaw?"

Jonathan was the only person Camille ever let get away with calling her *Red*.

"In the fridge," she hollered from the kitchen. "I can't have it sitting out getting warm." She grabbed it from the refrigerator and plunked it down on the table next to the pulled pork. "There you go."

Everyone grabbed a plate and dove into the delicious spread Camille and the girls had laid out, carrying their food into the family room. Every seat on the sectional was taken, as well as the easy chairs, leaving some to take their seat on the floor or the ottoman.

Emily glanced around the room with a satisfied feeling, watching them eating and chatting—she loved the closeness of her friends, like a big family, sharing a meal together.

Conversation flowed easily, but eventually it came around to the dead girl found in the river the night before.

"What can you tell us about the body that was found in the river last night, Colin?" Peter asked, sitting on the ottoman, balancing his plate on his knees.

Colin leaned back into the sofa and swallowed his food. "There's not much to tell yet. No more than the news has reported so far. We won't know anything more until we get the autopsy and lab reports back."

"I think she may have been a prostitute at one of those Thai massage parlors," Emily blurted out. She glanced at Colin next to her, and his frown told her he wasn't pleased with her reckless supposition.

"Really? What makes you say that, Emily?" Peter asked, his eyes and the tone of his voice showing his serious interest.

"Molly and I were at the Hilton Hotel a few weeks ago and ran into a young Asian woman crying in the restroom. She wouldn't talk to us, but she was all dolled-up like a teenager trying to pass as a grown woman—a very sexy grown woman. Then an older woman came in, scolded her in some Asian language, and pulled her out of the room. At the time, I chalked it up to a teenage girl being caught by her mom dressing up to appear older for some guy."

"Why would you think that?" Camille asked.

"Because that happened to me when I was fifteen," Emily replied.

"But now you don't think that's what happened?" Peter questioned.

"Molly and I saw the girl again not long after that, in the backseat of a car leaving a house in this neighborhood. Molly saw her more close up than me, and she said the girl had the saddest eyes she'd ever seen."

"She never mentioned that to me," Camille said.

"What else, Em?" Isabel asked.

"I was on a case where the wife thought the husband was seeing a prostitute, because of charges showing up on their credit card bill. I followed him to the Jade Thai Spa and found out later he was getting a lot more than a massage."

"What does that massage parlor have to do with the teenage girl?" Jonathan asked.

"I saw her again, not long ago, after I left here one day. She was in the backseat of the same car, with two other girls around her age. A stocky man was driving both times, and the woman from the restroom was in the front seat, the same as the first time Molly saw them. I had tried to tell Molly they were probably a family and the three girls in the backseat were sisters."

"Sounds like you don't believe that anymore," Peter said.

"The last time I saw them, I looked into that girl's face as they drove past me. She looked out the window, right at me, with her big brown eyes. Molly was right. They were the saddest eyes I'd ever seen. But more than sadness, I saw fear. So I decided to follow them."

"You never told me that," Colin said.

"Are you sure?" Emily asked.

"What did y'all see?" Maggie asked.

"They drove to the Jade Thai Spa, parked in the back, and they all got out and went inside. It was a little after four. The sign on the front door said they opened at five, so I banged on the door until someone answered."

"Now I know you never told me that," Colin insisted.

"So what happened?" Isabel asked.

"The older woman came to the door, but she wouldn't open it except barely enough to stick her head out. I stuck my foot in the door, hoping to keep her from closing it. I told her I wanted to buy a gift certificate for a massage, trying to get a peek past her. She said they don't sell them and they only take cash, which I know, based on my client's credit card bill, that wasn't true. I saw the teenager walk past behind her, but the woman kicked my foot out of the door and slammed it."

"Oh, my gosh!" Maggie exclaimed.

"I kept pounding, but she wouldn't open the door again."

"Emily, you shouldn't have gone there alone," Colin said. "I know you're a private eye, but have you ever heard of backup?"

Emily stared at Colin for a second, then went on. "With regards to the dead woman from last night, what if she was one of the three girls in the back of that car?"

"You got a look at the body last night. Was she the one from the hotel?" Alex asked.

"No, but it could have been one of the other two. Or maybe there are more being kept at that house."

"Sounds like you're watching too many movies, Em," Camille remarked.

"Actually, she could be onto something," Peter said.

"Please don't encourage her," Colin pleaded.

"I know it all sounds unreal, like something out of a movie, but I know what we saw. You can ask Molly." Emily glanced around the great room. "Camille, where's Molly?"

"She left a bit ago, said she was going on a bike ride in the neighborhood," Camille replied.

"Well, if Molly was here—"

"Did I hear someone call my name?" Molly bounded into the room.

"Yes," Emily shot up from her seat on the sectional. "I was just telling them all about the three Asian girls we saw."

"Funny you should say that," Molly said, planting her hands on her hips. "Just a few minutes ago, as I was riding past their house, they were backing out of their driveway. There were only two girls in the backseat this time, the one from the hotel and another one."

Emily's gaze shot to Colin, who seemed to be able to read her mind. He stood and faced her.

"Now, Emily, take a breath. Just because last time you saw three girls in the backseat and this time there were only two doesn't mean the girl in the river was the third one. That's a huge leap."

The whole room fell silent and all eyes were on the two of them.

"Isabel, tell her," Colin pleaded. "Peter?"

"It's certainly worth looking into," Peter suggested.

"I agree," Isabel concurred.

"Molly, did the driver or the older woman see you?" Emily asked.

"Maybe, but Emily, you really think they could have killed that girl? Why?" Molly asked, a tremor of fear lining her voice.

"Molly," Emily put a calming hand on the girl's shoulder. "My guess is that they are using these girls as prostitutes. Now, I could be wrong, but we need to know for sure what's going on. We know the people in that house are connected with the Jade Thai Spa, where prostitution is going on. And if that girl—"

"Emily, that's enough! Molly, I think this discussion is for the adults. Why don't you go busy yourself somewhere else and let us finish our conversation?" Camille advised.

"Mom, I'm not a child. I'm seventeen years old and I want to stay. If those girls are in trouble, I want to help."

"I think your mother's right," Jonathan added. "Find something else to do, please."

Molly's gaze moved from her dad, to her mom, then to Emily, as everyone held their tongue. Molly's eyes narrowed and her lips thinned. She stomped out of the room and the sound of the front door slamming echoed throughout the house.

"Sorry, Camille, Jonathan. I think I overstepped. I wasn't seeing Molly as a child."

"We know she's almost grown, but she doesn't need to be part of this conversation, talking about murder and prostitution," Jonathan barked.

"I think I'll go clean up the kitchen," Camille announced in a cool, even voice as she turned to leave.

"I'll help." Jonathan cast Emily a disapproving look as he joined his wife.

"Really, I am sorry," Emily called after them.

"Well, I'm stayin' put," Maggie said from her perch on the arm of the sectional. "I want to hear what's goin' on."

Emily brought her focus back to those remaining in the family room. "I was telling Isabel earlier today that we need a plan, some way to get inside that Jade Thai Spa and find out what's really happening." Emily gazed around the room, from face to face, to read their level of buy-in.

"What did you have in mind?" Colin asked.

Emily hoped that meant he was onboard to help.

"Okay, tell me what you guys think of this. What if one of you men went into the Jade Thai Spa to ask for a massage and see if in the course of that massage they make an offer for more than that?" Emily suggested.

"More than that? You mean sex?" Alex asked. "I'll volunteer," he said, raising his hand.

"Oh, no you won't," Isabel reprimanded, flashing him a sarcastic grin.

"Isabel's right. It should be Colin or Peter," Emily recommended. "They have more experience in working undercover."

"We'll need some kind of hidden camera," Peter said. "Emily, you're a private eye. Do you have anything like that?"

"No, nothing small enough to hide in this situation."

"Colin, can you get your hands on a tiny camera," Peter asked, "like a button camera, or something hidden in a pair of glasses?"

"Boy, I don't know." Colin shook his head. "Paradise Valley Police Department is pretty small, but maybe I can borrow something from my friends at the Boise PD."

"Or I may be able to get some equipment from the FBI, especially since they're going to be very interested in this case if you turn up anything," Isabel added.

"Oh, this all sounds so excitin'. What can I do?" Maggie asked.

"Just sit there looking pretty," Peter said with a

patronizing smile. "This could get dangerous."

Maggie's voice, which was normally upbeat and lilting, took on a stern tone as she looked Peter in the eye. "I know y'all don't know me very well, Peter, but I'm a lot more than just a pretty face. Maybe your sister hasn't told you, but Emily, Isabel, and I teach self-defense classes to women at the Y—I can take down a man twice my size."

"I'm so sorry. I must have sounded like a condescending jerk," Peter apologized.

"I'd say you stepped in it big time," Alex kidded.

"Can we get back to the plan?" Emily crossed her arms and paced a few times in the center of the room. "If the offer of sex is made, I want to make sure the madam is willing to bring the girl to you somewhere else."

"Like a hotel?" Maggie asked.

"Yes, excellent idea," Peter remarked, which made Maggie smile.

"But why do you want her to bring the girl somewhere else? Can't the police swoop in and arrest the whole bunch right then and there?" Maggie asked.

"To my way of thinking, divide and conquer is cleaner and safer for everyone involved," Emily replied. "You guys agree?"

The nodding heads assured her they were in agreement.

"We just need to decide who's going to be the patsy that goes in for the massage, because he'll have to be the same guy who meets the girl at the hotel," Isabel said.

"I volunteer," said Peter. "I want the story."

"Colin?" Emily asked.

"Let Peter do it, then I'll swoop in for the arrest."

The group spent the next half hour throwing ideas around for how and when they could work out the sting. If they were able to confirm the young Asian girls were being used for sex trafficking, then the FBI and the Boise PD SWAT team would need to be pulled into the operation quickly.

Isabel agreed to alert her FBI contacts to their plan, knowing they would want to be in charge of the operation. And Colin said he would inform his chief, as well as make contact with people he knew in the Boise Police Department to gain their involvement. If the operation was to proceed and the girls rescued, there would have to be a precisely timed orchestration of taking down this ring at several different locations simultaneously.

"We'll have to have a well-defined plan in place to move quickly if sex is offered and the madam agrees to bring one of the girls to the hotel," Colin said.

"My guess is she will. I'll bet that's what was happening when we first ran into the girl crying in the hotel restroom," Emily said. "The poor thing probably knew what was waiting for her and she didn't want to go."

"And we'll need time to get the hidden cameras, earbuds, and microphones together," Isabel pointed out.

"I don't want to wait too long. Every day we lose, those girls might have to prostitute themselves with who knows how many men," Emily said.

"From what I've learned, it could be up to ten a night," Peter added.

"Now remember, we're planning this whole thing on very little evidence," Colin pointed out. "Jade Thai

Spa could simply be a massage parlor."

"Now that's not completely true. My client's husband admitted they offered sex to him," Emily reminded them.

"You have a point," Colin admitted.

"I can't say for sure they're trafficking underage girls, but something is going on there. What if my gut is right about the girls and we ignored it and did nothing?" Emily asked. "I don't know how I could live with myself."

"Me neither," Maggie responded.

The rest nodded and muttered their agreement.

"Like I told Colin earlier, each one of those girls is somebody's daughter. We have to do something."

CHAPTER 13
Mr. Osterman's Discovery

AFTER AN EXHAUSTIVE CONVERSATION about their clandestine operation, and not much football watching, the gang decided to leave Camille and Jonathan in peace and call it a night. Those who would be involved agreed to reconvene the next afternoon to hammer out the details. Their best chance to go in for the massage, they agreed, would be Sunday evening. Depending on how things went, they could move on to the next phase of the operation Sunday night.

The evening was still early, around six o'clock. Colin and Emily decided to pick up some Chinese food to go at their favorite place, and head for her house.

"I'll get the plates if you'll pour the drinks," Emily said as she reached up into her kitchen cupboard. The cartons of Chinese delicacies waited on the table for them.

"What would you like?" Colin stooped over and

peeked into the refrigerator.

Emily glanced into the open refrigerator, and noticed a large bottle of sweet tea. "Iced tea is fine." She brought the plates, forks, and napkins to the table and laid the place settings out while he poured the tea. They took their seats at the table and began spooning out the various dishes.

"I was proud of you today," Colin said as he pulled a spring roll from one of the boxes.

"For what?" Emily stuck a piece of sweet and sour pork in her mouth and grinned.

"You really took charge of the discussion this afternoon."

"I suppose when you feel strongly about something, it sort of takes over and compels you to do something about it."

"I could see that. Pass me the fried rice, please."

Emily picked up the small box of rice by the wire handle and handed it to him.

"You just need to be careful you're on the right track. What if we find out there's nothing going on there?" Colin opened the box and scooped some of it onto his plate.

"There's definitely *something* going on in that place." She wagged her fork at him. "It may not be what I think, but it's definitely something."

Colin reached out and put his hand on hers. "If you're right, these people can be very dangerous. We need to be careful and do this thing by the book if we want any charges to stick."

"Yes, sir," Emily quipped.

"I'm not joking."

"Neither am I."

When dinner was over, they cleaned up the kitchen together and went to the living room to relax and watch a movie. They turned the TV on and scrolled through the Pay-Per-View choices.

"What do you want to watch?" Colin asked, pointing the remote controller at the television.

"Something romantic. How about—" Emily was cut off by the ringing of his cell phone.

"Sorry," he mouthed, grimacing, as he pulled the phone to his ear. "Colin Andrews."

She listened to his side of the conversation.

"He did? Where?"

He looked at Emily as he listened to the caller, then his gaze went beyond her, as if he was visualizing what the caller was saying.

"Okay," he replied, looking down at his watch. "I can be there in about fifteen minutes. Keep him there."

"What is it?" Emily asked, wide eyed.

"That was Ernie. Do you remember Mr. Osterman, one of the witnesses from the McCall murder case?"

"Yes, Delia's neighbor. Why?"

"Seems old Mr. Osterman has taken up a new hobby."

"A new hobby? What?"

"Using a metal detector to find buried treasures, Ernie said."

"So, what does that have to do with you?" Emily knit her brows together as she tilted her head.

"Well, our old friend seems to have found a gun half buried in the bank down by the river that flows past his neighborhood."

"Delia's neighborhood? Do you think—"

Emily's heart began to race and her mouth went dry. She could hardly get the words out she was so excited at the prospect that perhaps Mr. Osterman had found the gun that killed her late husband.

"Might be. I don't want you getting your hopes up, though. It could turn out to have nothing to do with Evan's murder."

"All right, I'll try to keep my exuberance in check."

"Ernie's detaining the old guy at the station 'til I get there, so I'm sorry, Babe, but I need to run."

"Let me get my shoes. I'm coming with you."

On the drive to the police station, Emily received a call from Isabel saying she had just been given some info on Jethro. She had spoken with an FBI agent on the human trafficking task force, part of the team that was watching the Jade Thai Spa, and he mentioned to her that he'd heard Jethro had been rushed to the hospital that afternoon. Knowing they had been friends, the agent thought Isabel would want to know.

"What's wrong with him?" Emily asked, looking over at Colin as he drove.

He glanced back at her.

"I don't know. The details are sketchy," Isabel replied. "I'm going to drop over there and see what I can find out."

Emily explained to Isabel where she and Colin were headed and why.

"If that *is* the gun, Em, this could be a huge break in

the case."

"I know," Emily responded, "but Colin keeps telling me not to get excited until we know for sure." She glanced over at him again and caught his gaze.

He grinned back at her. "You know I'm right."

"I'll let you know what we find out."

"Same here," Isabel promised. "I'm off to the hospital."

~*~

Colin and Emily breezed through the doors of the Paradise Valley police station. Being Saturday night, there was a uniformed officer behind the reception area, an unfamiliar one, who was not acquainted with Colin yet. He asked for his identification and Colin showed him his badge.

"Oh, sorry, Detective. Go on back."

Colin slid his key card through the slot and the door unlatched. He pushed it open and held it for Emily to pass through first. They turned the corner and went to Colin's office where they found Ernie, sitting in Colin's chair, with his feet propped up on his desk.

Mr. Osterman was seated in a chair across from Ernie, chatting about his latest metal finds.

"Hello, Mr. Osterman," Emily greeted as they entered the office.

The elderly man looked up over his wire-rimmed glasses and a smile spread across his wrinkly face. "Hello, there, Ms. Parker. It's good to see you again." He stuck out his hand and she shook it.

"You remember Detective Andrews, don't you?"

Emily asked.

The old gentleman pushed his glasses up on his nose and studied Colin's face. "Yes, I think I do. Nice to see you again, too, young man." He extended his hand to Colin, as well.

Colin shook his hand firmly then moved to the side of his desk. "Ernie?" Colin said as he turned toward the officer, raising an eyebrow.

"Oh, sorry." Ernie pulled his boots down off the desk and dragged himself out of Colin's chair. The burly officer stepped to the wall and crossed his arms as he leaned against it.

Emily took a seat in the other chair opposite the desk. She leaned forward, toward Mr. Osterman, and addressed him. "I hear you found a gun down by the river." She knew it was really Colin's job, but she could tell Mr. Osterman warmed up to her more than to Colin, so she took advantage of it. She hoped Colin didn't mind.

"That's a fact. Found it just this afternoon with my new-fangled whachamacallit."

"You mean the metal detector?" she clarified.

"Yes," he replied. "That's what you call it. It was mostly hidden in the mud at the edge of the river. If I'd been scouring the riverbank earlier this summer, the water would have been too high—I would never have seen it."

Luck was obviously on her side. She hoped her luck would hold out long enough for the county lab to determine this was the gun that was used to kill Evan. If so, she could finally move forward to solve the mystery surrounding his death.

"Where is the gun?" Colin asked Mr. Osternman.

"Bottom right drawer," Ernie replied, "already in an evidence bag and tagged. It's a Ruger P345."

Colin leaned over and pulled out the drawer to see the muddy gun for himself. "So it is. I'll get it over to the lab first thing in the morning." He closed the drawer and locked it. "I'd like to see where you found it, Mr. Osterman."

"Can't it wait 'til morning? I need to get home and tend to my dog. Snookie needs to be fed and walked."

"It's not far from your house, is it?" Emily asked.

"No, I guess not."

"Then it'll only take a few minutes, sir. I just need you to show us where you found it, then you can be on your way," Colin assured him, before turning his attention to his officer. "Ernie, I'm assuming you got the man's statement?"

"Yes, sir."

"Could you grab a couple of large flashlights on your way out, big guy, so we can see where we're going?" Colin requested.

"Yep," Ernie replied, pushing away from the wall.

Colin rose from his chair and motioned toward the door. "Lead the way, Mr. Osterman."

~*~

Isabel pushed through the doors of the St. Luke's Medical Center, on her way to find Jerry Banderas, hoping she wasn't too late for visiting hours. The young lady at the information desk told her he was on the fourth floor and suggested she check in with the nurse's station once she got up there.

As the elevator glided up to the fourth floor, Isabel thought back over the years she had known this man. He had been a stand-up guy, in her mind, almost a father figure, like an uncle she could go to for advice. It was hard to see him as a murderer, but she was resolute to find the truth of his involvement in Evan's death.

She had always known Evan as David Gerard, until he left the CIA to marry Emily and move to Paradise Valley, but she had worked hard to see him only as Evan after she followed him to this place. If she slipped up and called him David, Emily would question it, and the mistake could put his life in jeopardy. But he was no longer in need of her help to keep his anonymity—he was dead.

Still, she liked the person he had become as Evan. He was kinder, more caring of others. Picturing him in her mind, his dark blonde hair, those serious gray-blue eyes that could look right through you, and his engaging crooked smile—that was how she wanted to remember him.

The elevator doors parted and she stepped out, not far from the nurse's station. "I hope you can help me. I'm looking for a patient."

"Name?"

"Jerry Banderas."

"Banderas, Banderas, Banderas," the nurse repeated as she ran her finger down her computer screen. "Yes, room four twelve. Down this hallway," she gestured toward the corridor, "on your right."

Isabel turned to look down the hall and saw Delia McCall come out of a room on the right and turn the other direction, toward the stairs. She wondered if Delia had just been visiting with the same person she was there to see.

She walked down the wide, brightly lit hallway, as the nurse had directed, and came to room four twelve on the right. It was the same door she had seen Delia exit. Pushing it open, she saw Jerry lying in the bed, propped up on pillows, with his eyes closed.

"Jerry?" she said softly, not wanting to wake him if he was asleep.

His eyes opened slowly and a smile spread across his lips when he saw Isabel.

"Hey, Jerry. I just heard you were in here and I rushed over as soon as I could. What's going on? Why are you in this place?"

"Pancreatic cancer," he replied flatly.

"Oh, Jerry," she sighed. "How come you never told me?"

"I didn't want anyone feeling sorry for me."

"You never seemed sick to me, except at the lunch the other day I thought you looked kind of pale. But cancer? I had no idea."

"That's the way I wanted it. I only found out myself a couple of months ago. This type of cancer creeps up on you, and bam—you're a goner."

"Oh, Jerry, I'm so sorry." Isabel laid her hand on his as she fought against the tears that threatened to break through. With all her suspicions about this guy, he had been her friend for a long time. "What do the doctors say?"

"That I'm too far gone, there's nothing they can do but help me manage the pain. I don't have much time left."

"Do you have your affairs in order?" Isabel wondered if he would come clean about his involvement with Evan and his connection to Delia McCall, if he would want to get it off his chest before he passed.

"I think so. I don't really have much to leave anyone, except my pension. A life devoted to my work, in the end, didn't leave me room for much else, except four ex-wives."

"Four ex-wives? I thought you'd been married five times?"

"I was. One died."

"Sorry, I didn't know that."

"It was a long time ago."

"I seem to remember you had a couple of daughters. You used to talk about them when I knew him in DC."

"Yeah. One was killed and the other one has her own life. I didn't spend much time with my girls when they were growing up. Their mother was my first wife. She's the one that died years ago."

"You can be proud of the work you did at the FBI. You're a good man, Jerry."

"Not always so good, Isabel."

"What do you mean?"

"I'm really tired. I don't want to talk anymore. Hope you don't mind but I'd just like to sleep for a while."

"I understand." She patted his hands, as they lay folded across his stomach. "I'll come back and see you again later, all right?"

"Okay." He closed his eyes.

Isabel stepped out of the room and glanced up and

down the hallway, hoping to catch another glimpse of Delia McCall, but she was nowhere in sight.

As she drove home, with the window rolled down, the crisp fall air blew through her long dark waves. Isabel turned on some soothing music and wondered what her friend meant when he said he was not always so good. She suspected he might be referring to his actions concerning Evan, but without proof, and his death not far off, she may never know.

Maybe Delia could shed some light.

THE CHAIN OF LIES

CHAPTER 14
Meeting at the Morgue

EARLY SUNDAY MORNING, Emily woke from a deep sleep to the sound of her phone ringing on the nightstand. The sun was peeking over the horizon and shards of early light began to stream through her curtains.

Too sleepy to open her eyes, she fumbled around the top of the night table with one hand, feeling for her cell phone until she recognized the shape of it. "Hello," she mumbled.

"Good morning, sunshine," Colin said brightly. "Time to rise and shine. We're burning daylight."

"What?" She opened one eye and blearily peered over at her digital clock, trying to focus. "What time is it?"

"It's after seven."

"Seven in the morning? On Sunday? Are you kidding me?"

"Don't be like that, Emily. It's a beautiful day—let's not waste it. There's lots to do."

"Why are you so chipper?" She propped herself up on one arm, trying to open her eyes.

"I'm finally back in the saddle and it feels good. We have this new lead in Evan's murder and I got a call a few minutes ago from Dr. Walters. He's finished with the autopsy and the test results are back."

Emily plopped back against her pillows, raking her fingers through her curls. "You dragged me up and down that riverbank 'til the middle of the night. Can't I have a couple more hours before we jump into the day?"

"It wasn't the middle of the night, only twelve thirty."

"Well, it felt like the middle of the night."

"Sorry, I'm just excited to be back to work, not to mention the three cups of black coffee I've had so far."

"Coffee? That sounds really good." She laid the back of her hand against her forehead, closed her eyes, and smiled. "Mmm, coffee," she purred.

"Tell you what, I'll stop by Starbucks and pick you up a tall mocha cappuccino. I'll be over in about twenty minutes."

"Twenty minutes," she repeated drowsily, her eyes still closed. "Uh-huh."

"See you then."

"Okay," she mumbled. "See you in twenty minutes."

She reached over, with her eyes shut, and set her phone down on the nightstand, then rolled back over and laid her head against her pillow. "Twenty minutes," she muttered again.

"Twenty minutes!" She sat up with a start. The words had finally sunk in. She dragged herself out of bed, stumbled into the bathroom, and turned on the shower.

By the time Colin arrived, she was ready to go. The shower had helped to revive her, as did the thoughts of what the newly found gun would mean.

"Good morning." Colin waltzed through the door, planting a soft kiss on her lips. "A tall mocha cappuccino, as promised." He held out the box that carried her hot drink. "And a couple of slices of your favorite pumpkin bread."

"You sure know how to sweet talk a girl." She took her coffee from the box, then lifted a slice of bread and a napkin from it. She wandered into the living room and curled her bare feet under her as she sank down onto the sofa.

Colin followed her to the couch and set the box on the coffee table. Pulling the other slice of pumpkin bread out, he tore off a piece. "As soon as we're done eating, I'd like to get down to the county M.E.'s office. Doc Walters said he has some info to share." He popped the piece of bread into his mouth.

She took another sip of her coffee. "On a Sunday?"

"Murder doesn't sleep, Emily. Doc said he worked most of yesterday and was back in his office this morning at six a.m."

"Too early for me." She shook her head and pulled a small piece of bread off. "But it'll be good to have some news from the doc. Don't forget we have that meeting this afternoon about the Jade Thai Spa sting."

"I emailed my contact at the Boise PD about that,

and he wants me to be part of the meeting this afternoon. If we do need the SWAT team involved, he can mobilize them pretty quickly. Do you know if Isabel made contact with the FBI agents who are watching that place?"

"Only what she said last night when she called—remember when we were driving down to meet with Mr. Osterman. She mentioned she'd spoken to someone about it, and that agent told her Jethro was in the hospital."

"That's right. I'd forgotten about that."

"I haven't heard from her this morning, but it's still early—*very early*."

"Okay, okay, I get the point."

"If she said she'd call me and let me know what she found out, she will. Besides, she'll be at the meeting this afternoon, too." Emily wiped the napkin over her lips, crumpled it up, and tossed it in the box. She leaned over and kissed Colin lightly before standing up. "Thanks for breakfast."

"My pleasure." He rose from the couch and followed her to the door.

She slipped on her flats that sat in the entry. "I'll finish my cappuccino in the car."

"Grab your purse then and let's roll."

~*~

"What do you have for us, Doc?" Colin asked as they stood around the body of the young Asian woman on the steel table, draped from the shoulders down with a white sheet.

"It's hard to determine time of death, since she was

in the cold water when she was found. Likely a day or two. She had drugs in her system, like Valium, but not enough to kill her. I believe the cause of death was that she had been beaten to death. She suffered blunt force trauma to the head and had quite a bit of internal bleeding in her abdomen too."

"That poor woman," Emily sighed.

"The saddest part is that she was about six weeks pregnant," Doc added. "Such a shame. Two lives cut short—and for what?"

"That's what we need to find out." Colin pursed his lips and shook his head with disgust. "What about her fingerprints? Did they turn up anything?"

"No, she wasn't in the system."

"Had she been sexually assaulted?" Emily asked.

"It's hard to tell. She did appear to have quite a bit of tissue damage, scarring really, and I was able to extract some semen. But I won't have DNA results back for days. They don't come back as fast as they do on TV, you know."

"Any gut feelings, Doc?" Emily asked.

"I have seen this before, the tissue damage and scarring, I mean. It was on a prostitute that had been murdered a few years ago here in Boise."

"You think this girl could have been a prostitute?" Emily shot Colin a look.

"It's possible, with this type of damage."

"How old would you say this woman was?" Colin asked.

"I would hardly call her a woman, Detective. Based on various markers, I'd say she's no more than eighteen, maybe younger."

Emily grabbed Colin's forearm when she heard the medical examiner's words. This was exactly what she was afraid of. If she was one of the girls working at the Jade Thai Spa and she was being forced into prostitution, so were the other girls in that house.

Colin patted her hand. "We'll do our best to get the S.O.B. that did this to her." He pulled out his phone and took a photo of the girl's face. "Maybe someone will recognize her."

"Anything else, Doc?" Emily asked, willing herself not to cry.

"Not at the moment. I'll let you know when I have more test results back."

~*~

"Since we didn't have much of a breakfast, let's grab some lunch real quick," Emily suggested.

"Sounds good. Where would you like to go?"

"We can get a sandwich pretty fast at Hugo's Deli. It's right up here on the right."

Colin swung his Jeep into the parking lot and they went inside and ordered. Finding a table on the outdoor patio, they unwrapped their sandwiches and dug in.

"After talking to Doc Walters, I'm feeling more certain than ever that we're on the right track." Emily took a bite of her turkey on whole wheat.

"It's starting to look that way," Colin agreed, chomping down on an all-meat marvel.

"Once Peter gets inside and has a look around, we'll know more."

"Actually, we'll all get a look inside if Isabel's able

to get the FBI to loan us a micro-camera. We can hook up the feed to the media van and watch what's going on."

"That'd be great. We'll get enough on those people to nail them to the wall."

"Whoa! We don't even know what's happening in there yet."

"We do to a point. My client's husband admitted he accepted their offer for sex during his massage, so we know prostitution is going on. What we don't know is if these girls are underage and possibly being forced to perform."

He nodded his agreement as he took another bite.

"And if we can tie them to the murder of that girl—

Emily was interrupted by the sound of her phone ringing in her pocket. She dug it out and saw it was Camille calling. "Hello, Camille."

"Oh, Emily. I'm so glad I caught you. Something terrible has happened."

"What's happened?" Emily shot a concerned look at Colin.

"Molly didn't come home last night."

"Oh, Camille."

"I know she was mad when we sent her out of the room. We didn't want her hearing about murder and prostitution. I had assumed she went to a friend's house to cool off."

"You weren't concerned when she didn't come back last night, before you went to bed?"

"No, Molly's a responsible girl. Jonathan and I were both exhausted, so we went to bed early. We assumed Molly would come home at a reasonable hour and we'd talk to her in the morning, but she never came home." Emily could hear Camille attempting to stifle her sobs.

"Let's not jump to conclusions. Maybe she stayed the night at a friend's house."

"I already called around to all her friends, but no one's seen her," Camille replied between sniffles. "What are we going to do?"

"Maybe Colin can put an ATL out on her car." Emily looked at Colin again and he nodded.

"No, it's still in the driveway. She must've taken her bike."

"She couldn't have gotten far on her bicycle. Does she have her cell phone?" Emily wondered if Colin could track her by it.

"No. I tried calling it but I heard it ringing in her room. She was so angry when she went out that she must have forgotten it."

"Perhaps she went to see a friend you don't know." Emily wracked her brain for plausible possibilities.

"Anything's possible," Camille sadly conceded.

"I tell you what, Colin and I have a meeting this afternoon, but I'm free for the next couple of hours. Let me come over and we can talk this through, see what we can do to find her."

"I'd really appreciate that, Em," Camille said, sounding as frightened and as small as Emily had ever heard her. "I'm going to call Maggie and let her know."

"And I'll phone Isabel. She'll want to know too, I'm sure. Don't worry, Cam, we'll find her."

"You're a good friend, Emily."

Emily said good-bye and made her call to Isabel.

Colin drove Emily home to pick up her car so she could head to Camille's house while he went to his office. He urged her to have the Hawthornes come in and file a missing person report.

"I will." Emily unbuckled her seatbelt as Colin pulled into her driveway. "I want to get Camille settled down and see what we can do to locate Molly. It's not like that girl to stay out all night and not let her folks know where she's at. She's headstrong, but she's pretty responsible and level-headed."

"Doesn't sound like you think she spent the night at a friend's house." He reached out and took her hand.

She shook her head. "I'm worried, Colin. It isn't like Molly to just run off."

"I'll be at the station all afternoon if you need me. Have Camille and Jonathan come in."

"If we don't find Molly soon, I will." She climbed out of his Jeep.

"Don't forget our meeting with Peter and the others at three—my office," he called out before she shut the door.

"Not a chance I'd forget," she replied as she waved good-bye.

CHAPTER 15
What Happened to Molly?

"OH, EM! I'M SO GLAD you're here." Camille greeted her at the door and threw her arms around Emily, holding damp tissues in one hand. "Come in, come in."

"Any word from Molly?" Emily asked as Camille walked her to the open kitchen area.

"None. Not a single word. I'm so worried, Emily." Camille wiped her nose with a tissue.

Emily glanced from the kitchen to the family room. "Where are Jonathan and Peter?"

"They're driving around to places Molly might have gone. We've phoned all the friends we found in her phone, but no one's seen her." Camille's normally brilliant blue eyes were swollen and almost as red as her hair. "I'm so scared, Em."

"Colin wants you or Jonathan to fill out a missing person report at the station. Will he be back soon?"

"So Colin thinks she's missing, too." That

acknowledgement brought a flood of tears to Camille's eyes. Picking up a box of tissues from the breakfast bar, she went into the family room and plopped down on the sofa.

Emily followed and sat beside her. "It's just a possibility, Cam, and it has been twenty-four hours since she took off. Let's go through the appropriate steps—it can't hurt."

"I guess you're right."

"Make sure you bring a recent photo of her, too."

Camille and Emily turned their heads at the sound of the front door opening and closing, and they heard voices coming down the hall. Jonathan and Peter had come through the doorway, with Maggie following close behind.

"Did you find her?" Camille shot to her feet as Maggie rushed to hug her.

Jonathan almost spoke, but his eyes grew watery and his lips trembled as he tried to form the words.

"No, no sign of her," Peter replied, stepping in to answer. "But we'll keep looking."

"Emily said Colin wants us to come down to the station and file a missing person report." Camille went to stand by her husband and he put an arm snugly around her shoulders.

"Then he can put her picture and profile out to all his officers and the state's law enforcement agencies." Emily rose from the couch and stepped closer to Camille and Jonathan. "We should move quickly on this."

"Don't forget the Amber Alert, too," Maggie added.

"Sorry, these circumstances wouldn't qualify," Emily said. "But law enforcement can't do anything until the report is filed."

"Then what are we doing standing here?" Peter asked. "Let's load up and get down there."

Emily turned to Maggie and put her hand on her friend's arm. "Maggs, I think you should stay here in case Molly returns on her own."

"Would you please, Maggie?" Camille pleaded with sad eyes.

"All right." Maggie released a sigh of resignation as she crossed her arms and pursed her lips. "I'd rather come with all y'all, but I understand. Whatever I can do, Cam."

"Staying here is a big help," Camille assured her.

"Call us if she shows up," Peter said.

Jonathan and Camille took their car and Emily invited Peter to ride with her. As they drove down the street, away from the Hawthorne house, Emily noticed the garage on the mysterious family's home going up. The Mercedes was approaching from the opposite direction and beginning to turn into their driveway. Emily caught a glimpse of the inside of the garage before the car obscured her view. It looked like a normal family garage, she thought, fairly empty with a few boxes on shelves along the side wall. She noticed the back end of a bright red and yellow bicycle leaning against the shelving deeper into the space.

"See that house there?" Emily nodded in the direction of the house. "Where that car just pulled in?"

"Yeah."

"Write this address down."

Peter pulled a small notepad out of his jacket pocket and Emily handed him a pen.

"Five two three three Somerset Drive."

He scribbled down the address. "Why did you want me to do that?"

"That's the house where Molly and I saw the young girl from the hotel restroom. Later I saw that girl in the car that just pulled in, and I followed it down to the Jade Thai Spa. If I'm right about the prostitution ring, the woman who poses as the mother in that house is really the madam at the spa."

Emily glanced over at him and saw he was furiously scribbling down what she was telling him.

"This will be great info for my story. After we take down this ring, Emily, I want to sit down with you and get all the details, no matter how small."

"I'd be happy to do that, I just wish Molly hadn't taken off yesterday. We can't focus all our energy and resources on nailing these scumbags if we have to find Molly first. She couldn't have picked a worse time to run off."

"There's never a good time for your kid to go missing," Peter reminded her.

"Sorry, I didn't mean to sound insensitive, I just meant having one thing on top of another makes succeeding at either a lot more difficult."

"From what my sister tells me, you're up to it."

"What do you mean?" Emily glanced at him with a smirk.

"Camillé talks about you like you're Wonder Woman."

"Believe me, I'm no Wonder Woman." Emily rolled her eyes. "I'd say your sister's a bit prone to exaggeration, Peter."

"And Maggie? What's her story?"

"You mean to tell me Camille hasn't given you every detail of Maggie's life yet?"

"Not every detail."

"Why so interested?"

"I like her. She's beautiful and sweet and smart. I feel something stir when I'm near her."

"Geez, Peter, I can't imagine why." Though Emily's comment was a bit sarcastic, she was glad to hear he liked her friend, but the timing could be a deal breaker.

"Is she seeing anyone?"

"No. It hasn't been that long since her last relationship ended—very badly. I'm not sure you should start making advances toward her when you're leaving town soon."

"Seattle's not that far away—an hour and half by plane."

"So you'd be up for a long-distance relationship?"

"I would if Maggie and I hit it off. Do you think she would?"

"Don't know. You'd have to ask her." Emily was pretty sure Maggie would be open to it, eventually. Peter was a great catch, but she wasn't about to speak for her.

"I think I should ask her out to dinner first, though," Peter joked.

"Good idea."

~*~

When Emily and Peter arrived, Colin was ushering Jonathan and Camille into the conference room, balancing his laptop in one hand and a cup of coffee in the other. He set the laptop down on the table and motioned through the glass for the two to join them.

Emily sat on one side of Camille, taking her hand, and Jonathan on the other. Across the table sat Colin and his computer. Peter pulled a chair out next to him and deposited himself.

Jonathan gave Colin the initial information, full name, address, and so on, but when it came to physical description, Camille stepped in.

"Five foot five, a hundred and twenty pounds, long red hair, green eyes. She has a light sprinkling of freckles across her cheeks." Camille's fingers fluttered across her own face as she described them.

"Any birthmarks or tattoos?" Colin asked.

"A small birthmark on her right shoulder—looks like a kidney bean," Camille replied, pointing to the area.

"Tattoos?"

"No," Jonathan answered.

Camille shook her head.

"Well," Emily interrupted sheepishly, "she does have a small butterfly on her right hip."

Molly's parents both craned their necks and looked at Emily with surprise.

"She does?" Camille asked. She looked over at her husband and shrugged. "I didn't know."

"She got it this past summer," Emily explained. "I'm sorry, Molly didn't want me to tell you. She showed me the other night when we went shopping. We were trying on clothes, and well, you know."

"What else did she not want you to tell us?"

Jonathan asked, his eyes widening with irritation.

"Oh, Em, was Molly doing things behind our backs?" Camille questioned.

"Not that I know of," Emily replied with a slight shake of her head. She looked into her friend's searching eyes. "But you know teenagers. Didn't you do things you never told your parents?"

"Yeah. There are plenty of things I did that my folks still don't know anything about," Peter remarked, "and I plan to keep it that way."

Colin stifled a chuckle.

Camille shot her brother a quizzical stare. "Like what?"

"You all can sort that out later, let's get back to the report," Colin said. "Emily told me Molly's car is still at the house."

"Yes," Camille replied, moving her gaze from Peter to Colin. "She must have gone off on her bike because it's missing from the garage."

"Can you describe it?" Colin asked.

"It's one of those Fat Tire cruiser bikes, bright red with yellow fenders. She loved going on long rides along the green belt," Camille described, her eyes welling up as she talked about her daughter.

Emily's thoughts flew to the back end of the bicycle she saw in the garage of the suspicious Asians' home. She started to open her mouth, almost blurting out that fact, but she bit her lip to keep quiet about it awhile longer.

"Was there something you wanted to add, Emily?" Colin asked, noticing she was about to speak.

"No." Emily noticed how he was getting good at

reading her, picking up on the slightest facial expression, seeing the gears moving in her mind. She hoped he'd let it drop until she was ready to share what she was thinking.

"Do you have the photo?" Colin's gaze bounced from Camille to Jonathan and back.

She scooted it across the table to him.

"Okay, then. I think I have all I need to file this report in the National Crime Information Center and get Molly's picture out to the media. That way the whole country will be on the lookout for her." Colin stuck the photo in his file before pushing back from the table.

Emily patted Camille's hand and smiled weakly at her.

"Why don't you guys go home?" Colin stood and picked up his laptop. "We'll let you know the second we find out anything."

"We'd appreciate that, Colin." Jonathan rose and helped Camille up. "The very second you know anything."

"Peter, are you coming?" Camille asked her brother, as he remained seated.

"No, I have a meeting here in a little while, so I'll catch a ride home with someone."

"Oh, yeah, I almost forgot—the all-important sting." Camille rolled her eyes and her sarcastic voice cut like a razor blade, as she pulled another tissue out of her purse to blot the tears from her eyes.

Is she blaming us?

"Don't worry." Emily put her arm sympathetically around her friend, knowing her suggestion was futile. "We'll get Molly home."

Camille looked Emily in the eye and paused, as if she wanted to say something but thought better of it. Jonathan took Camille's hand and led her out of the room.

Emily stood in the conference room doorway and watched as the couple meandered down the hall. She couldn't remember ever having seen her friends so upset or worried. She didn't have children of her own, but she could imagine how terrifying it would be if one of them was missing. Her heart broke for them as she thought of their frightening situation.

Colin stood beside Emily as she watched them go. He laid his arm warmly around her shoulder and she leaned into him. He lightly kissed the side of her head. "It's best if you don't make promises you might not be able to keep."

"Agreed, but there's something you should know." She pulled away from him and walked back to the table.

"What?" Colin followed her.

"I didn't want to say anything while they were here, but I think I saw Molly's bike."

"Where?" Peter and Colin asked simultaneously.

"Peter, the house." Emily and Peter's eyes met.

"What house?" he questioned.

"You know...the house down the street from Camille and Jonathan's. I had you write down the address."

"That house?" Peter's brow furrowed.

"Emily, explain to me what you're talking about." Colin crossed his arms and shifted his weight to face her.

Emily looked at Colin with eyebrows raised, giving him clues as to what she was talking about. "The house where Molly and I saw the Asian girls in the backseat of the car…the girl from the hotel…the vehicle I followed down to the Jade Thai Spa."

He nodded. "When did you see it?"

"Just a little while ago, after we left Camille and Jonathan's."

"I don't understand. How were you able to see the bike at their house?" Colin asked.

"When Peter and I drove past, the garage door was up. I saw a red Fat Tire bike near the back of the garage. It was leaning against the shelves and it had bright yellow fenders."

"I don't want to be the party pooper here, but it could belong to someone who lives in the house, couldn't it?" Peter asked.

Colin's gaze locked on Emily's and she knew they were thinking the same thing—if she was right about what was going on, it was highly unlikely anyone in that house ever went on a bike ride for pleasure.

"It's possible," Colin replied. "Assuming—"

"Assuming Emily's wrong about her suspicions." Peter finished the detective's sentence. He glanced at Emily, whose eyes were narrowing at him. "But that's not likely, is it?"

"It seems to me the more we discover, the more it looks like I'm right."

"It's beginning to look that way," Colin agreed.

Emily turned her wrist and looked at her watch. "The others should be here pretty soon for our next meeting, so I'm going to make a quick coffee run. Anybody want anything?"

THE CHAIN OF LIES

~*~

When Emily returned, Colin's superior was standing near the conference table talking with him and Peter. They all turned in her direction as she walked in, carrying a cardboard tray full of coffees.

"Emily," Colin said as he put his hand out to her to draw her in, "you remember the Chief of Police, don't you?"

The Chief was a tall man with dark skin, dressed in a navy blue suit, with curly gray hair clipped short and neat.

"Yes, we've met a couple of times. Nice to see you again, Chief Nelson." She extended her hand.

"Nice to see you again, too." His large hand grasped hers and shook it. "Last time was when you helped solve the Wakefield case, right?"

"Yes, that's right," she replied.

"I know you've been a big help to Colin and Ernie, and I've had my eye on you. Have you ever thought about joining us as a consultant?"

"A consultant? You mean like you pay me to help your department?"

"Yes. Seems crime is on the rise, so we could use you on a case-by-case basis. It would save Paradise Valley some money and we'd have two detectives whenever necessary. Colin speaks very highly of you and your skills. Ernie, too."

"Hmmm." She glanced at Colin, who was grinning widely at her, then her gaze moved back to his boss. "I'll have to give it some thought, Chief. I just might take you up on that."

"Well, I'm going to grab a coffee and find a seat," Peter said, reaching for a cup.

Within minutes, Isabel arrived at the Paradise Valley police station with FBI Special Agent Tony Ellis in tow. Ellis had a commanding presence, standing well over six feet tall with neatly trimmed dark hair and the typical FBI dark suit and tie with spit-shined shoes.

Right on their heels, Colin's friend, Captain Ray Decker, from the nearby Boise SWAT team, strode into the conference room. He was dressed in police blues and his light brown hair was buzzed short, military style. He had been a Marine, like Colin, and appeared to be all about discipline and force.

Introductions were made around the room, and Colin suggested they all have a seat and get down to business.

"Emily, why don't we begin this meeting with you explaining to us what precipitated this gathering and what you've discovered so far," the Police Chief proposed.

"Of course." She stood and described everything she had witnessed, from the young Asian woman in the hotel restroom, to the family in Camille's neighborhood, to her experience with the Jade Thai Spa, including her client's husband who verified there were sexual favors offered at that massage parlor.

Ellis confirmed there had been numerous complaints of prostitution to the Boise Police Department and the Feds were brought in because of the suspicion of moving prostitutes across state lines.

Colin pointed out the seriousness of this meeting in light of the young Asian woman who was recently found murdered.

"We suspect the dead girl may be tied to what's going on at the Jade Thai Spa," Emily added, glancing from Special Agent Ellis to Captain Decker.

"And we've had a troubling new development, gentlemen, since we made the arrangements for this joint task force to meet," Colin informed Ellis and Decker.

Ellis's head tilted and both his and Decker's eyes lit up with interest. "What kind of new development, Detective?"

"My friend's daughter, Molly, has gone missing," Emily blurted out. She went on to explain Molly's connection to the case, in detail, and how she had seen what she believed was Molly's bicycle in the suspects' garage earlier that day.

"That does put an urgency to our plan," Captain Decker said, rubbing his jaw.

"If they took the girl because they think she knows too much," Special Agent Ellis explained, "assuming they really do turn out to be traffickers, she could be whisked out of the country within forty-eight hours."

Isabel and Emily shot a terrified glance at each other. This was Molly they were talking about.

"Maybe we should nix the joint task force and let my men handle this," Ellis said. "It sounds to me like it's clearly a federal case."

"Sounds to me like the FBI will benefit from having the different agencies involved," Isabel remarked. "We have a better chance of success that way."

"I don't know." Ellis shook his head.

"Let me remind you, Tony, I've had a lot of years of experience—at the CIA and the FBI—so you know, that I know, what I'm talking about. Besides, you can still take all the credit when we take this ring down."

He stared at Isabel, obviously thinking through the possibilities, and everyone around the table fell silent, waiting for his response.

"All right, Martínez, but if this thing goes south, it's your butt, not mine."

"Now that we have that out of the way, how old is Molly?" Decker asked.

"Seventeen," Peter replied.

"Description?"

"About five five, a hundred and twenty pounds, long red hair, green eyes, very pretty," Isabel answered.

Decker and Ellis both made notes of her description.

"How long has she been gone?" Ellis questioned.

"Since about six o'clock Saturday night," Emily responded.

"A girl like that would fetch a good price," Decker noted.

"Molly's my niece, Captain. I'll do whatever I have to, to get her back." Peter's voice was serious and determined. "I've done some investigative reporting on human trafficking and a bit of undercover work. If you'll get me a small video camera, I'll go into the spa as a customer and see if I can get the proof you need to bust these S.O.B.s."

"I can't have a reporter in the middle of an operation. I'd rather have one of my agents—"

"She's my niece! Please, let me do this."

"You're asking too much," Ellis insisted.

"I could just go in there on my own, as a potential

customer, and see what I can find out," Peter suggested.

"Oh, no you don't," Ellis responded.

"It's what I do, Ellis. But with the right equipment, I could be a lot more effective."

"What do you think, Detective?" Ellis focused on Colin, then turned to Chief Nelson. "Chief?"

"It's your call, Andrews." The Chief leaned forward in his seat. "You've got more experience with these big city crimes."

Colin looked at Peter as he thought about it. "I think he can handle it, if you get him wired up and hooked up." Colin crossed his arms and leaned back in his chair. "Can you provide the equipment we need, Special Agent Ellis?"

"Yeah, I can get it, and more. Make a list. But if something happens to this reporter, it's on your head. I'm not going to be hung out to dry over this."

"I'll take that chance," Colin replied, standing his ground.

Captain Decker stood and leaned forward over the table. "When are you planning this little shindig?" He looked Colin in the eye first, then Peter.

"This evening, around five o'clock. That's when the spa opens."

"Yeah, that's right." Ellis sat back. "We've been watching that place for a few weeks, working on gathering evidence of interstate prostitution. My people were actually planning a raid when Isabel called me."

"But human trafficking, Ellis, that'll be a much more significant collar for you than simply interstate prostitution," Isabel reasoned.

"I can't argue with that," he agreed. "All I need to

do is say the word and my people will jump into action."

"Okay, then. Let's stop wasting time and nail this plan down," Decker ordered.

Emily began, "My idea was that—"

"Whoa, little lady," Special Agent Ellis cut in. "We can't have a civilian running the show."

"Not a civilian," Chief Nelson corrected, "a consultant."

Emily flashed a slight grin in gratitude at the Chief for standing up for her before she turned her attention back to the smug FBI special agent. "I'm only sharing my thoughts, sir."

"Well, consultant or not, I want to make one thing perfectly clear to all of you. The FBI is in charge of this operation and everything goes through me. Agreed?"

"Yes, everything goes through you," Emily concurred.

With nodding of heads, everyone around the table agreed to Ellis taking the lead.

"Now, let Emily explain, Special Agent," the Chief ordered, rising to his feet, "then you all can decide on the best plan of attack, but hear her out." He glared around the table, almost daring anyone to contest his words. "Emily, proceed." He motioned toward her with his hand and sat back down.

"All right. What do you got?" Ellis asked.

"Colin goes in first as a customer, wired and with a tiny video camera," Emily explained. "He'll try to get as many faces on that video as he can. If and when they offer sexual favors, he will decline."

"I decline?"

"Yes, just listen," she said before proceeding with

her plan. "Then, a little while later, Peter goes in, also wired with a video camera, going through the same routine, but this time, when sex is offered, he'll tell them he would like sex, but not there. He only wants it to be at a nice hotel. If she can bring the girl to him, he'll pay more."

"Explain how that makes them bring Molly to me?" Peter asked.

"Tell the woman you're partial to American girls, especially redheads and blondes, and you'd be willing to pay more for one of them, especially if she's young."

"Why not just a redhead?"

"Don't you think that would make them suspicious?" she asked.

"I guess, assuming they don't also have a blonde hidden somewhere too."

"I hadn't thought of that." Emily grimaced. "Geez, I hope not."

"No, I don't think you should say anything about blondes or redheads," Decker disagreed. "That'll make them suspicious and scare them off. Just tell them something like no offense to Asians, but I prefer Caucasian girls. It's doubtful they'll have any other white girls on hand."

"I agree with Decker. This ring seems to keep with Asian girls, particularly Thai." Special Agent Ellis glanced around the table. "But getting back to the plan, if they're keeping girls at the house and at the spa, we'll have to execute this plan with split-second accuracy. We'll need to take down all three locations simultaneously so they don't have time to warn the others."

"Good idea," the Chief agreed.

"Decker, your team can take the house," Ellis asserted. "The FBI will take the spa, since we've been getting ready to move on it anyway, and Colin and his team can handle the arrests at the Paradise Valley Hotel."

"What about the warrants?" the Chief asked.

"I've already got federal warrants in the works for the spa and the house," Isabel declared.

"Sounds like a plan," Decker agreed.

"Yeah, it all sounds good to me, too," Colin said.

"I'm all in," Peter added. "Let's do it for Molly."

"But what if it turns out Molly's not at *any* of those places?" Emily asked, nervously considering that might be the case.

"We'll have to figure that out when we come to it," Decker said. "For now, let's stay positive and hope we can rescue her in one of the sweeps."

Before ducking out, the Chief praised Emily for her insight and plan, and he said he was looking forward to working with her as a consultant. She hadn't given him an answer yet, but she figured he said it to give her more credibility with the other agencies, particularly Special Agent Ellis.

After hammering out a few more of the finer points of the plan, they all agreed to meet back at the Paradise Valley police station in two hours. Ellis confirmed he and his team would bring all the technical equipment they would need to pull off the plan, including the media van to monitor the audio, video, and radio contact.

"Let's do this thing!" Decker hollered with a loud clap of his hands.

CHAPTER 16
The Jade Thai Spa

EMILY SQUIRMED IN HER SEAT inside the FBI van, parked half a block from the Jade Thai Spa, as she and Isabel watched the monitor with anticipation. Special Agent Ellis ably ran the equipment.

He had outfitted Colin with a tiny video camera embedded in the button of a vest the FBI provided, complete with a microphone woven into the fabric. Colin was dressed down, jeans and a button-down shirt with his cuffs rolled up to complement the vest.

Ellis had provided Colin an earbud for two-way communication in case Emily recognized any of the girls on the video monitor. After doing a test run to make sure the equipment was working and the camera was pointed in the right direction, Ellis turned Colin loose.

Peter was also wired and given a micro-video camera. He was dressed in a suit, with his necktie loosened and the top button of his shirt undone, as if he had just come from a long, exhausting business meeting. His shtick would be that he was a business man from out of town, in Boise for a series of high-level meetings. He wanted a massage to unwind and de-stress from his tiring day.

Waiting for his turn to go in, Peter took a seat on the other side of Emily.

"I'm walking up to the front door," they all heard Colin say as they watched the monitor, seeing him approach the front door of the massage parlor. It was five fifteen in the late afternoon on a crisp, sunny fall day.

He pushed open the door and casually strolled up to the reception desk. The monitor showed there was a middle-aged Asian woman with shoulder-length black hair behind the counter. She was looking down at the desk when Colin entered. The name plate on her lapel read *Ratana*. She raised her head when he came in.

"That's the woman! That's the woman! I think she's the madam," Emily excitedly exclaimed into the microphone so Colin could hear her.

"Ow." Colin winced, apparently at Emily's loud voice in his ear.

"Hello, mister. Can I help you?" she asked in a thick accent.

"Yes, I need a massage. I have this terrible pain in my neck." He grimaced and rubbed a hand on the back of his neck.

"Happy to help. We have Thai neck and shoulder massage, twenty-five dollar, or full body massage for sixty dollar. Which you like?"

"Which one do you recommend?"

"Ooh, full body is very relaxing. I think you like."

"Full body it is, then."

"You pay first, then we go. Cash only."

"I thought you took credit cards."

"No. We used to, but change policy. Now, only cash."

"I wonder if that's a clue they suspect the FBI is onto them," Ellis commented.

Colin pulled his wallet out of his back pocket and handed her three twenties. "Your name badge says *Ratana*. That's a pretty name. What country are you from?"

"I am from Thailand," she answered with a smile.

She unlocked the cash drawer, laid the money inside, and relocked it before walking away from it. "Follow me. This way."

The four of them watched as the monitor showed Colin following the woman down a dimly lit hallway. It was clear this establishment had been a house at one time and the massage rooms had been bedrooms.

A young woman with long black hair came out of one of the rooms and turned toward Colin. She scurried past him and the older woman. The girl had looked at Colin ever so briefly then lowered her face toward the floor as she dashed past him.

"I think that's the girl from the hotel!" Emily exclaimed into the microphone.

"Ow," Colin muttered, putting his hand up to his neck to cover.

"Massage will take care of that," the woman said, opening the door to one of the rooms.

"You sure, Emily?" the special agent asked.

"Not totally sure. She only looked up for a second. It could be her, though. Can you rewind it?"

"We might miss something crucial if I do. We'll replay it in slow motion when he's out of there."

Colin turned his body, keeping it in line with his eyes, as he scanned around the room. On the monitor, a massage table could be seen in the middle of the room with a couple of large white towels folded and stacked on one end of it. A twin-sized bed, covered with a red satin comforter and an array of colorful pillows in daybed fashion, was pushed against one wall. A straight-backed wooden chair sat next to it.

"You have a few minutes to get undressed. Put your clothes over there." She motioned to the wooden chair. "Climb on table, face down, and put towel over yourself, if you like."

"Thank you, ma'am."

The woman left the room and closed the door after herself.

"Colin, this is Special Agent Ellis. Can you see any video cameras?" He could tell by the movement on the screen that Colin looked around the room for any signs that what happened in the room was being recorded.

"Nope." He spoke softly as he grabbed a towel off the table. "Now to get undressed and climb on the table without exposing myself to the world." He walked over to the chair, took the vest off first, and pointed the buttons away. "I'm taking the rest of my clothes off and leaving them on the chair. After I wrap the towel around myself, I'll reposition the vest."

"Got it," Ellis replied.

"How's that?" Colin whispered.

"That's good. I can see the whole table clearly."

"Since I know you're all watching, I'll try to climb on this table as modestly as I can. You might want to look away until I get in position."

"Not a chance," Isabel muttered.

"Isabel!" Emily scolded possessively under her breath.

"Nice abs," Isabel remarked.

"All right, I'm in position."

There was a knock at the door.

"Come in," Colin called out.

The door opened slowly and a young Asian girl, likely late teens, came in wearing her jet-black hair down past her shoulders, a tight white smock over black short shorts, and obviously little else. "I start with your shoulders."

"Okay," Colin replied.

"Is that the same girl?" Isabel asked Emily.

"No, looks like a different one." Emily squinted at the screen. "But she may have been in the car when I saw the three of them."

The masseuse applied a light layer of oil and began working it in as she massaged his back and shoulders, then worked on his neck.

"That feel good?" she asked.

"Yeah...great."

"You have tension in your neck and shoulder." She continued to knead the muscles.

"It's my job, gives me a lot of stress."

"What your job?"

"My job?" he asked, as if he suddenly realized he couldn't say he was a cop and he fumbled for an answer.

"Tell her you're a construction worker," Emily suggested into the mic.

"I'm a construction foreman. Lots of stress running a crew."

"A crew? What that?"

"My workers," Colin replied. "By the way, my name is Colin. What's yours?"

Emily and the gang in the van leaned forward, waiting for her answer.

"Icannot say."

"Really? Why not? What if I want to ask for you the next time I come?"

"No, sorry, you cannot. Madam will bring you the girl available."

"That's too bad. I'd like to ask for you. You're doing a very good job. Can't I at least get a first name?"

"No," she whispered.

"The way she glanced around, she must suspect she's being watched," Ellis noted.

The girl massaged down his back and his extremities. "You want to turn over and I do the front."

"This should be interesting," Isabel remarked, glancing around to the others in the van.

Emily held her tongue, wondering what he would do to keep from giving her and her fellow van members a peep show.

"I think I'd like to stay on my stomach. I'm so relaxed that I feel like going to sleep."

Emily and the others watched the monitor, seeing the girl look at the door, then look around the room.

"Mr. Colin—"

"No, just Colin."

"If you turn over, I can do much more for you."

"What do you mean?" Colin asked.

Emily and Isabel held their breaths as their attention was glued to the monitor. The men also seemed to be silent and drawn to the video.

"If you let me massage the front too, I think you will have much pleasure." She glanced toward the door again.

"She's trying to excite him sexually, isn't she?" Emily squirmed in her seat.

"It appears to be what she's expected to do before offering him—"

"Sex?" Emily cut Isabel off. A little embarrassed by her outburst, realizing Colin probably heard her. She lowered her voice. "Poor girl looks nervous."

"No, I'm happy with the back massage," Colin responded.

"There seems to be a thought-out plan the madam enforces for her girls to stimulate clients toward wanting sex, at a price of course," the special agent remarked.

"Are we done?" Colin asked.

"I do good job. *Please*, Mr. Colin. You will like it."

Emily felt a knot twisting in her stomach at the girl's pleading. She reached out and grabbed Isabel's hand to steady herself. It was clear this young girl was expected to push the male clients to have sex with them. She wondered what the consequence was for failing. Was this what Molly could be facing if they can't find her in time?

"Guess that's what I have to look forward to." Peter sat back and crossed his arms, an uneasy smile quivered on his lips. "Glad I got to observe what I'm getting myself into."

"I thought you had undercover experience." Ellis shot a questioning glance at Peter.

"Undercover investigating, not investigating under the covers."

"Sorry, no," Colin replied. "Not this time. But don't worry, I will be back."

The masseuse wiped her oily hands on a white towel, her head hanging down as if she had failed somehow. "Thank you, Mr. Colin. You very nice. Please, come back. Please." She turned, her shoulders slumped, and she walked out the door.

Colin pulled the towel around his waist and carefully climbed down off the massage table. Turning the buttons on the vest away, he grabbed his clothes off the chair and quickly pulled them on. As he was buttoning the vest, there came a knock at the door.

The four in the van watched the screen intently.

"Come in."

The door opened and the madam stepped into the room, leaving the door open. "I just want to make sure you are happy with your massage?"

"Yes, very happy." Colin faced her and his camera caught one of the young masseuses walking past. The girl briefly looked toward the open door.

"That's definitely the one from the hotel." Emily gasped as she lunged forward, toward Special Agent Ellis and the microphone.

"Are you sure?" Ellis turned to face her.

Emily nodded.

The older woman moved farther into the room. "You still have time you already pay for, but you are leaving early. I want to make sure everything okay?"

"Yes, great." Colin fastened the last button on his vest.

Emily instructed Colin, through the earpiece, to make sure the woman knew the girl did everything she could for him.

"Your girl did an awesome job. I feel very relaxed."

"But you have more time. She can do more for you."

"I have to get to an appointment, ma'am, so I've used all the time I can spare. But I will come back again another time." Colin skirted around her and backed toward the door. "She was very good with her hands. I simply need to get going."

"Okay. I want to make sure you are happy."

"Very happy." Colin backed all the way out the door. "Thank you." He turned and made his way to the front area.

"As you can all see, I'm out of that place and on my way to you." The monitor showed Colin climbing back in his car and driving around the corner to the media van. Opening the door, he climbed into the increasingly cramped space.

"Nice abs," Isabel commented.

Colin looked at her, then at Emily. "Thanks."

Special Agent Ellis stood at the front of the van, speaking to Captain Decker on his cell phone. He reported on the operation so far and directed him to get his SWAT team together and stand by, ready to raid the home at twenty-one hundred hours, assuring him they would be in close radio contact. The timing of the operation would hinge on what happened at the hotel.

"Nice work, Detective," Ellis praised as he stuck his phone in his pocket and walked back toward Colin and the others. "Good legwork, so now Peter here has a better handle on his role."

While the men discussed what they'd discovered so far and what the objective of Peter's performance would be, Emily leaned over to speak quietly to Isabel. "How's Jethro doing?"

"He's pretty sick, pancreatic cancer."

"I thought he looked different at lunch the other day, thinner than the first time I met him."

"Funny thing, though. I saw Delia at the hospital, too. She's got to be related to him in some way."

Emily looked into Isabel's deep brown eyes. "You think she's his other daughter?"

"Could be. She's probably too young to be one of his ex-wives."

"I hadn't thought of that. He did say he'd been married five times. When I read Delia Banderas McCall, I assumed Banderas was her maiden name, but it could have been a previous married name."

"Maybe she was the Las Vegas party girl he was married to briefly." Isabel covered her mouth to stifle a chuckle.

"Can you imagine sophisticated and demure Delia McCall as a party girl?"

"What are you girls laughing at?" Colin stood behind Emily's chair.

"Just girl talk," Isabel replied.

Emily rose and turned to him, lacing her hands around his waist. "Good job." Standing on her tiptoes, she gave him a soft peck on the cheek. "Now, it's Peter's turn."

Emily's phone chimed in her pocket. Pulling it out, she saw it was Camille. "Hello," she answered, glancing from Colin to Isabel.

"Emily, I'm so glad I reached you. Any word yet?" Camille pleaded in a tone filled with desperation.

"No, hon, sorry not yet." Emily could hear the high anxiety behind each of Camille's words and her chest felt heavy and tight at having to tell her no.

"But it's been several hours. No word at all?"

"Camille, sweetie, listen to me. We are doing all we can to find Molly." Emily couldn't tell her she had seen her daughter's bike and she was, in all probability, being held by sex traffickers. She fought against the desire to blurt out the truth, needing to keep that news from her for now. "It'll take some time. I promise to call you as soon as we have anything at all to tell you."

"Okay." Camille backed off. Her voice was weak and shaky.

"Is Maggie still there with you?"

"Yes, she's been here since we got back, but I haven't seen Isabel."

"Isabel's helping Colin find Molly. She'll be in touch. Can you put Maggie on the phone?"

"She wants to talk to you," Emily overheard Camille say.

"Hello."

"Maggie, I need you to listen carefully. I know Camille and Jonathan are beside themselves with fear. I'm counting on you to be strong for them and try to keep them calm."

"I will."

"When they start playing the blame game, and you know they will, make sure they know this was not their fault. Can you do that for me?"

"I'll take care of them. They've taken care of me plenty of times. Don't you worry yourself, I'm here for 'em."

Emily couldn't help but agree that Maggie was right about their having taken care of her. Camille and Jonathan had stepped up numerous times over the years to help Maggie and her son, Josh.

Maggie had grown up dirt-poor in Texas and had dragged her toddler to Hollywood seeking fame and fortune. When things didn't turn out the way she had planned, she took her little boy and moved to Paradise Valley where her brother and his family lived.

Most recently, in the months previous, Maggie had endured a life-shattering event, and it was Camille, with Jonathan's help, who became a regular fixture at Maggie's house until she could get back on her feet. Though she appeared to be a soft and lovely Southern belle, she had forged a backbone of steel as she fought to leave poverty behind and make a better life for herself and her son.

"That takes a load off my mind, knowing you're there, Maggs. Tell Jonathan and Camille that it'll probably be hours before we know anything, but I will call as soon as I have something."

"Got it."

CHAPTER 17
Peter's Performance

TO MINIMIZE ANY SUSPICIONS, Special Agent Ellis had Peter wait half an hour before sending him into the Jade Thai Spa. With his dark blue suit, complementing his auburn hair and deep blue eyes, and a classy gold tie, Peter was dressed for the part of successful businessman. He had already loosened the tie and unbuttoned the collar, but now he stuck the fake black-framed glasses on his face. A tiny micro-video camera was hidden in them.

Peter patted his pants pocket. "Hey, what about the money?"

Ellis handed him a stack of cash, folded in half inside an expensive-looking money clip. "There's more there than you need, Peter. Just make sure the woman sees you have plenty of cash to spend for later."

Peter shot him a wry smile as he took the money and shoved it in his pocket. "Thanks, Ellis."

"What about a car?" Emily asked while rummaging through her handbag.

"What do you mean?" Peter tilted his head and quirked an eyebrow.

"Wouldn't they expect to see a nice car in the parking lot, if he really was a successful businessman?"

"I already thought of that." Ellis dug in his pocket. "My car's down the block a little ways. Black Lexus sedan. Here's my keys." He gingerly tossed them to Peter.

Ellis had Peter test the video camera in the bridge of the frames to make sure the feed was coming through to the monitor, as well as the microphone that was embedded in the corner of the glasses. Peter slipped an earbud into his right ear as he walked to the end of the van and spoke a few test words.

"Everything looks good, Peter. I'm about to begin recording." Ellis adjusted the sound level from his perch in front of the control panel. "Are you ready?"

"I'm ready. Let's do it." Peter pushed open the back door and stepped out into the cool dusk.

Colin took Peter's seat in the van as the four of them crowded around the screen, watching Peter get into Ellis's Lexus. Once Peter started the engine and began driving away, his monologue began.

"This is Peter MacKenzie reporting to you from Boise, Idaho. I'm going undercover into a suspected sex slave brothel to see if I can gather enough intel to prompt an arrest and to rescue the young women, girls really, that are forced to prostitute themselves to an avalanche of men every single night."

Those seated in the media van looked questioningly

at the monitor and then at each other, many with their mouths gaping open, shocked into temporary silence.

Colin was first to break the silence. "What the—"

"He is a reporter," Emily added. "He can't help himself."

"I guess it won't hurt to let him intro the footage that way, as long as he doesn't do any of that posturing once he's inside," Ellis said.

"I can hear you," Peter responded evenly as he approached the building.

"Stick to the plan and we'll be good," Ellis said.

Peter parked the car in one of the few spaces in front of the Jade Thai Spa and climbed out. "I'm coming up to the door." The monitor showed him opening it and stepping inside. The same woman stood behind the reception counter.

She looked up at him, appearing on the video as if she was looking directly into the camera. She smiled pleasantly. "Good evening. How can I help you?" she asked in her thick Thai accent.

"I need a really good massage. I've been in meetings all day and my shoulders are one big knot."

"Meetings all day on Sunday?" She continued to smile, apparently hoping to glean more information from him.

"Yeah, I'm from out of town and have had one meeting after another all weekend. We're finally done and now I can take a break and relax, that is if I can get these kinks worked out of my shoulders."

"We take good care of you. Thai neck and shoulder massage twenty-five dollar and full body massage sixty. Which one you like?"

"I'm pretty wound up. I better take the full body one."

"That will be sixty dollar. We only take cash."

"Now flash the cash, MacKenzie," the special agent ordered.

"No problem." Peter tugged the loaded money clip out of his pocket and peeled off a fifty and a ten. He made sure she saw there was quite a bit left.

"Look at that vulture," Emily muttered to Isabel. "I think she's salivating."

She accepted the cash with a grin, stuck it in the drawer, and locked it. "This way, mister."

From the monitor, Peter could be seen following close on her heels down the same hallway Colin had taken. She opened the door to a different room, one more plushly appointed.

"Looks like she knew Peter had more money than I did." Colin hunched forward, resting his forearms over his knees. "This should be good."

From the camera's view, the screen showed the massage table again in the center of the room, but the chair was an upholstered overstuffed one sitting next to a queen-sized bed covered in a high-quality comforter set. A tri-fold screen with gold shirred silk fabric stood in the corner as a place for the customers to disrobe, with hooks on the wall to hang their clothes.

"You can undress there," the woman said, directing him to the tri-fold screen. "There are fluffy towels on the table if you like to cover yourself. Your masseuse will be in shortly. Enjoy." She backed out of the room and pulled the door shut.

"Let's see if he'll be as deft as you were with the

towel," Emily kidded.

"Peter," Ellis spoke into the mic, "nonchalantly take a gander around the room for anything that could be a video camera."

Peter grabbed a white towel off the table and stepped behind the screen, slinging part of the towel over the top of it. As he took off his jacket, shirt and tie, he casually glanced around the room, as well as behind him and up on the ceiling. He took his glasses off and the monitor showed the camera swinging haphazardly. "I'm putting the mic near my mouth, lowering my head," he whispered. "Video camera above the door, watching me."

"Then you'll need to be careful what you say to us or you could blow the whole thing," Ellis said.

He stuck his glasses back on his face and pulled his shoes and pants off.

"Don't look down at your feet, man," Colin advised.

"Why? Oh." The monitor screen showed the camera suddenly swing up to the top ridge of the tri-fold and higher. "Thanks," he whispered. "I can hear those giggles." Peter wrapped the towel around his midsection, then set his glasses on the night table between the chair and the bed, facing the massage table and the door.

"Perfect view," Ellis said.

With one smooth motion, he mounted the table.

"Good job, Peter," Isabel teased.

He loosened the towel under him so it laid flat over his backside.

There was a soft knock at the door and a young woman's voice asked if he was ready.

"Show time," Ellis announced.

"Come in."

The young Asian woman entered, dressed in a similarly seductive uniform to the one that worked on Colin.

"That's her," Emily exclaimed. "That's the girl from the hotel."

"You're sure?" Ellis asked.

"Yes, absolutely sure."

"You know what to do, MacKenzie," Ellis said.

"Good evening. Are you ready to begin?" the masseuse asked in her heavy accent.

"Oh, yeah. I'm so knotted up I feel like a pretzel."

"What is pretzel?"

"A piece of bread that's all tied up in knots."

"Oh, yes," she replied, unconvincingly.

She poured a layer of oil over him and began massaging his back and shoulders, working up to his neck and head. "That feel good?"

"That feels amazing."

"Peter, remember why you're there," Ellis reminded him.

"My name is Peter, by the way. What's your name?"

"No, no. I cannot say," she uttered firmly, "but Peter is a nice name." She continued to massage his back, then switched to his feet, working her way up his legs.

"Your hands are fantastic. How can I ask for you next time I come if I don't know your name?"

"No, sorry," she said with a shake of her head. "Does that feel good?"

"Like heaven."

"You want I do your bottom?" she asked, patting it lightly. "I do good job."

"Uh, no, I have no knots there."

"Okay, you turn over and I do front."

Emily's head jerked to Colin and she raised her eyebrows at him, wondering what Peter would do next.

Colin grinned at her and patted her leg. They had talked about this. He had to go farther than Colin did and he had to make it believable.

"Oh, my," Isabel muttered under her breath.

The girl raised the towel just enough for him to roll over beneath it before she laid it back down on him. She worked his arms and his chest muscles.

"We're watching you," Ellis reminded Peter.

She once again massaged his feet, working her way up his calves to his thighs. "That feel good, Mr. Peter?"

"It feels wonderful," Peter replied in a dream-like voice.

She kneaded his thigh muscles, putting her hand a little way up under the towel to reach them. Then her hand moved farther up and Peter's eyes grew wide. His body responded to her touch and he sat up on the table.

"I think that's enough," he said, gathering the towel tightly around him.

"Oh, Mr. Peter, I'm sorry. I do something wrong?" Her voice had a trembling quality that spoke of fear. "Other men like it when I do that."

Emily stared at the monitor, trying hard to swallow the lump that had formed in her throat. She wondered if the others were feeling the same. No one spoke until Ellis broke the silence.

"Peter, remember you're doing this for Molly," Ellis chided him. "Make the deal."

"No, I'm the one who's sorry," Peter said. "You did nothing wrong. I just wasn't expecting it."

"Can we continue? I can make you happy."

"What do you mean when you say *make me happy*?"

The young girl motioned with her hand toward the lavishly decorated bed. "I can make you very happy."

"For extra money?"

"Yes, three hundred dollar," the girl replied.

Peter looked at the girl, then at his glasses, staring right into the camera. Even at a distance, it was an unmistakable look of anger mixed with sadness over the plight of this young soul.

"What is wrong?"

"I would like to make a deal with your boss. Could you go and get her for me?"

"She will be angry with me."

"No, she will be happy. I promise."

The girl left and Peter slid off the table, standing with the towel secured around his waist. In a few minutes the girl returned with the woman named Ratana.

"What can I do for you?" the woman asked.

"This lovely young woman offered to have sex with me on that bed for three hundred dollars."

The woman glowered at the girl, who in response lowered her gaze. "She do something wrong?"

"No, no, nothing like that." Peter shook his head.

"You want to have sex with her? She is very pretty girl." The woman cupped the girl's chin and lifted her face. "She will show you good time."

Peter looked at the girl cowering next to the woman. Then he turned his attention back to the madam.

"I would like to have sex in my own hotel room, not here. I'm sure I would enjoy it a whole lot more."

"But she is here, you are here, the bed is ready. What is problem?"

"I want you to bring a girl to my hotel room. Can you do that? I'm willing to pay extra."

"How much extra?"

"I'd pay five hundred dollars."

"Five hundred?" The woman's eyes widened at the number.

"Yeah, but she has to be an American. No offense to you Asians, but I really prefer a Caucasian girl, you know, a white girl. I'd be willing to pay you twice that, but she has to be young. I don't want any worn-out hookers."

"One thousand dollar?" She sounded incredulous. "You pay me one thousand dollar if I bring a young American girl to your hotel room?"

"Yes, that's what I want."

The woman looked hard at Peter for a moment, then she looked at the girl cringing beside her. "You give me half now and half when I bring the girl."

"Five hundred now and five hundred tonight?" Peter asked, rubbing his jaw. "Let me see."

"Do it, Peter," Ellis directed. "You have enough on you, but make her work for it."

"Let's say I give you the first five hundred dollars but then you don't show up? I'm out five hundred big ones."

"You know where you can find me. No worries, I

show up," she assured him.

"Still, I'm taking a risk here."

"No, no, you have my word. I am honest business woman."

"Oh, brother," Emily sighed.

"I don't know," he stalled, fidgeting with his towel.

"Peter, don't make her work that hard. Close the deal," Ellis said.

"All right, lady, you have a deal."

"Very good, mister."

"Now let me get dressed, and I'll give you the cash and my hotel information on the way out. Okay?"

"Okay." The woman grabbed the girl by the arm and all but dragged her out the door.

Peter's hidden video camera caught the girl casting a fearful glance over her shoulder at him as he stood watching her leave, wearing nothing but a towel. As soon as she was out of sight, he turned away and stepped behind the tri-folding changing screen, grabbing the glasses on his way. He quickly dressed and left the room, finding Ratana waiting for him behind the reception desk.

As he stepped up to the desk, he heard the crinkling of paper behind him in the small waiting area. Peter turned to see a stocky Asian man, dressed in black slacks and a black polo shirt sitting in a chair reading a newspaper.

"That's the driver!" Emily bolted out of her chair. "He brings the girls from the house down to the massage parlor."

"Peter," Ellis called out, "try to get the guy to look up at you so we get his face on tape."

"Mister," Peter said, "is that today's paper?"

The man looked up briefly and nodded his head at Peter.

"You want newspaper?" Ratana asked.

"Nah, that's okay. Now that I think of it, there's probably one in my hotel room."

Peter dug the full money clip out of his pants pocket and pulled off five one hundred dollar bills. She handed him a pad of note paper and a pen, and he scrawled down the name of the hotel and his room number.

"There you go." He held out the money and the note but did not release them when she tugged on them, getting her attention. He lowered his voice to a quieter, more serious tone and dipped his head down closer to hers. "You will bring the girl to my hotel room at nine o'clock tonight, right? Because I don't like being made a fool of."

She leaned to the side and peered around Peter, presumably at the man in the waiting room. Was she seeking his confirmation?

"Yes, yes, I bring her. Nine o'clock." Ratana yanked the money and note out of Peter's hand as he loosened his grip on them. "No worries. I bring her."

CHAPTER 18
The Hotel Sting

PETER STEPPED UP into the FBI van to a round of applause. With one hand in front of his waist and one hand behind, he took a dramatic bow.

"Great job, MacKenzie," Ellis praised.

"It was all for Molly."

"You could always become an actor if the reporter thing doesn't work out," Colin kidded as Emily elbowed him lightly in the side.

"I'd say Oscar worthy," Isabel added with a few claps of her hands.

"Too bad you couldn't get that girl's name," Colin said.

"I think the girl knew she was being watched," Peter said. "You know, the camera over the door."

"Yeah, you have to be very careful when a camera is on you," Colin smirked, clearly referring to Peter looking at his shoes. "Forgetting can leave you, shall we say, *exposed*."

Peter's cheeks flushed red.

"Oh, Colin, stop that." Emily playfully slapped his leg. "Peter, you did a great job."

"Now, about my car." Ellis stuck out his hand and Peter tossed the car keys to him.

Emily swiveled her seat to face Tony. "Now what?"

"Now we move on to phase two." Ellis stood and addressed the group. "We mobilize our respective teams, stick to the plan, and we rescue those girls."

Molly's image flashed in Emily's mind. A stillness fell over the van like a hush. From the somber looks on the others' faces, she suspected they were likely thinking about her, too. Time was ticking away. As important as it was to set the other girls free, if they didn't rescue Molly that night, she may be lost to them forever.

~*~

Colin, Emily, and Peter got in position at the Paradise Valley Hotel. Colin had called earlier in the day and made arrangements for the hotel to clear a block of eight rooms on the third floor, hoping to keep any other guests from traipsing through their operation. He brought along three of Paradise Valley's young police officers, dressed in street clothes.

FBI Special Agent Tony Ellis took charge of the entire operation, and he had outfitted each of them with state-of-the-art earpieces with embedded microphones. Peter retained his glasses, both for continuity and for taping their end of the takedown.

Emily sat in the lobby with two of the plain-clothes

officers, out of the way but with a clear view of the entrance, anxiously waiting for Ratana to deliver Molly. Colin waited with Peter and the other plain-clothes cop in the third-floor room. The plan was for Colin to move to one of the vacant reserved rooms as soon as Peter was alerted their guests had arrived. The plain-clothes cop was to hide in Peter's closet until he was needed.

At five minutes to nine, Ratana and one of the Thai girls walked through the hotel's entry, escorted by the husky Asian man. Seeing Molly was not with the woman, Emily's heart began to race and her palms became sweaty, horrified at what that might mean.

"Colin," Emily said as she faced one of the officers seated next to her, leaning toward him as if she was having a conversation with him, "Ratana is here but she did not, I repeat, did not bring Molly with her." Her voice cracked as she fought against the tears that rushed to her eyes. "She brought one of the girls from the spa."

"Damn!" she could hear Colin shout.

"She didn't bring Molly?" Special Agent Ellis asked through the earpiece.

"Oh, it gets better. She brought a body guard. Colin, you better alert Peter and get out of there."

~*~

"I heard you, Emily." Peter stared at Colin. "Now what?"

"Agree to accept the girl, but I have to get out of here before they show up." Colin walked toward the door and the other cop stepped into the closet. "Heads up in there. Not a peep. I'll let you both know what to do next through the earpieces."

The officer slid the closet door shut as Colin slipped out and down the hall.

Within minutes there was a knock at Peter's door.

"They're here," he said quietly into the mic before he opened the door. "Hi, come on in."

Ratana pushed passed him, pulling the dolled-up girl behind her. The Asian man remained in the hallway.

"What's this? I told you a white American girl. You promised me."

"I know, I know. I don't have one for you. I know you want American, but not possible. So sorry."

Peter crossed his arms and glared at the woman, then at the girl, showing his displeasure at the change. In truth, he was trying to cover his mounting fear and crushing disappointment at the diminishing chances to rescue his niece. This would have been his opportunity to save her, but now her rescue was in question.

"But this one will give you great pleasure. And it will only cost you five hundred dollar. See, I save you money this way."

Peter looked at the girl whose eyes were lowered. She was dressed in a short, tight, red satin dress with black stilettos and way too much makeup. Her midnight-black hair was pulled up in a twist, held in place by two chopstick-like mahogany picks. She reminded him of a little girl trying to play dress-up.

He put two fingers gently under her chin and slowly lifted her face, revealing her big brown eyes. He was certain what he saw in them was utter fear and soul-wrenching pain. "Okay, she can stay." If he couldn't save Molly, at least he could save this one.

"I leave now. I be back in one hour."

"One hour? Five hundred dollars for only one hour?" Peter feigned surprise. In reality, he was glad to have the ordeal over in an hour instead of dragging it on through the night.

"You want longer, it will cost more."

"No, one hour is fine."

Ratana said something to the girl in her native language and the girl nodded, then the woman was out the door.

"Did you get that?" Peter asked, knowing Tony Ellis was monitoring the video feed.

"Got it."

Peter looked out the peephole to make sure Ratana and the man were both gone. All he saw was the back of the man's broad head. "That woman left the hulk to stand guard outside the door."

"We'll put our heads together and get rid of the guy," Colin said.

"I've tapped into the hotel's video feed. I can see the woman in the elevator," the special agent informed the group. "Andrews, make sure one of your men in the lobby watches for her when she gets off the elevator and stays with her. We have to keep eyes on that woman."

"He's already been given his orders, Ellis."

Peter turned back to the girl who was seated on the edge of the bed, unbuttoning her dress. "No, no. Don't do that," he said, waving his hands at her.

"I don't understand." Her expression told of confusion mingled with fear.

"I'm not having sex with you. I'm going to help you."

"Help me?"

"That's right."

"No one can help me," she said sadly with a slight shake of her head.

"What's your name?"

She shook her head again, looking down at her hands worrying in her lap.

"Trust me, no one will hurt you."

She raised her head and looked into Peter's face, as if she was considering whether to believe him or not. "Maliwan," she said softly.

"Okay, Maliwan, just sit tight. There'll be people coming and going, but you're safe here with me. Understand?"

She nodded.

"And you might hear me talking to myself, but I'm actually talking to someone else in my ear." He pulled his earpiece out and showed her.

Her eyebrows wrinkled together and she cocked her head, then she sat in uneasy silence.

"Peter, this is Colin. I have a plan, but I need you to distract the hulk so I can sneak out of this room."

"What do you want me to do?" Peter asked, distancing himself from the girl.

"Take the ice bucket to the door and ask the guy to get you some ice. Of course, he won't, but it will sway his attention for a few seconds."

"I can do that," Peter replied.

The girl watched as he grabbed the ice bucket off the dresser and went to the door. As Peter opened it, the large man spun around and glared at him. Holding up the bucket, he asked, "If it's not too much trouble, big guy, would you mind getting us some ice? I think the machine might be by the stairs, but I'm not sure. Here's the bucket." Peter held it out to him.

"Me get ice? No. You want ice, you get it." He shook his head as he turned back around and retook his post.

"Never mind." Peter slowly shut the door.

"Give us a few minutes, Peter. Emily and I have a plan. You might hear a ruckus outside your door for a second. Don't panic."

"You have things under control over there, Andrews?" Ellis asked.

"Yes, sir. We'll give you an update as soon as we get this goon out of the way."

~*~

The elevator tone dinged as the doors slid open. Out stepped Emily clinging to Colin, pretending they'd had too much to drink and were on the way to their room. Laughing and staggering down the hallway, they kept an eye on the Asian hulk. They stopped at the room directly across from Peter's.

"Where's your key card?" Colin asked with a drunken slur.

"Shoot!" Emily screeched, stamping one foot for emphasis. "I forgot my purse in the bar." She giggled then hiccupped like a woman who had had too much bubbly.

"All right, sweetie," Colin said. "You wait right here and I'll go down and get it for you." He stumbled away.

Emily wandered over to the man standing guard and attempted to start up a conversation to distract his attention. "Why are you standing out here? You locked out of your room?" she asked, swaying and slurring her words only inches from his face.

"Go away, lady."

"Okay," she sang, before unleashing her fury. In a matter of seconds, Emily stomped hard on his foot with the sharp heel of her boot, then she jerked her knee up into the man's groin. As he bent over in mind-numbing pain, she jabbed her elbow in his face.

Without giving him a moment to recover from the surprise attack, Colin had the muzzle of his Glock pressed against the man's neck. "Get your hands up!"

The man did as he was ordered, seething with anger, blood dripping from his nose.

Emily gingerly reached inside the man's jacket and pulled out the handgun he had in a holster under his arm. "What about his phone?" she asked, pulling it out of his breast pocket.

"Pesani, Cleaver, I need you out in the hallway to take the trash out," Colin ordered as he grabbed the man's hands, one at a time, and brought them down and cuffed him. He took the man's gun from Emily and stuffed it in the back of his belt.

One officer stepped out of Peter's room and the other came sprinting down the hall from the stairway toward them.

"Take him into room three eighteen and gag him. We can't have him warning the woman," Collin called after the cops as they took the man down the hall.

"We make a pretty good team," Emily said,

grinning up at Colin.

"We certainly do, but we ought to get inside, don't you think?" He tapped on the door.

"Good work Colin and Emily," Ellis praised through their earpieces.

"Thanks, boss, but it's not nearly over. We've got to find Molly." Emily entered Peter's room and Colin followed.

"SWAT has an unmarked surveillance van already in position near the house. I've been given word they're picking up four bodies on the heat sensor, two moving around on the main floor and two stationary upstairs."

"My man, Mason, is down in the lobby keeping watch over the woman," Colin reported. "She went in the bar. He'll let us know when she's on her way back up."

"She's probably in there sipping a mai tai, waiting while her girl does her dirty work." Emily growled between clenched teeth.

"She said she'd be back in an hour, so we only have to wait until then," Peter said, checking his watch. "Another twenty-three minutes or so."

"You do realize she'll be expecting to see the man she left outside your door?" Ellis pointed out. "You better come up with a plan quick to deal with that."

"Already thought of it and have it covered." Emily walked over to the young girl and settled on the edge of the bed next to her. She slipped off her cardigan and pulled the sweater around the girl's shoulders. "Don't worry, sweetie, we're here to help you. Do you understand?"

She nodded, fear still pooling in her dark eyes.

"Her name is Maliwan," Peter informed Emily.

"I need you to help me, too."

The girl stared silently into Emily's eyes.

"Will you help me, Maliwan?" Emily returned her gaze and looked kindly into the girl's face, hoping to allay her fears.

She nodded again, her eyes brightening a bit.

~*~

After her brief talk with Maliwan, Emily returned to Colin and Peter. She began to tell them that the girl thought she may have caught sight of Molly that very morning at the house.

"You forget you're mic'd, Emily," Ellis cut in. "We all heard the whole thing."

"Then you must have heard her say she saw a girl with long red hair lying on a mattress in the upstairs bonus room."

"We hope to God one of those four heat spots is Molly."

Ellis typically sounded professional and by the book, but every once in awhile Emily swore she could hear his voice quiver as he spoke of Molly. "As soon as you have the madam in custody, I'll give the signal to move on the house and the spa. If we move too soon, someone could text her a short one-word warning and she's in the wind, guys."

"One word?" Emily asked.

"Like *run*."

"Got it." Emily looked from Colin to Peter. "Now, we don't have much time, fellas, let's all get in position.

You heard the plan."

"We're on it," Peter replied.

"Maliwan," she said, casting a glance over her shoulder, "you know what to do, right?"

"Yes," she replied in a small, nervous voice.

Colin stepped into the closet and Emily went down the hall, just past the elevators, and waited around the corner in a small alcove. "We're all in place, Ellis." She reached back and felt her gun snuggly fitted in the back of her waistband, under her shirt.

"Ellis, is my video feed coming through okay?" Emily heard Peter ask.

"A-Okay."

"The elevator just dinged," Emily informed everyone. "Open the door, Peter. Cue Maliwan."

The doors glided open and the madam stepped out, turning toward Peter's room. She only took a few steps before she halted abruptly. Emily crept out of the alcove and tiptoed behind her, watching as the madam realized the man she'd left there was gone. The woman spun around and took a couple of steps toward the elevator, but Emily stood between Ratana and her escape.

"Oh, I'm so glad I found you," Emily gasped, her arms spread out to keep the woman from going around her. "There's a girl in the room down there that's been crying for her mother." Emily pointed toward the room. "She looks a lot like you, so I'm assuming that it's you she's been calling for?"

"That stupid girl," the woman spat under her breath, looking down at the floor. Then she raised her head and her expression softened. "Yes, I am her mother. Where is she?"

"Right down here." Emily laid one hand on the woman's shoulder and motioned down the hall with the other. She walked her to the room where Peter held the door open.

"I'm so glad you're back," Peter said. "Your girl has been crying her eyes out ever since you left."

The woman marched into the room, past the bathroom and closet. The girl was resting on the edge of the bed, her head bent down, weeping.

"There, that's the girl," Emily exclaimed, following the woman into the hotel room. Maliwan lifted her head as Ratana approached her.

Ratana barked something to the girl in Thai, motioning for her to leave with her. The girl replied something in her language, shaking her head no. The woman grabbed the girl by the arm and yelled at her again, yanking her to her feet.

Maliwan looked at Emily, pleading for help with her eyes.

Peter leaned against the dresser, watching the events unfold. "Are you getting this?" he whispered.

"Loud and clear," Ellis responded.

"Let her go!" Emily hollered, stepping toward the woman. "You're hurting her!"

"Peter, Emily needs a distraction, quick," Colin whispered into his mic from inside the closet.

The woman dropped her hold on the girl's arm, reached into her purse and drew out a small handgun. "The girl, she leave with me." Ratana pointed the weapon at Maliwan.

Peter glanced around. He picked up a glass from the dresser and hurled it against the closest wall, shattering with a loud crash.

The woman's head jerked toward the sound long enough for Emily to seize her opportunity. She grabbed the woman above the wrist, stepped in, flipped her over her hip and flat on her back on the floor, twisting the gun out of her hand. She dropped down and planted a knee on the woman's chest. "You're not going anywhere."

Colin rushed in and stood over them, his gun drawn, with a slight grin on his face. "Great job, Emily."

"And we got the whole thing on tape," Peter exclaimed, positioning himself to record the arrest.

"Paradise Valley Police," Colin shouted, flashing Ratana his badge while keeping his Glock leveled at her. "You're under arrest for prostitution and human trafficking, and anything else I can find to charge you with. Roll over on your stomach and put your hands behind your back."

Emily pulled her knee off the woman and sprang to her feet. "She's all yours."

Peter turned to watch as Colin clamped the cuffs on her and pulled the madam up.

"Why is it always my job to take the garbage out?" Colin marched the woman out of the room, reading her her rights as they went. Peter followed to get the whole thing on video.

"Stop complaining, Andrews," Ellis chided in their ears.

One of the doors across the hall opened and the two officers escorted the stocky man out, as well. The woman screamed a string of indiscernible words at the man in their native tongue and he barked a few back at her as they marched down the hallway.

"You heard all of that, Ellis, right?" Emily asked, touching her ear as she sat beside the girl on the bed.

"I did and I've already given the order to storm the spa and the house."

"I'm heading over to the house right now," Emily reported. "I'm keeping the girl with me for the time being."

"Not a good idea," Ellis said. "Let one of the officers take custody of her."

"She's just a kid, Tony, and she's been through a lot. I can't simply hand her over to another man she doesn't know." Emily thought she'd get some push-back from the Special Agent, but he must have understood she wasn't backing down. "Besides, we're already on a fast-track out of the hotel. I'll turn her over at the house, so have someone meet me, ready to take her. I want to be there when they bring Molly out."

"You mean *if* they bring Molly out. There's no guarantees here, Emily," Ellis said.

"I have to believe she's there, Tony, because if she's not, it would be better for her if she were dead." Emily glanced over at Maliwan, and the girl nodded sadly as she released a long sigh.

"She's there," Peter insisted. "We have to believe she's there."

"Keep the faith, Emily. I'll meet you at the house," Colin assured her.

CHAPTER 19
The Hidden Room

EMILY RACED TO THE HOUSE where Molly was suspected to be, with Peter in the passenger seat and Maliwan belted into the back. Special Agent Tony Ellis had stayed in their earpieces and she and Peter could hear, blow by blow, what was happening.

The FBI had raided the Jade Thai Spa, rounding up the girls and the customers. Ellis assured Emily they would all be sorted out and the girls would be held and looked at closely to determine if they had been forced into prostitution.

The SWAT team had surrounded and stormed the house, finding three of the four people who had shown up as hot spots on the infra-red heat sensor. The upstairs was being torn apart, Ellis had reported, trying to find the fourth, hoping it was Molly.

"She must be stuck in some hidden spot, Emily," Ellis said. "The scanner shows there's another heat source in the house, in an immobile and reclining position. I just hope it's the person you're searching for."

"We're about a block away. Where are you, Ellis?" Emily glanced over at Peter, meeting his gaze.

"I'm in the van and we're headed that direction, but still probably twenty minutes out."

"This is Colin. I'm just a few blocks away."

"Let me ask Maliwan if she knows anything." Emily peered upward, into the rearview mirror, and asked the girl about any hiding places in the house.

"Are you talking to the man in your ear, too?" the girl asked.

"Yes, how did you know?"

"Mr. Peter."

"Do you know about any hiding places in the house?"

"Bonus Room, there is small door to storage area," Maliwan replied.

"Did you get that, Tony?"

"The men have been all over that room."

"Behind big dresser," Maliwan clarified.

"Tony, ask them if they moved the big dresser. Our young friend says there is a small door behind the dresser. Molly's got to be there. I'm pulling up to the house now."

"Hold on, let me ask."

Emily, Peter, and Maliwan jumped out of the car and the girl stuck close to Emily as she and Peter marched to the front lawn of the house. Two SWAT members faced them from the porch and would not let anyone enter.

Ellis could be heard asking Decker what was happening, then he came back to Emily. "They're doing it, they're doing it. They've found the door."

"They found the door," Emily whispered to Maliwan. The two stood frozen, grasping each other's hand. Peter stepped closer to the porch to get a better view with the camera.

"Opening, opening, shining flashlight," Ellis continued. "She's there! Emily, did you hear me? She's there!"

"Oh, my God!" Emily gasped.

"What is it?" the girl asked anxiously.

"They found her. They found Molly." Emily could no longer contain her tears and a few broke free and trickled down her cheeks. She turned to the girl and threw her arms around her in her excitement.

Emily drew in a deep breath to calm herself. Releasing her hold on the girl, they turned and stared expectantly at the front door, waiting for the men to bring Molly out. Emily noticed one of the officers stationed on the porch was communicating with someone on his radio.

"Tony, what's happening?" Emily asked.

"They're calling for an ambulance, from what I can overhear." The special agent repeated what he was picking up on the radio. "She was found in the crawl space, lying on a pile of blankets, she's unresponsive, probably drugged."

Emily spun around at the sound of a siren blaring from an emergency vehicle, growing louder as it approached. "Peter! The ambulance!" she called out, pointing toward the flashing red lights in the distance, the scream of the siren intensifying as it moved closer.

She's going to be okay. She has to be. Oh, God, please let her be okay.

A uniformed officer moved one of the patrol cars crowding the residential street, to make room for the ambulance. Two young men in stiff white shirts and navy blue pants sprang from the vehicle and sprinted to the rear, pulling a gurney out of the back door.

"Make way!" one of the officers ordered. His hands furiously directed them, and the small crowd that had gathered on the lawn moved aside.

The paramedics bolted up the few stairs and disappeared, with the gurney, into the house.

Emily willed herself not to cry. This was not the time or the place to break down. It was a time to be strong for Molly and for Camille.

Oh, my gosh—Camille. Should I call her?

It was all she could do to hold it together. If she had to explain the situation to Camille right now, she knew she'd lose it. But Camille and Jonathan had a right to know.

She dug her phone out of her pocket and stared at it, wondering what she should do, what she would say.

"Emily!"

Over the din of chatter from the crowd, she heard her name called. She turned toward the sound and saw Colin sprinting toward her from the street.

"Colin!" She yelled and waved him over.

"Ow! Some of us still have earpieces in, Emily," Ellis scolded.

"Sorry." She grimaced.

Colin rushed to her and pulled her into his arms.

"Did they find Molly? I saw the ambulance. Is she okay?"

"Yeah, they found her. They're bringing her out, but she's unconscious so they're rushing her to the hospital. Didn't you hear about it in your earpiece?"

"No, I took it out when I left the hotel. I had to deal with the madam and her thug."

"Why is it taking so long?"

"Be patient, Emily. Let them work."

"Well, Maliwan has been keeping me company while we wait to see Molly."

Colin released his hold and stepped aside, keeping one arm protectively around her waist. "Maliwan, hello." He offered her a friendly smile.

The girl gave him a small, guarded smile in return.

"You were very brave back at the hotel."

"Yes, you were," Emily added.

"I need you to be brave a little while longer. I've asked one of the female officers to take you to the police station."

Maliwan's dark eyes grew wide and the fear that had begun to drain from them was instantly refilling.

"No, no, you don't have to be afraid," Emily said, in an effort to console her.

"We need to do some paperwork, you know, get your story," Colin explained slowly. "Then you'll be staying at a women's shelter in town. They'll take care of you for the next few days until we can sort this thing out."

"Shelter?" Maliwan repeated.

"Yes, it's a safe place to sleep with plenty of food to eat. They'll take care of you there." Emily wasn't sure the girl understood all of what she and Colin had just said, but she nodded compliantly.

"It will be okay, Maliwan. Those bad people can't hurt you anymore."

She nodded again. A smile began to bloom on her face. It was clear that she understood that.

"Here comes the officer now." Colin motioned her over with the rotation of his hand. "Officer Sanchez, this is Maliwan…I'm sorry, what is your last name?"

"Willapana."

"Sanchez, this is Maliwan Willapana. Could you please escort the young lady down to the police station and take her statement? Sherry Howard from City Lights will be picking her and the other girls up when you're done."

"Yes, sir. Right this way, Miss Willapana." Officer Sanchez gestured toward her cruiser. "What a pretty name."

The girl hugged Emily quickly before leaving. "Thank you."

She waved at Emily and Colin as she went with the police woman. Emily didn't want to take her eyes off of her until she was safely seated in the squad car.

"Emily, have you called Camille and Jonathan yet?"

"Just about to," she replied, turning her gaze from the car back to Colin. "I hope I don't break down and blubber my way through it." With the emotional roller coaster she had been on all day, she could sense her tears bubbling very near the surface again.

"Why don't you let me do it?" Before she could give him an answer, Colin whipped out his phone and ventured beyond the driveway for some quiet space.

THE CHAIN OF LIES

Emily observed him as he put the phone to his ear, grateful he took the initiative to handle it for her. She imagined his words to her friends and their relieved, yet horrified reaction. Maybe she should have gone and told them in person, but then she might miss their bringing Molly out. Her boots felt nailed to the ground. She had to stay.

Colin made his way back through the crowd until he returned to Emily's side. "They're on their way. Fortunately, they're only a few blocks away. Maggie's coming, too."

"Emily!" A female voice shouted from the street.

Emily turned to see who had called her name and spotted Isabel cutting through the swelling crowd.

"I got here as fast as I could." Isabel squeezed Emily warmly. "I heard they found Molly."

"They should be bringing her out shortly." Emily's voice trembled. "She's unconscious, Is."

Isabel rested a comforting hand on Emily's arm. "She's a strong girl, Em, a lot like you. We'll see her through this."

Emily nodded and lowered her eyes. "I feel somehow responsible."

"Why on earth would you say that?" Colin asked.

"She and I talked about this house and what might be going on here. I should have known she was too young to discuss this kind of thing. Me and my big mouth. If I hadn't—"

"This is not your fault," Colin insisted. "Tell her, Isabel."

"He's right. This is not your fault. These people were committing crimes against young girls, and Molly must have tried to do something about it. She's a courageous girl to try to take these people on."

"I hope Camille and Jonathan see it that way."

"You hope we see what that way?" Camille and Jonathan walked up behind Emily and the small cluster of friends.

Emily looked their way, her mind racing for a good answer. No words would come, a hug would have to do. Emily reached out and pulled Camille into a firm embrace, which Camille returned. Isabel stepped up and softly patted Camille's back, glancing over at Maggie, who had joined the group.

"They'll be bringing Molly out any minute," Colin remarked. "Like I told you on the phone, she's unconscious, but alive."

"I don't understand," Jonathan said through clenched teeth, staring at Colin, "why was she in this house in the first place?"

"We'll sort it all out when Molly regains consciousness," Isabel replied.

"If I hadn't ordered her out of the room yesterday, none of this would have happened," Camille cried, dabbing her eyes and wiping her nose with tissue.

"Don't blame yourself, Cam," Maggie said.

"If you want to blame anyone, blame the criminals that abducted her." Isabel stroked Camille's shoulder.

"Where's Peter?" Jonathan asked, glancing around the yard.

"Up there by the door." Emily pointed to him standing at the foot of the porch. "He's videotaping them bringing Molly out."

Maggie looked confused. "Videotapin'? But he

doesn't—"

"Look! Here they come!" Isabel shouted over the chaotic roar from the crowd on the lawn.

"Step aside, make way," one of the officers commanded.

The crowd parted as the paramedics brought the gurney out the front door and down the few steps to the walkway.

"Stop!" Camille hollered, running up to the gurney.

"Step back, ma'am," the officer ordered, sticking his hand out to block her.

"That's my daughter!"

"Hold up, fellas," the policeman requested, dropping his hand.

Camille bent over her daughter and stroked her matted red hair. "You're going to be okay, Molly, sweetie. Daddy and I are here for you."

Jonathan stepped to the gurney as well, his eyes glistening, wiping his sleeve across his face, while Peter stood at the foot of the metal contraption, continuing to tape.

"Ma'am?" One of the paramedics lightly touched Camille's arm. "We need to get her to the hospital. Would one of you like to ride with her?"

"You go, honey," Jonathan suggested. "I'll bring the car. We'll need it later."

Camille nodded appreciatively. Her hand remained fixed on Molly's shoulder as she stayed beside the gurney, keeping up with the paramedics as they rushed to the ambulance.

"I'll be right behind you!" Jonathan called after her.

"Are you sure you wouldn't rather have one of us

drive you, Jon?" Colin asked.

"That's probably best. Peter, can you drive me?" Jonathan's voice was noticeably shaking.

"Absolutely. Let's go."

"I wanna come too," Maggie said. "Camille's gonna need me at the hospital."

"The rest of us will get there as soon as we can." Emily set her hand on Jonathan's shoulder. "We all want to be there for you and Camille."

"Okay, let's roll." As Peter walked away with Jonathan and Maggie, he pulled his high-tech glasses off and he turned them around to face toward himself. "This is Peter MacKenzie signing off. You got that, Ellis?"

"Loud and clear."

CHAPTER 20
The Hospital Visit

IT WAS ALMOST MIDNIGHT when Colin and Emily made it to the hospital. The visitors area was overrun with their close circle, waiting for any news about Molly. Tests had been run, vitals monitored, but nothing yet to report except that she had still not woken up.

Alex came strolling down the hallway with a box full of coffees.

"Thank you, hon." Isabel took a cup from her husband.

"Anyone else?" He set the box down on the coffee table. "I made sure there are packets of sugar and creamer in there, too."

The doctor pushed through the heavy swinging doors. "Mr. and Mrs. Hawthorne?"

"That's us." Camille and Jonathan bolted from the chairs and rushed over to the doctor.

"I'm Dr. Reed. Your daughter has not gained

consciousness yet, but she seems to be resting comfortably. If you'd like to come in and see her for a few minutes, that'd be all right."

"Yes, please."

"Can any of the rest of us see her, too?" Emily asked.

"For now, let's just take her folks in."

Camille and Jonathan clasped hands and followed the physician.

Watching her friends hurry away, Emily was unable to shake the feeling that she was partly responsible for their daughter lying in that hospital bed. She wrapped her arms around herself in a self-comforting gesture.

Colin must have sensed her need because he placed his arm around her shoulders and drew her in. Responsively, she wrapped her arms about his lean torso and laid her cheek against his chest. Clinging to each other, he gently kissed the top of her head as they stood in contemplative silence.

"Emily?" Isabel softly laid a hand on her friend's arm.

Emily raised her head and extended her hand to Isabel, who took hold of it.

"Alex told me that when he went to the cafeteria for the coffees he saw Delia down there."

"Why would she be here? Especially this late?" Emily looked up at Colin.

"Remember I told you Jerry Banderas was in the hospital," Isabel replied. "I'm guessing it has something to do with him. I wonder if he took a turn for the worse."

"Can you check on him?" Emily asked.

"I'm not family, but maybe I can play the FBI card

and wrangle some details out of the nurse."

~*~

Isabel took the elevator to the fourth floor. An older, heavy-set African-American nurse was reviewing papers on her desk when Isabel strode up to the counter.

"Good evening, ma'am."

The woman peered at Isabel over the top of the glasses sitting low on her broad nose. "Hello, may I help you?"

"I'd like to check on Jerry Banderas. Would it be possible for me to see him?"

"Sorry, no." She shook her head. "It's way past visiting hours, dear, and I'm quite certain he's asleep. You'll have to come back tomorrow." She returned her gaze to the papers on the desk in front of her.

"Can you at least tell me how he's doing?"

"Are you family?" she asked, not bothering to look up.

"No, but—"

The woman raised her eyes and peered at her again over her rims. "I'm sorry, but I can't give out that information if you're not family."

Isabel slapped her FBI badge down on the raised counter a little harder than she intended, causing the woman to jump in her seat.

"Sorry, ma'am, but this is important. I'm with the FBI and I need to question him regarding a case." It may not have been an FBI case, but it was an open police case.

The hefty nurse stood to her feet, placed her hands

on her desk and leaned forward, staring into Isabel's face. "That kind of bullying might work on other people, young lady, but it doesn't fly with me. You either come back tomorrow during normal visiting hours or you bring me a warrant."

"Can you at least tell me if his daughter was here earlier?" Isabel toned down her attitude.

"Like I said, warrant."

Isabel backed away from the nurse's station, clipping her badge back onto her belt. "I'll see you in the morning, then." She headed to the elevator and pushed the button, keeping one eye on the nurse. While waiting for the doors to open, she noticed the nurse was called away to one of the rooms in the opposite direction from Jerry's room. Once she was out of sight, Isabel snuck down to Jerry's room. "Stop me now, Nurse Krachit."

Finding room four twelve, Isabel slowly pushed open the door. The room was dark except for the dim nightlight plugged into one of the walls.

"Jerry," Isabel whispered, walking nearer to his bed. "Are you awake?"

He did not respond.

"Jerry," she tried again. He moaned something indiscernible. She hoped in a half-asleep state that he might be unguarded and candid with her. She walked to the side of his bed and gently shook his shoulder. "Jerry."

"Go away, nurse. Let me sleep," He mumbled and shrugged one shoulder, his eyes still closed.

"Jerry, it's Isabel. Wake up. I need to talk to you."

"Isabel?" he slurred, not yet opening his eyes.

"Do you remember David Gerard?"

"Gerard?" he repeated quietly as if he was floating between being asleep and awake.

"Yes, David Gerard."

Jerry's face had been relaxed as he slept, but at the name Gerard it began to contort into an angry scowl.

"What did David Gerard do?" Isabel asked in her calmest, most soothing voice in response to the change in his facial expression.

"Gerard, he killed my baby."

"Natalia?"

"Natalia," he mumbled. "My baby."

"Did you kill Gerard?"

"Kill Gerard," he repeated in a dreamlike voice.

Now we're getting somewhere.

"Yes, that's right. Did you kill Gerard?"

"Kill Gerard," he said again.

Isabel was uncertain if he was simply repeating what she said, or if he was answering her. She decided to come back to that question later. "Is Delia your daughter?"

"Delia?" His eyes were still closed as he shifted in his bed.

"Yes, Jerry. Is Delia your daughter?"

"What are you doing in here!" the large nurse screamed from the doorway in the loudest throaty whisper Isabel had ever heard. "Do I need to call security?"

"I'm leaving." Frustrated, Isabel knew there was nothing more she could do until the morning.

As she turned to leave, she felt someone grab her hand. She looked back and saw Jerry clinging to her. "Isabel?" The boisterous nurse bursting in must have fully awakened him, she suspected.

"Yes, Jerry, it's Isabel." Her voice was low and soft. "I wanted to see how you're doing. I'll be back in the morning." Isabel patted his hand lightly and pulled her fingers free knowing the insistent nurse with angry dark eyes was impatiently holding the door open for her.

~*~

Isabel returned to the waiting room. The air was thick with anticipation and anxiety as her friends sat hoping for news from the doctor. Jonathan and Camille had not returned yet from Molly's room. Peter and Maggie sat beside each other, huddled quietly in what appeared to be serious conversation. Colin snuggled up to Emily with his arm around her, as she leaned against him silently.

Alex stood and approached Isabel as she entered the waiting room. "I need to shove off, Is. I've got court in the morning. Are you going to stay?"

"For a while. No news on Molly, I'm guessing." Isabel looked around at the gang.

"No. It could be quite some time before they know anything."

"I'm not ready to call it a night, hon. I have my own car."

"All right. Call me if you need anything." Alex kissed his wife lightly and left.

Isabel took a seat beside Emily.

Emily sat up straight in her chair and turned to Isabel. "Any luck?"

"Not much. The nurse up there was a real peach."

Isabel grimaced.

"That's too bad."

"I'll try again tomorrow."

"Do you mind if I tag along?" Emily asked.

"I don't know. Jerry might be more forthcoming if I can talk to him alone."

"You're probably right." Emily patted Isabel's leg. "Let me know if he gives you anything of importance."

"You know I will."

"And I'll get that gun to the county lab first thing tomorrow," Colin said.

"What are you talking about? I have the gun," Isabel said, looking confused. "I'm taking it to the FBI lab in the morning."

"The other gun, Is," Emily replied.

"What *other* gun?"

"I'm sorry, Isabel, but I think in all the drama over Molly and the Jade Thai Spa, we haven't kept you in the loop about the other gun," Emily said.

"A neighbor of Delia's found a gun by the river Saturday, a Ruger P345. Emily and I interviewed him Saturday night and we had the man show us where he found it."

"You think it might be the weapon used in Evan's murder?" Isabel asked.

"It might be," Emily replied with a nod. "It's been mostly submerged in mud for the past year, but we're hopeful the lab can get some prints off of it."

"Make sure they check to see if there are any bullets left in it. Maybe they'll be able to get a print off of one of them," Isabel suggested.

"I had that same thought," Colin said.

"As far as the gun I have, I'm planning to ask the lab to put a rush on it," Isabel remarked. "Jerry doesn't have much time left, so if the Beretta pistol from Evan's safe deposit box was his, I'd like to get a confession out of him before he passes away."

"Good idea," Colin agreed.

Emily grew silent and pensive, staring blankly off to nowhere, her thoughts somewhere else. She felt Isabel take her hand.

"I know the handgun you left with me isn't the one that killed Evan, but it could get us closer to the truth."

Emily nodded, bringing her gaze down to meet Isabel's.

"On the other hand, the Ruger found at the river might actually reveal the killer," Colin added. "Then we can finally put an end to all the questions surrounding Evan's death."

Emily looked into Colin's kind hazel eyes and saw how much he wanted that for her, to put an end to the investigation so she could move on with her life. She nodded again. "Once and for all."

Everyone jumped to their feet as Camille and Jonathan came back to the waiting room.

"How is she?" Emily asked, but her words were drowned out by Maggie's abundant exuberance.

Maggie rushed in and threw her arms around Camille. "Oh, Cam, did Molly wake up?"

"She's still not conscious," Jonathan replied.

"She looks so peaceful, like she's sleeping," Camille answered, dabbing a tissue under her eyes once Maggie released her.

"What does the doctor say? Anything new?" Isabel

asked.

"No change yet. They're doing all they can to find out what's in her system and counteract it." Jonathan wiped his moist, red eyes with his fingers. "She may simply have to let the drugs wear off, the doctor said. Apparently her kidnappers were trying to keep her sedated."

"What can we do?" Emily asked.

"You've done enough," Camille replied flatly to Emily.

Emily wondered what Camille had meant.

Camille turned her attention to the rest. "You should all go home and get some rest. There's really nothing to do now but wait."

"Camille and I are staying the night." Jonathan put his arm around his wife's shoulder. "They're bringing a cot into Molly's room and we'll take turns in the chair."

"If you're stayin', we're stayin'," Maggie insisted.

"That's right," Peter agreed.

"No, no, go on home, please," Camille pleaded. "We appreciate your wanting to stay, but we'd feel better knowing you all went home. We'll phone you if there's any news in the night."

CHAPTER 21
Daughter Delia

EMILY'S CELL PHONE BEEPED on her nightstand, alerting her to a new text message. She rolled over in her bed and felt for her phone. Through bleary eyes, she could see the time on her digital alarm clock—which she purposely did not set—read eight thirty-five. It was almost three in the morning when she had finally crawled into bed, and she was having a hard time opening her eyes and focusing, even in the bright morning light.

Pulling herself up against her pillows, she worked to get her tired eyes to adjust to the tiny screen on her phone. The text was from Isabel. *Took gun to lab. Results asap.*

Flipping the comforter back, she dragged herself out of bed and wandered into the sunny kitchen, in her bare feet and oversized t-shirt, to make her morning coffee. Her phone buzzed again. Her eyes were still adjusting to the sunlight streaming in through the kitchen window over the sink, but she was beginning to focus.

The text was from Colin this time. *Morning, Sleeping Beauty. Gun in lab, will have results today. R U up?*

Emily texted back. *I'm up. Not awake, but up.*

She pulled herself up on a stool at the breakfast bar, ran her fingers through her curls, and waited for the coffee machine to do its thing.

Be there in 10 minutes, his next text read.

"Shoot!"

No time for coffee.

As she sprinted down the hall to throw on some clothes and a dab of makeup, the tone on her phone signaled another text. It was Colin again.

She paused in the doorway of her bedroom and looked at her phone. His text read *Gotcha! LOL! Stuck at work. Meet 4 lunch?*

We'll see, she shot back, bristling with annoyance as she padded back to the kitchen to get her cup of coffee.

Opening the cabinet, she pulled a coffee mug out and poured the steaming dark liquid into it. Since Colin was stuck at work for the morning and Isabel apparently was too, Emily decided she'd drop by the hospital and see if there was any news on Molly.

She ripped open a packet of sweetener and emptied it into her cup. As she swirled it around with her spoon, she thought about Jethro, who was also in the hospital. Should she call him Jerry, now that she knew who he really was? Should she pay him a surprise visit? Terminally ill or not, if he was Evan's murderer, she had to know.

How could she approach him without seeming insensitive to a dying man?

Her thoughts flew back to the gun Evan had hidden away at the bank and the note she'd found bundled in the center of a banded wad of money he had kept secret from her. She recalled the handwritten note said he had wrestled the gun away from someone who had tried to kill him but slipped away when Evan fought back. *Could that someone be Jerry Banderas?* Had he returned and finished the job? Did he blame Evan for his daughter's death and so took his life as payback?

The Beretta was now in the hands of the FBI lab, Isabel saw to that, and she would have some answers soon.

As she sat on a stool, drinking her coffee, her phone shrilled on the counter and she jumped at the noise. She had been lost in her thoughts, but she was instantly pulled back to reality by the ringing. She picked up her phone off the breakfast bar, noticing the caller was Maggie this time.

"Good morning, Maggs," Emily answered brightly. "Any news on Molly?"

"That's why I'm callin'. Peter and I stayed at the hospital all night, hopin' that girl would wake up—and she finally did."

"Oh, Maggie, that's great news!" Emily slid off the stool and stamped her feet in a little happy dance, spinning around with joy and relief. Abruptly, she stopped. "She is going to be all right, isn't she?"

"The doctor believes so, but they want to keep her another day or two for observation. She had some heavy-duty sedatives in her system."

"That poor girl. I want to get her story, find out how she ended up inside that house and what they did to her." She knew Colin, Isabel, and Peter would as well, for their own reasons.

"Peter already asked her if he could interview her, but Camille pushed him right out of the room and gave him what-for."

"Thanks for the warning. But I would like to come by and say hello, see if Camille and Jonathan need anything."

"Now that she's awake and doin' okay, the doctor sent them home to get some rest. They didn't get any sleep last night at all in that flimsy cot and uncomfortable chair. Heck, y'all can hardly get any sleep in the hospital bed with all the noise and lights and nurses comin' in every couple hours to check y'all's vitals."

"I'm going to stop by anyway. This is my fault. She wouldn't be in the hospital if it wasn't for me."

"Don't say that, Em. Y'all couldn't have known what would happen."

"It's not just me. I get the feeling Camille blames me, too."

"Why on earth would y'all say that?"

"Last night, when I offered to do anything I could to help, she told me I had done enough. I'd say that was pretty clear."

"I'm sure she didn't mean anythin' by it. She was tired and upset."

"Maybe. Somehow I need to make it up to her—and to Molly."

"I think your puttin' those traffickers behind bars was doin' plenty in my book."

"It wasn't like I did it single-handedly."

"From what I heard from Peter, y'all were a big part, though. Don't worry about Camille, hon, she'll calm down and all will be back to normal before we know it."

"Sounds like you and Peter are getting pretty cozy," Emily remarked.

"Cozy? No. I'm not ready to jump into another relationship just yet, but we are on friendly terms. He's very interestin' and very easy to talk to. We'll see where it goes."

"Friendly terms, huh? I saw how he looks at you. I'd say the man is smitten."

"Ya' think?"

"I do."

~*~

Mid-morning, Emily boarded the hospital elevator with a vase brimming with yellow Shasta daisies in one arm and a stack of Molly's favorite magazines under the other. Trying to balance her load, she awkwardly bent forward and pushed the button to go to level three, trying not to spill water on her jeans.

The doors glided open and Emily gingerly stepped out, catching sight of Maggie and Peter strolling down the corridor toward her. Maggie's white V-neck sweater set off her bronze Hawaiian tan. She waved as soon as she noticed Emily and hurried toward her.

"Here, let me take those flowers," Maggie offered,

reaching for the vase.

Emily gladly relinquished them with a smile. "Thanks, Maggs. How's our girl?" Emily shifted the stack of magazines and cradled them in front of her with both arms.

"Holding her own," Peter replied. "We'll walk you back to her room, then Maggie and I are shoving off."

"Peter's offered to drop me off at my house on his way to Camille's," Maggie said as the three of them started down the hallway.

"What a gentleman," Emily replied, glancing over at Peter who wore an impish grin.

"I do my best." Peter pushed the door to Molly's room open for the two women.

Maggie led Emily in, carrying the vase of daisies. "Look who the cat dragged in," Maggie said, setting the flowers down on her night table.

A smile blossomed on Molly's face when she saw Emily step from behind Maggie. "Emily!" she squealed, extending both arms to her.

Emily set the magazines down at the foot of the bed and bent down to give Molly a hug. She kissed the side of her head and stroked Molly's hair a couple of times before she released her embrace, wishing she could take the last few days back.

"I'm so glad you came, Emily. I heard it was you that rescued me."

"No, sweetie, it wasn't me."

"Don't be so modest," Peter chided. "It was the SWAT team that pulled her out of the hidden crawlspace, but none of this could have happened if it hadn't been for you."

Heat rushed to Emily's cheeks and she gently shook her head in denial, making her loose curls tickle the back of her neck. "You give me too much credit, Peter."

Molly reached out and took one of Emily's hands. "You saved my life, Em." The girl's vivid green eyes were moist with tears, her bottom lip quivered as she spoke. "And you saved those other girls, too."

"Like I said, it wasn't just me. I only played a part in it." Emily squeezed Molly's hand lightly before letting it go. "Your uncle Peter, now he was amazing." Emily glanced over at Peter, who was standing next to Maggie on the other side of the bed.

"I can't wait to see the video footage." Maggie smiled admiringly at him. "From what you told me—"

"There's video?" Molly asked, her eyes brightening at the prospect.

"Absolutely." Peter seemed to bask in the glow of their admiration. "It's going to be a compelling story once I edit it and make it ready for media release."

"You're going to have to wrangle it away from the FBI first," Emily pointed out.

"Special Agent Ellis promised I'd get a copy, so if he's a man of his word, it shouldn't be too long."

"Can we put it on YouTube?" Molly asked. "Then everyone can watch it. I bet you'd get over a million hits on something like that."

A chubby middle-aged nurse with frizzy blonde hair bustled into the room. "Sorry to break up the party folks, but this gal needs her rest. Doctor's orders."

"We'll be back, sweetie." Emily leaned over and kissed the top of Molly's head. "You get some rest. And if you get bored, I brought some magazines for you."

Maggie and Peter skirted around the bed and they all headed out to the hallway.

"We'll be off then," Peter said. "Shall we walk you out, Emily?"

"No, I'm not leaving yet. There's someone on the fourth floor I want to pay a visit to."

"Who would that be?" Maggie asked.

"No one you know. He's involved in another case I'm working on," Emily replied. "I'll walk with you to the elevator."

"One case after another. You're a firecracker, Emily Parker," Peter remarked as they began to walk. "I'll bet that Colin Andrews has his hands full keeping up with you."

"A firecracker?" Emily raised her eyebrows at him.

"Land sakes, Peter, I'd say they both have their hands full with each other." Maggie giggled and winked at Emily. "Am I right?"

They reached the elevator and Emily quickly pushed both the up and down buttons, wishing she could worm out of the conversation. As luck would have it, the doors for the elevator going up slid open almost immediately and Emily stepped in and spun around. "You're right, Maggie," she said, waving good-bye as the doors glided shut.

Emily felt the lift as the elevator took her to the next floor up. The doors swept open and she went to the nurses' station directly ahead. A young brunette in light blue scrubs sat behind the counter, typing something on the computer's keyboard. She looked up as Emily approached.

"May I help you?"

THE CHAIN OF LIES

"Can you tell me which room Jerry Banderas is in?"

"Banderas, let me see," she replied, typing his name into the computer. "Room four twelve."

"Thank you, ma'am." Emily spun on the spiky heels of her black-leather boots and headed toward his room. She remembered Isabel mentioning she would come and see him that morning, and when Emily asked if she could tag along, Isabel told her it would be better if she went alone. That didn't mean Emily couldn't pop in on her own, though.

Emily read the room numbers as she meandered down the corridor until she found room four twelve. She pushed the door open slowly, judging if anyone else was in the room. Not hearing any voices, she pushed it open all the way.

Jerry's eyelids raised as she approached, likely hearing the click of her heels on the hard surface of the floor. His face remained expressionless.

"Hello, Jethro. Or should I say Jerry?" Emily forced a friendly smile onto her lips.

"How did you know?"

"I figured it out. It's what I do."

"I'd forgotten you were a private eye."

She found that hard to believe.

"I hear you're pretty sick, Jerry. I'm sorry to hear that."

He raised his eyebrows in doubt. "Really?"

"Why would you think I wouldn't be?" She knew exactly why, but she wanted to hear him admit it. She cast him a sad look. "I would never wish you any harm, Jerry. You were trying to help me to find out my husband's true identity. I'm grateful for that."

"Did you ever figure out what to do with that hypothetical gun you asked me about?"

"As a matter of fact, I gave it to Isabel and she turned it in to the FBI lab, like you suggested."

She saw disappointment in his eyes—or was it fear? The gun was no longer within his reach.

"We should have results later today, then we'll know who the gun belonged to, maybe even who killed my husband."

"That couldn't have been the gun that killed him," he said with a slight shake of his head.

"How do you know that?" Emily toyed with him. She knew it wasn't the gun, but she wanted to rattle him, get him wondering how close she and Isabel were to figuring things out.

"If that gun had been used to kill him, then how did your husband manage to hide it away? I remember you saying the gun was hidden away."

"I was only speaking hypothetically," Emily reminded him.

"Hypothetically my eye. I never believed that for a minute, girl."

"Was it your gun, Jerry?"

"That's enough!" Delia shouted from the doorway, her deep brown eyes almost glowed with anger. "The man is sick and I won't stand by and let you rile him up with your questions, Emily."

Emily turned in shock. "Delia, what are you—"

"It doesn't matter." Delia cut her off. "This interrogation is over."

"But we were just having a little chat, weren't we, Jerry?" Emily smiled sweetly at the man in the bed, patting him softly on the arm. She noticed the wrinkles around his eyes were more pronounced than she remembered, and his skin was more sallow.

"We were talking about my late husband." Emily turned her attention back to Delia. "Someone killed the man I loved and has been tormenting me for the past few months. I hoped Jerry could help me figure out who that might be."

"I can't let that happen, Emily. He's too ill to be badgered into helping you."

"Delia, I thought we were friends. I helped you get through your own husband's murder investigation, and I found the killer, not all that long ago. If I hadn't, you'd be rotting in prison right now. Can't you and your dad do the same for me?"

"You know he's my father?" Delia's eyes widened for a moment, then they narrowed as if she realized that Emily knowing that fact now put her in jeopardy somehow.

"Delia, let me tell her," Jerry pleaded.

"No," she said firmly. "Emily, you need to leave." Delia walked to the door and held it open, avoiding making eye contact with her.

Emily started to walk through the doorway, but paused as she reached Delia. Standing toe to toe with her, she searched the woman's face for any sign that they had ever truly been friends. "This isn't over, you know."

"I know," Delia replied, pressing her perfectly painted lips tightly into a straight line, still refusing to look at her.

DEBRA BURROUGHS

CHAPTER 22
Jetho's Interview

IN THE CRISP, COOL AUTUMN AIR, Emily leaned against a pillar near the main entrance of the hospital, tugging her cropped black-leather jacket closed. She raked her fingers through her curls in aggravation at Delia stopping her from pulling a confession out of the man she suspected of murdering her husband.

She dug her phone out of her jacket pocket and dialed Isabel's number.

"Hey, Emily, what's up?"

"You told me last night you were going to stop by the hospital and see Jerry Banderas this morning. I was wondering when you were planning to do that."

"Let's see." Isabel paused and Emily imagined she was looking at her watch. "It's almost eleven. I can be there in about thirty minutes. Are you there?"

"I am."

"But I told you I want to talk to him alone."

"I'm not asking to go in with you. I already warmed him up for you."

"Tell me you didn't."

"Actually, I was doing a pretty good job of it, too, if it hadn't been for Delia walking in and ordering me out of his room."

"Oh, boy. I'd like to have seen that." Isabel chuckled at the thought. "You really think you warmed him up for me?"

"Yes. He wanted to talk, but Delia put the kibosh on that. So we'll need to put our heads together and come up with a plan to keep her out of his room while you sneak in and talk to him."

"She's a pretty sharp cookie. It'll have to be plausible."

"I have an idea. Let me call Colin and get him over here. Can you arrange for one of those fancy hidden cameras to record his confession?"

"I believe so. Give me a few minutes to make a quick call to line that up."

~*~

Colin came as soon as Emily called, meeting her and Isabel in the agreed-upon spot—the hospital gift shop.

Emily pointed to the elevators through the wall of glass that faced the hospital foyer. "We've been watching the elevators from here and—"

"Delia came down about ten minutes ago," Isabel finished.

"I called her, like you asked. When she gets to my

office and I'm not there, she's going to be pissed." Colin looked to Emily and then to Isabel.

"That's the plan." Emily said.

"A guy from the FBI should be here any minute to bring me a brooch with a hidden camera and mic in it. He'll monitor the recording from his vehicle." Isabel looked through the wall of glass, searching for the man. "Here he comes."

A young man, no more than twenty-five, with closely cropped red hair, dressed in a polo shirt and khakis, strolled into the gift shop with something under his arm that looked like a small laptop. He glanced around and made a beeline to Isabel as soon as he spotted her. "Hey, Izzy."

"Emily, Colin, this is Buzz. He's a wizard with technology."

They exchanged pleasantries and Buzz helped Isabel pin the daisy-shaped brooch in place on the jacket of her navy blue pantsuit at an angle that would most advantageously capture Jerry's position in bed. "To turn it on, just twist the stem of the daisy to the right."

"Let's test it." Isabel twisted the stem and walked around the store, commenting on different items, and Buzz watched and listened on the monitor.

"Good?" Isabel asked.

"Roger that. Twist it back the other way to turn it off," Buzz instructed as she walked back toward him. "I'll be out in my van waiting to see it come on."

He tucked the monitor under his arm again and began to walk away. Stopping short, he spun back around. "Oh, by the way, Izzy," he said, shaking his pointer finger at her, "I was supposed to tell you something. Guess your phone's been off 'cause of the hospital, but Benson's been trying to reach you. The fingerprint results are back. Give him a call." With a light wave of his hand, Buzz ambled out of the building.

"Let me step outside and call him. It'll just take a sec." Isabel hurried out as the front doors *whooshed* open.

"That was fast," Colin said.

Emily slung her bulky handbag over her shoulder and moved toward the door. "I wonder what they found."

Colin followed her out into the foyer. "We'll know in a minute." He gestured toward Isabel putting her phone away as she walked back inside.

"Well?" Emily asked impatiently.

"The gun belongs to Jerry Banderas." Isabel turned and went to the row of elevators.

"According to the note Evan left in the safe deposit box, Jerry had to have been the one who attempted to kill him that night, not very long after we moved to Paradise Valley. If Evan hadn't wrestled the gun away from him, Jerry certainly would have shot him to death back then." Emily nervously shifted her purse and ran her fingers through one side of her curly mane. "He's probably the one who eventually did murder Evan."

"Looks that way." Colin reached over and pushed the up arrow for one of the elevators.

"Isabel, you need to put the screws to that man," Emily ordered, grabbing her friend's arm. "We need him on tape admitting what he did."

Colin glanced at Isabel and she met his gaze, mirroring his look of puzzlement and concern at Emily's stress level.

"Don't worry, Em." Isabel patted her hand, then pried Emily's fingers off her arm. "I'll do my best."

"I want to go in with you." Emily's voice took on a nervous intensity. "I'm afraid you'll go too easy on him. He's been your friend for a long time and he's dying, so how can you be expected to treat him like any other murder suspect?"

"I will. I promise."

"Let her do her job." Colin wrapped an arm loosely around Emily's shoulders. "Jerry may be her friend, but Evan was her friend, too. You're going to have to trust her."

Emily looked into Isabel's deadly serious face, searching her dark eyes. Isabel stared back and nodded at Emily, reaching out and taking her friend's trembling hand. "I won't let you down, Em."

Emily paused, processing Isabel's response. "We're in agreement then. Isabel will be the only one to go inside Jerry's room—that is, until she signals us to come in."

The elevator tone dinged and one set of doors slid open. "After you, ladies."

They boarded the elevator and rode it up to the fourth floor. Stepping off, they all turned to the right and marched down the corridor, stopping right before reaching Jerry's room.

Isabel turned the stem of her daisy pin to the right. "Buzz, I'm on," she said, dipping her chin toward her lapel as she spoke. Her eyes flashed to Emily and Colin. "Wish me luck, guys." She stood up straight, pulled in a quick breath, and gently pushed the door open.

~*~

"Good morning, Jerry," Isabel said in a light and friendly voice.

"Isabel." Jerry tried to pull himself up on his pillows. "Is this a social call? Or—"

"Some of both. How are you feeling this morning?" Isabel moved to the foot of his bed, making sure she had a good angle for the camera.

"A little better."

"You look better. What do the doctors say?"

"Oh, you know doctors. I could have a month, I could have a year. All I know is I can't beat it."

"I really am sorry to hear that. We've been friends for a long time, Jerry."

"Going on fifteen years, but I don't think you stopped by to take a walk with me down memory lane. What's on your mind?"

"Remember the gun Emily talked to you about the night we stopped by her place together?"

"You mean the hypothetical one?"

"Only I knew you didn't believe it was only hypothetical. You kept pressing me to see it."

"So now you're saying the gun is no longer hypothetical?"

"That's right, it's no longer hypothetical. It's a Beretta 92FS pistol."

Jerry's eyes narrowed a bit at the description.

"I had that gun run through the system this morning and turns out it belongs to you."

"Damn!"

"You've been searching Emily's house for it, haven't you?"

"Maybe."

"Have you been tailing her?"

"Why do you ask?"

"Why are you being so evasive, Jerry? We're not going to charge you with breaking and entering—with you being so sick, I mean. What would be the point?"

"Then why are you pressing the issue?" He crossed his arms and glared at her.

"I merely want to know, and I want to be able to put Emily's mind at ease. With the gun located, we won't be seeing any more of that behavior, will we?"

"All right, you've got me. I was just trying to get that freakin' gun back—I didn't want it connected to me. Guess I'm getting too old, too rusty to work undetected. It sucks to get old, Isabel."

"I have to agree with you there. So, now that we have that mystery resolved, let's move on to why this gun was so important."

"What do you want to know?"

"Because we're friends, Jerry, I'm going to give you the chance to tell me what happened. You can ask for a lawyer to be present, that's certainly your right, but since you don't have long to live, it isn't likely you'd ever be held accountable for any of it. It wouldn't be financially prudent to pursue a case against you. I'd simply like to know what happened to David Gerard before you're no longer able to tell me."

Jerry turned his head and stared out the window, biting on his upper lip.

Isabel wondered if he was thinking over his options.

He turned back and met her gaze. "Okay, I'll tell you."

"Everything?"

"I might as well. What do I have to lose at this point?"

"I just want to make sure you understand that you're telling me all of this under no duress whatsoever, that no one is pressuring you to do it."

"No, none."

"Do you want a glass of water before you start?"

"No, I'm good."

"Okay, then. Tell me what happened to David Gerard."

"All right." Jerry cleared his throat. "I was working in DC about seven years ago and got word my daughter, Natalia, had been killed in France. She'd been going to school there. An accidental shooting I was told. I never could really get a straight answer. Then, a couple of years later, a friend of mine in the CIA told me he'd read a report that said she had been killed in a shoot out between David Gerard and an enemy spy. She and David had been seeing each other and an operative from one of the unfriendly countries opened fire on them."

"So you think it was David's fault your daughter was killed?"

"I know it was," he snapped.

"Even if he didn't pull the trigger or purposely put her in harm's way?"

"David Gerard was a CIA operative. He had no business getting involved with a civilian and putting her life in danger. He should have known better, instead of letting his Johnson make his decisions for him."

"So you decided to do something about it? Avenge your daughter's death?"

"By the time I found out the truth, he'd left the CIA and moved west with his new wife, but I didn't know where."

"Then how'd you find him?"

"I was here in town visiting someone, thinking of retiring here. I went to lunch with a colleague from the FBI's Boise office and saw Gerard eating on the patio of a restaurant with his wife, laughing and enjoying the fresh air." He shook his head. "While my Natalia lay cold in her grave, he was laughing and enjoying the sunshine with somebody new. It wasn't fair."

Isabel noticed her ailing friend's eyes fill with tears at the mention of his daughter's name.

He wiped his hand across his eyes and drew in a deep breath. "I don't know what's wrong with me. Must be allergies."

"You had two daughters, as I recall."

"Yes, that's right."

"Is Delia McCall your other daughter?"

"Why are you bringing her into this?"

"Just wondering. She did hire David to work for her."

"Yeah, but she only knew him as Evan. Do you want to hear my story or not?" He seemed to bristle at her questions about his older daughter.

"Sorry, Jerry. Go on, please."

"Like I said, I saw him at the restaurant and I followed him back to his office. I sat in my car for a long time, wondering what my next move should be. I had plans for dinner with Delia, so I decided to keep an eye on him and wait for an opportunity to confront him."

"Then what happened?"

"A few nights later, I was driving by his office and noticed him through the lit window. I parked my car around the corner and snuck into his building. I opened his office door just enough to see him and stick the nose of my gun in. I took a shot, but the phone rang and he turned away toward the darn thing. The bullet must have whizzed past his head. Before I knew it, he slammed the door on the gun and my hand and wrestled it away from me. He fired a few shots at me, hitting me in the shoulder."

"So he shot you with your own gun?"

"You don't have to remind me. I ducked behind the next building and raced to my car. I phoned Delia to come to my hotel room and help me."

"Why didn't you go to her house?"

"She had that good-for-nothin', pretty-boy husband. She didn't want him or the housekeeper knowing anything about the gunshot. The bullet went through and through, so she brought all the medical supplies she needed to patch me up—and some painkillers, to boot."

"But David had your gun."

He nodded. "Afraid so."

"Did you tell Delia what happened? Why you were there? That you had tried to kill David and he was defending himself?"

"Well, I tried not to involve her. I wasn't a very good father when she and Natalia were growing up. Travelled a lot with the job, you know how that is."

"Yeah, I know."

"She's a good girl and she's all I've got left in the

world. I didn't want to burden her with the sordid side of my life. She deserves to be happy."

"So you're saying you never told Delia that Natalia died because of David Gerard?"

"What good would it have done, Isabel?"

"All right, let's move on. So what did you do then?"

"After holing up in my hotel room for a week or so, I had to get back to Washington, back to work. I'd had my chance to avenge Natalia's death and I blew it, so I high-tailed it back to DC, hoping David would never find out who the gun belonged to."

"So tell me about David's murder a year ago. Did you decide to come back and give it another try?"

"You think I killed David Gerard?"

There was a knock at the door before it swung open. Colin popped his head in and told Isabel he had some news.

Isabel turned her face toward the door, consciously keeping her chest pointed at Jerry.

"The lab said the ballistics are in on the second gun and they're a match. The fingerprint results will be back within the hour. Just thought you'd like to know that."

She thanked him and he left.

"Wow, did you hear that?" Isabel studied the man's facial expression for any tells. However, as a seasoned agent, he had been trained to keep his feelings and outward expressions under control—his face remained still as stone.

"What second gun?" he asked in an emotionless tone. "A match to what?"

"A Ruger P345 pistol that was found on the riverbank Saturday night." Again, she watched his expression, particularly his eyes, for even the most subtle hint. She thought she saw a flicker in his eyes, for the briefest moment, so she pressed him. "The gun that killed Evan Parker. Sorry, I mean David Gerard. Is there something you want to tell me about that gun?"

"Like what?"

"Jerry…are we going to find your prints? Did you kill David Gerard?"

He did not answer, his face twisted into a snarl. "Whatever he got he had coming to him."

"Let me remind you we have the ballistics proving it's the murder weapon, and confirmation of the prints will be in soon. If you admit it right now, I'll see that you don't go to prison for this. You don't have much time left. Wouldn't you rather spend it with Delia?"

"Delia." He spoke her name and blankly looked off in the distance—Isabel imagined he was seeing Delia in his mind, perhaps as a happy little girl running into his arms.

"So, I'll ask you again, did you kill David Gerard?"

He paused and stared at her with laser intensity, as if his glare could bore right through her. "Yes, Isabel." His words were slow and calculated. "I killed David Gerard. I went to his office and shot him for what he did to my daughter."

"Tell me exactly, step by step, what happened the night David Gerard died." Isabel stood motionless at the foot of his bed, capturing the entire confession on video.

After drawing in a deep breath, Jerry took her through each action, how he set David up, how he shot him, and why.

"What's going on in here?" Delia burst through the

door.

"Your father has just confessed to murdering David Gerard. You knew him as Evan Parker."

"Oh, Dad, no!" Her head shook violently as tears sprang to her eyes.

"I'm afraid so, Princess." His eyes were brimming with tears, as well, and he reached out to his daughter. She rushed to the side of his bed and grabbed his hand, leaning over to rest her head on his chest. He stroked her long, dark hair.

Colin and Emily silently slipped just inside the door. Isabel turned away from Jerry and Delia and stepped over to her friends. She bent her head down toward the brooch and whispered, "I'm turning it off for now, Buzz, but stand by. I'll be back on in a few." She raised her head and looked to Colin. "You're up."

He moved closer to Jerry's bedside. "Delia, I'm sorry I didn't get back to my office in time to meet with you, but I—"

"You asked me to come to your office so Isabel could get in here and talk to my father, didn't you?" Her normally refined manner had melted under pressure, exposing the raw anger seething below it. "I want you all out of here! Now!"

"Whoa, lady. You're not in a position to be giving orders. I still need to talk with you, preferably down at the station." Colin rolled his wrist and read his watch. "Let's say in one hour?"

"I have nothing to say." She spoke slowly, through clenched teeth, looking Colin in the eye.

"Then why so defensive, Delia?" Emily crossed her arms and glared at the woman whom she had once considered a friend. Now she was more of an enemy combatant.

"My father is dying and I don't want to leave him." A knot seemed to catch in her throat and she swallowed hard.

"Delia, go with the man," her father encouraged. "I'll be fine."

"No, I don't want to leave you."

"It's okay, go."

"Should I bring an attorney?" Delia asked.

"Only if you have something to hide," Colin replied.

Delia glared at Colin, then her eyes narrowed as she pinched her lips together. "All right, Dad, I'll go," she said, turning her gaze back to her ailing father. "But I'm coming back just as soon as we're done. Okay?"

"Okay, sweetheart." Jerry closed his eyes. "Now, if you all don't mind, I'd like to get some shuteye."

Delia stalked out of the room first and stomped down the hallway as Isabel stood with Colin and Emily in the hall, right outside the door.

"Where's she off to in such a hurry?" Colin asked.

"She probably didn't want to get stuck in the elevator with the rest of us." Emily remarked. "I've never seen her so ruffled."

"That's a good thing," Colin remarked. "She'll be more likely to blurt out the truth under pressure. I'm going to give ADA Laraway a call and bring her up to speed on what's happening."

"Give her my regards," Emily muttered with a hint of sarcasm as Colin pulled his phone out and walked down the hall. The polished blonde with a take-no-prisoners attitude had all but thrown herself at Colin when he'd first arrived in Paradise Valley.

"Time for me to head back in." Isabel twisted the daisy stem and turned her brooch back on. "Buzz, I'm back on. After I'm finished this time, I'll need a copy of this entire recording ASAP." She raised her head and grinned at Emily. "I'm not through with Jerry yet. You guys may want to stick around for the show."

THE CHAIN OF LIES

CHAPTER 23
Killer Trapped

ISABEL BREEZED BACK INTO Jerry's room. "Knock, knock."

Colin and Emily waited out in the hall as Isabel let the door swing silently behind her. She hoped Jerry didn't notice the lack of sound when the door did not close all the way—Emily had stuck the toe of her pointy black boot there so they could listen.

"What the—"

"Sorry, it's just me again, Jerry." Isabel moved to the foot of his bed once more.

"I thought we were done. You got your confession. What else do you want?"

"There was something else I need to tell you."

"What's that?" he asked, rubbing his eyes.

"Like I told you before, the ballistics verified the gun that was found by the river was the one that killed David Gerard. Unfortunately, the lab says there were no usable fingerprints on it. It had been in the mud too long."

"So you're saying I confessed for nothing?"

"As luck would have it, there was a bullet still in the gun and the lab was able to pull a beautiful print off of it."

"No kidding." Jerry crossed his arms over his chest and stared at her.

Isabel wasn't sure if he was really interested or simply being sarcastic. "Want to take a wild guess who the print belongs to?"

He pinched his lips together and waited, turning his head and staring out the window at the cloudless blue sky. Did he have an idea who it belonged to but didn't want to say?

"The print belongs to Ricardo Vega." For a millisecond Isabel thought she saw a look of surprise flash in his eyes before his expression went flat again.

"Delia's late husband?"

~*~

Isabel grabbed a thumb drive from Buzz in the hospital's parking lot. It had the video confession recorded on it. She handed it over to Colin. "The ball's in your court now, Detective."

Emily rode with Colin back to the police station, and Isabel followed in her own car.

"I can't wait to question Delia," Emily said, excitedly squirming in her seat. She rolled the window down and let the cool fall breeze whip through her hair.

"You can't officially question her, Emily. You're

not law enforcement."

"Can't I at least be in the room while you interrogate her?" She sat up straight in the seat and twisted her shoulders, leaning toward Colin. "You know how important this is to me."

"I don't know." He paused and shook his head. "It's a pretty small room," he teased.

She playfully smacked his arm and grimaced.

"Okay, since the Chief wants you on board as a consultant, I'll let you be in the room, but you can't ask any of the questions. I mean it." He down-shifted the red jeep and came to a stop at the light. He looked over at her, waiting for a response.

She leaned back in her seat and looked away from him, out the open window.

"Emily..."

"I'm thinking." She gazed back at him and grinned. "Okay, I promise I'll be as quiet as a church mouse."

"Where have I heard that before?" Colin rolled his eyes. That's what she had promised him in the interrogation he had conducted in New York City on the first case they ever worked together.

He was questioning a Russian mobster about his role in Ricardo Vega's murder, and it was more than she could do to keep her mouth shut. He chuckled to himself as he thought of it. She couldn't keep that promise then and she likely wouldn't keep it now. Although, he did have to admit that in the New York interrogation she had asked a pivotal question, so he had quickly forgiven her.

Yes, that was his Emily—pretty as a peach and as hot and hard to handle as a firecracker.

~*~

"Hey, Stella," Emily greeted as she strolled through the front doors of the Paradise Valley police station with Colin.

Stella stood up behind her desk and smiled. "Hello, Emily. Good to see you, dear. We're all so pleased Colin is back."

"Me too." Emily gave Colin's hand a squeeze.

"Isabel Martínez should be coming right behind us. Send her back to the interrogation room as soon as she gets here." Colin and Emily walked to the door leading to the back offices and he swiped his security pass to let them in. "Oh, and Delia McCall will be here soon. Have her wait out here and I'll come and get her when you announce her."

"Yes, sir, Detective," Stella replied with a hand salute.

He grinned at her. "Cut the formalities, Stella. *Yes, Colin,* will do just fine."

At the sound of the *buzz-click*, Colin pushed the door open for Emily and followed her through it. He led her back to his office and went directly to his laptop which sat open on his desk. He pushed the *on* button and sank down into his black-leather office chair. He waited for the programs to come alive before sticking the thumb drive in an available USB port.

Emily stood across the desk and placed her hands on the edge, craning her neck to try to get a glimpse of the screen. "Do you think we have time to watch the video before Delia shows up? All we know is that Isabel was able to get a confession, Colin. We haven't seen any of the video ourselves yet."

"We all agreed to the plan, so if Isabel stuck to the script, there shouldn't be any surprises."

"Surprises? What surprises?" Isabel asked, standing in the doorway. "We don't want no stinkin' surprises."

"Very funny." Emily spun around, crossed her arms, and sat back against the edge of the desk.

"Emily was wondering if we should watch the video before Delia shows up," Colin said. "I stuck the thumb drive in and it's all queued up."

"Let me give you the short version. I told Jerry if he confessed before the prints came back from the lab, I wouldn't have him arrested."

"How can you promise that?" Colin asked.

Emily grinned at her girlfriend. She knew how Isabel's mind worked. "It's easy, Colin. She didn't say *you* wouldn't arrest him, she said the Feds wouldn't arrest him."

"Ahh—I get it. Evan was murdered in my jurisdiction. It's not a Federal case. Very clever, Isabel."

"I do have my moments. Although, he'll probably be in the grave before it ever got to trial, so what would be the point?"

"True," Colin had to admit.

"Now, back to the video. Jerry did confess to the murder, but when I told him Ricardo's prints were on the bullet still in the gun, he started to backpedal."

"Why would he confess then think he could recant?" Emily asked.

"We'll need to figure that out," Colin replied. "Hopefully we can squeeze something out of Delia."

"Colin," a female voice blared from his desk

phone's intercom speaker. "Delia McCall is here to see you."

Colin depressed a button and spoke toward the phone. "Tell her I'll be right out." He released the button and rose from his chair. "It's show time, ladies."

~*~

Emily and Isabel were already seated at the table in the conference room when Colin escorted Delia in, dressed in her customary tailored suit and expensive jewelry. Her long dark hair floated around her shoulders in waves.

The laptop sat open in the center of the table, ready to play the video of Jerry's confession, alongside a gun sealed in a clear plastic evidence bag.

"Have a seat, Ms. McCall." Colin pulled a chair out for her, then he took his place at the table and set a file folder down on it.

"Thank you, Detective." She eyed the gun and computer as she sank down onto her chair. Her gaze rose to Colin. "But you can call me Delia. It's not like we don't already know each other." She set her purse on the floor and scooted her seat up to the table. "Hello, Emily, Isabel."

"Hi, Delia," Emily replied pleasantly.

Isabel looked at her with a deadpan expression.

"I didn't expect all of this." Delia gestured around the table with her open hand. "I thought you simply needed to ask me a few questions to clear something up. What's going on?"

"I do have something I want to talk to you about,

and I thought it'd be best if Isabel and Emily were here."

"All right, I'm listening," she replied, with a hint of hesitation in her voice.

"Several years ago, someone tried to kill Evan Parker. Did you know that?" Colin asked.

"No." Delia shook her head. "I only knew he was murdered about a year ago."

"From what we've discovered, he managed to wrestle the gun away from the perpetrator during the attempt. He hid the gun with a note saying he hoped one day he could use it to identify his attacker."

"I don't know anything about that, Colin."

"Obviously, the gun has surfaced, along with the note, or we wouldn't be talking about it," he said.

"The FBI lab traced that gun back to your father, Jerry Banderas," Isabel added.

"Oh, my." Delia put a freshly manicured hand to her chest. "I had no idea. Really."

"You had no idea?" Isabel crossed her arms and leaned forward on the table, staring into Delia's dark eyes.

"No, none." Delia pursed her perfectly painted lips.

"Jerry confessed that he attempted to shoot Evan that night," Isabel said.

"He never told me—honest."

"I videotaped his confession, Delia. He stated Evan wrestled the gun away from him and shot him in the shoulder as he escaped." Isabel watched Delia's expression, but she remained stone faced. "He said he called you and you came to his hotel room with everything he needed to dress the wound."

"Uh—well, um—I didn't know it was Evan that

shot him. He just said he'd been shot. I assumed, with his work in the FBI, it had something to do with one of his cases."

Emily sat silently, her arms crossed and her lips pressed tightly together, fighting against the urge to say something.

"I'm not sure your story is lining up with Jerry's," Isabel said. "Let's play the video, shall we?" Isabel reached over and pushed the play button.

Delia watched as her pale and sickly father reclined in his hospital bed and confessed to trying to kill Evan—David Gerard—several years ago, and why he did it. He told how he had called Delia to bandage his wound after David shot him in the shoulder.

In the video, Isabel's voice could be heard asking questions and moving the confession along to the night Evan was killed.

"Tell me what happened the night David Gerard died," Isabel was heard to say.

"I made an appointment with him, pretended to be someone who wanted to hire him for a job. I showed up at his office that night, and we chatted for a while about this and that. We'd never worked together in Washington, so he didn't know me—but I knew him. I knew he was the reason my Natalia was dead."

Delia watched the computer screen as Jerry's voice cracked and his eyes grew moist. He ran his hand across his eyes to wipe the tears then continued.

"I'd hated that man for so long, I couldn't help myself." His voice quivered with emotion. *"I didn't care what he was calling himself at the time, I wasn't going to give him another opportunity to wrestle the gun out of*

my hand. When David went to get something from the file cabinet, I jumped on the chance to put a bullet in the back of his head."

"Did you act alone?"

"Yes, completely alone."

"You're saying your daughter, Delia, knew nothing about what you had done."

"You think I had something to do with that?" Delia shrieked, her eyes wide, shooting a questioning look at Colin.

"That's right. She had nothing to do with it. It was all me," Jerry replied on the video.

Isabel paused the video play.

"Is that the gun?" Delia asked, casting a glance at the bagged weapon that lay on the table.

"Yes. That's the gun that was used to murder Evan Parker." Colin leaned forward in his chair, studying her face. "And you just heard your father confess to doing it."

"You aren't going to charge him, are you?" Delia's eyes widened as her hand slapped the table in Colin's direction. "He'll be dead long before he comes to trial. He's given his life to the FBI, sacrificed his own family for this country."

"You want us to believe you don't know anything about this, Delia?" Emily snapped, then looked sheepishly toward her lap. "Sorry," she whispered to Colin.

"Of course I don't, Emily. Don't be ridiculous!"

"I have a file here with the results from the lab." Colin patted the folder as he said it.

Delia sucked in a gasping breath and her eyes

flickered in surprise for a moment. She quickly regained her composure and calmly folded her hands on the table in front of her, meeting Colin's gaze with a steely one of her own.

"The fingerprint results came back on the gun—because it sat in the river mud for a year and began to rust, no usable prints could be taken from it."

Emily noticed a faint look of relief in Delia's eyes.

"However," Colin continued, "there was one bullet left in the gun and it had a well-defined thumbprint on it that belonged to Ricardo."

"You think my late husband killed Evan?"

"We considered it, but no," Colin said. "Your father insists he did it. He says he's dying and he wants to clear his conscience. So I believe what happened is that Ricardo had loaded the bullets in the gun at some point, but who knows when that might have been. It could have been months or years before. I don't believe he's the one who pulled the trigger."

"Why not?" Delia asked.

"Because Evan was investigating him," Colin explained. "If Ricardo knew Evan was onto him and came to his office to kill him, to cover up what Evan had discovered he'd been doing, it doesn't make sense Evan would ever have trusted him enough to turn his back on the man. No, it had to be someone he felt comfortable with. Your father said he met with Evan under the guise of hiring him to do some work for him."

"Please don't arrest my dad. I don't have him for much longer. You've seen how sick he is—he'll die before he even steps foot in a courthouse." Tears began to trickle down her cheeks as she pleaded for her father's life. "He must have been out of his mind with grief when he pulled the trigger. He didn't know what he was doing."

"Delia, this file has something else very interesting in it." Colin picked up the folder and shook it at her as he said it.

She dug a packet of tissues out of her purse and carefully dabbed at her eyes. "What else?"

"The lab found a small piece of flesh stuck in the hammer of the gun. Fortunately, it did not degrade too much in the water because it was encased in the gun."

"What does that mean?" Delia's eyes narrowed and a small frown line formed between her perfectly plucked brows.

"When an inexperienced shooter fires a gun, they're not used to the kickback. The gun grabs a tiny piece of skin from the wenis."

"What's a wenis?" Emily questioned. Just as quickly, her hand flew over her mouth as she glanced at Colin, who shot her a disapproving glance.

"Some call it a thenar space, that area between your thumb and your index finger." Isabel held her hand up and pointed to the area.

"Why are you droning on about something I couldn't care less about? My dad already confessed."

"With all his years in the FBI, he wouldn't have let that happen to him." Colin threw the folder on the table with a smack.

Delia jumped at the sharp noise.

"But you're not used to shooting a gun, Delia." Emily scooted forward in her chair and rested her elbows on the table, lacing her fingers together, consciously avoiding eye contact with Colin. "What if I told you the DNA test shows those skin cells belong to you." She knew the test wasn't back yet, but she hoped to bluff Delia into thinking it was.

Delia bolted from her chair. "I didn't do it!" she hollered. "My father already told you he did it. Why are you trying to pin this on me? Do I need to call a lawyer?"

"Oh, I'm sorry," Isabel said. "I forgot to show you the rest of the video." She pushed the play button again.

On the video, Isabel could be heard explaining to Jerry that the fingerprint on the bullet belonged to Ricardo Vega.

Delia watched intently, sitting absolutely still with her gaze riveted to the computer screen.

"Ricardo? Then I take it back." Jerry squirmed in his bed. *"If the print is Ricardo's, you know I couldn't have done it. That no-good son-in-law of mine, so he was the one that killed David. Must've been because he found out the guy was investigating him. Ricardo obviously didn't want him to spill the beans to Delia about what he was up to."*

"Yes, must've been, but Jerry...why did you say you did it if you knew you didn't?" Isabel could be heard to ask.

"I only said I did it to cover for Delia—I figured she must have done it. I don't have much time left, but she has her whole life ahead of her."

All eyes were on Delia as she sat in frozen silence for a moment, her gaze still focused on the computer screen.

"I'm not saying another word. I want my lawyer,"

Delia demanded.

"Now, I know you're not talking about my husband, Alex," Isabel snapped. "He defended you once, but he's not taking this case, lady."

"They can get you a nice public defender, if you like," Emily offered.

"I'm fully capable of hiring my own attorney, thank you."

"Delia, you have the right to remain silent…" Colin went on and read her Miranda rights.

"Am I under arrest?" she interrupted.

"If you cannot afford an attorney, one will be appointed for you. Do you understand your rights as I have explained them?"

"Yes, but—"

"Delia, I want some answers! You can clam up until your lawyer arrives, that's your right. Or you can waive your right to an attorney and make a full confession," Colin said, rising from his seat and coming to rest next to her on the edge of the table.

"Now, why would I do that?" Delia asked, looking up at him.

"Because we have you dead to rights with the DNA evidence proving you were the last person to fire that gun," Emily pointed out.

"Emily, please, let me handle this." Colin turned back to Delia. "You can choose to remain silent, but you need to know that we already have the ballistics matching this gun to the bullet that killed Evan. Hard evidence doesn't lie."

Delia sat silently staring at Colin.

"If you want to go to trial, make no mistake, the DA

will also charge your father with aiding and abetting. With the proof we have, your father's last weeks or months will be miserably spent in jail awaiting trial and you'll be given the death penalty for sure."

Delia dabbed at her eyes again and shook her head slowly. Her lips moved, but no words came out.

"I've already spoken to the District Attorney's office about this," Colin went on. He pushed off from the table and went back to his seat. "If you decide to plead guilty to second-degree murder, they'll consider taking the death penalty off the table and not charging your father. He can live out his last days in peace."

Delia looked directly at Colin for an extended moment, her face as set as stone, likely processing what he just offered to her. She glanced at Emily, then back to Colin, pulling in a deep breath.

"Yes, I did it." Her normally strong and commanding voice was shaky. "I killed Evan Parker."

Instantly, Colin was on his feet, stepping behind the suspect's chair. "Delia McCall, you are under arrest for the murder of Evan Parker, also known as David Gerard. Please stand up and put your hands behind your back."

She rose slowly, her head down, and Colin clamped the handcuffs on her delicate wrists.

"Why, Delia? Why?" Emily demanded, shooting out of her chair, which flew back from the force. Her eyes welled with tears as she stared across the table, thinking of Evan, his life—their life together—cut short by this woman.

"He deserved it for killing my little sister! Everyone keeps saying she was caught in the crossfire, but Dad found out from a CIA buddy that it was really Evan's gun that shot her."

Emily's eyes widened. "Evan killed Natalia?"

Isabel stood and placed a protective hand on Emily's shoulder, silently urging her to sit back down. "Actually, Delia, that's not the whole story."

Emily took a seat again at Isabel's urging.

"I received a call a couple of days ago from one of *my* CIA contacts. He said the file on the official investigation says your sister had been recruited by a terrorist group in Spain and David Gerard had killed her in self-defense. Apparently, their supposedly chance meeting at a Paris café wasn't by accident, according to one of the CIA's in-country assets. Natalia's assignment had been to get close to him, see if she could learn anything, and then take him out because he was working an operation to expose them."

"That can't be." Delia shook her head, disbelief simmering in her dark eyes. "The CIA is just saying that to cover up what he did—that's what they do."

"Well, you'll have the rest of your life to mull that theory over, Ms. McCall." Colin grasped her upper arm to take her away.

"Wait!" Emily had one more question.

"What is it?" Colin asked.

"Delia, why did you hire me to investigate your husband? I don't get it."

"Remember the night you phoned me, told me you'd found my name and number on a scrap of paper in Evan's old sweatshirt? I figured hiring you would help me discover if Evan had hidden any other information about me. Keeping you close helped me keep tabs."

"I thought we were friends."

"Pretending to be your friend simply made it easier."

Colin led Delia out of the room and down the hall to booking.

Emily sat speechless, stunned by what Delia had just admitted and what Isabel had recounted. Her eyes filled with tears as visions of her husband's murder flashed in her mind, much like the recurring nightmares she had endured. Only now she knew the identity of the dark shadowy figure that held the gun.

"I'm so sorry, Em." Isabel pulled a chair out and sat next to Emily. "I didn't know how to tell you."

"But his letter said he felt responsible." Emily wiped a few tears with her hand.

"Look at it from his point of view. He had to kill a vibrant young woman he had feelings for. My contact told me the psych evaluation in his file said that something broke in him that day—he was never the same. He blamed himself for not reading her better, not rescuing her from the ones who'd recruited her."

"So I got the broken version of him?"

"No, Em. I'd say you got the better version. Remember, I worked with the guy. He was all about his operations and the next assignments before Natalia died. After that, he didn't have the heart for the spy game anymore. He was on his way out of that life when he met you."

Emily's lips turned up into a small, grateful smile, her eyes still moist with tears.

"I recall the day he came into the office at Langley and told me about meeting you." Isabel brushed a stray curl back from Emily's face. "There was something different about him. He had a spark in his eyes that I hadn't seen in a very long time."

"I appreciate you sharing that with me, Is." Emily put an arm around her friend's shoulder and gave her a quick hug.

"He really did love you a lot, Em."

She nodded slightly. "Maybe now I can finally move on without having to keep looking over my shoulder."

"I'm sure Colin will be glad to hear that."

THE CHAIN OF LIES

CHAPTER 24
COLIN'S SURPRISE

THE NEXT DAY, MOLLY WAS scheduled to be released from the hospital around noon. Camille let all her friends know and hoped they would help with a small welcome-home party for the girl. Since Camille and Jonathan would be at the hospital most of the morning with Molly, she asked Maggie to handle all the party arrangements.

Happy to help, Maggie took care of the food while Peter decorated the entry and family room with pink and purple balloons and streamers. He strung a big welcome-home sign across the garage doors with a couple of balloons on each side.

With Maggie in charge, the menu would not be up to Camille's high standards as a chef, but Cam wasn't there to prepare it. Maggie figured the food should be what Molly liked, so she arranged to have a variety of different pizzas delivered and she bought all the fixings for a help-yourself ice cream sundae bar. As a personal trainer, this was the type of food Maggie usually worked hard to avoid, but this party wasn't about her. It was all about Molly.

Colin swung by Emily's house and picked her up. When they arrived at Camille's, Isabel and Alex were already there, helping to lay out the stack of dishes, glasses, and silverware on one corner of the table where the pizzas would sit.

"Hey, guys," Emily said with a bright smile as she and Colin breezed into the house. "Everything looks fabulous!" Emily gave Maggie and Isabel a quick squeeze.

Maggie was setting out a variety of toppings for the sundaes along the breakfast bar, leaving room for the multiple selections of ice cream.

"What can we do to help?" Colin asked.

"Hello, Colin." Peter shook his hand.

"Hey, Andrews," Alex called out, perched on a stepstool, retrieving a bowl from the top shelf of one of the tall kitchen cabinets. "Glad you could make it."

"I think we're just about set, Colin." Maggie replied to his offer. "Camille called and said they're on their way from the hospital, and the pizza should be here any minute."

"Pizza and ice cream. Camille's not going to like that," Emily teased.

"It's not about Camille, it's about Molly, and y'all know that girl loves her pizza and ice cream."

"Always has," Peter added.

"Oh, to be young and able to burn up those calories," Isabel lamented.

"Too bad some of her friends couldn't be here," Emily said.

"Remember, it's a school day," Isabel reminded her.

"Not to worry. Camille said her friends are planning somethin' for her tomorrow night." Maggie set a bowl of colorful M&Ms on the breakfast bar. "Oh, my. I think I just heard a car door shut."

The gang moved toward the living room to check. The front door opened and Molly walked through first.

"Molly! You're home!" Maggie gushed, giving her a big hug.

Emily and Isabel took their turns welcoming her home, as well, and greeting Camille and Jonathan. Alex and Colin both shook Jonathan's hand.

Peter stepped up and pulled his niece into a warm bear hug. "Glad to see you home, pip-squeak."

The doorbell rang and Maggie rushed to answer it. Standing there, with a stack of pizza boxes, was the delivery man.

"That'll be eighty-six dollars and twenty-eight cents."

Maggie dug in her pocket for the money. Peter stepped up behind her. "Let me get that, Maggie." He handed the man two fifty dollar bills and took the pizzas from him. "Keep the change."

"You didn't need to do that." Maggie smiled as she tucked the cash back in her pocket.

"It was my pleasure. Besides, Molly's my favorite niece. What kind of uncle would I be if I didn't take care of her?"

"Y'all did take care of her, Peter. Y'all saved her life."

"No, not me alone. It was a joint effort." He turned sharply, balancing the stack of boxes, and headed back toward the kitchen. "We'd better get these pizzas eaten before they get cold."

Maggie followed Peter into the open kitchen where he set the stack on the counter. She and Camille took care of setting them out on the table in the dining area. The rest of the gang had congregated in the family room.

"Pizza's ready! Dig in!" Camille announced.

"Molly, you go first," Peter suggested.

Eventually, they all filled their plates and settled in to easy conversation. Before they were ready to bring the ice cream out, Isabel and Emily collected everyone's plates and took them to the kitchen.

"Em, I'm glad we have a minute away from everyone else."

"Why's that?"

"I spoke to Special Agent Ellis this morning and he told me some things he learned from the lead interrogator about the Jade Thai Spa and the ring of sex traffickers."

Emily's eyebrows raised in curiosity. "What?"

"Apparently, according to Ratana—that awful woman who ran the spa—Molly was scheduled to be transported and sold the next day. A rich businessman from Thailand was supposed to fly in on a private jet and Molly would have been whisked out of the country. A young, fair-skinned beauty, especially a redhead, would bring a high price."

"Oh, Isabel. I can't even imagine how horrific that would have been."

"It was unclear whether the businessman wanted her for himself or if he had plans to sell her to someone else on the open market. He would have gotten a lot of money for her, I'm sure."

Emily rubbed a hand over her stomach. "Oh, Is, I feel

sick at the thought."

"Let's just be grateful we were able to rescue Molly."

Emily peeked over the breakfast bar and into family room, watching Molly smiling and laughing as she talked with Peter and Maggie. She was thankful Molly was safe now, and glad they were able to rescue the other girls in that house, but a nauseating feeling continued to roil in her gut.

"What about all the others?" Emily wondered about the thousands whom they could not save.

"I guess all we can do is try to keep our eyes open, watch for others who might be caught up in it."

"I totally agree."

"Turns out most of the Thai girls had been kidnapped from their villages and snuck into the US."

"What about the dead girl in the river?" Emily asked.

"Your girl, Maliwan, confirmed she was one of the girls from the house, but she didn't know why she had been killed."

"Probably because she turned up pregnant."

"Maybe," Isabel supposed. "Oh, before I forget, Jerry admitted he had been the one breaking into your house. He was searching for the infamous hypothetical gun. I hope that helps to put your mind at ease."

"It does." Emily nodded. "I assume that means he won't be following me anymore either, right?"

"I don't know why he would."

"Emily?" Molly interrupted, standing across the breakfast bar.

Emily turned and smiled at her.

"I wanted to thank you for believing me about that sad Asian girl…and for rescuing me."

"You're welcome, Mol."

"You wouldn't have had to do it if I hadn't screwed up." Molly rested her forearms on the breakfast bar and pursed her lips.

"What do you mean?" Emily cast a sideways glance at Isabel.

"If I hadn't been snooping around that house, searching for clues—I only wanted to be part of the investigation, of saving those girls."

Emily flew around the breakfast bar and flung her arms around Molly. "You're a brave young woman, Molly Hawthorne, to attempt something so dangerous, but you could have gotten yourself killed."

"Honey, please don't do anything like that again," Isabel added.

"You guys don't get it." Molly pulled back from Emily's embrace. "I was only trying to help, to be more like you."

"Hush, Molly," Emily warned in a low tone, putting her hands on the girl's shoulders as she glanced around to make sure Camille wasn't within earshot. "Your mom will kill me if she hears you talking like that. She's already mad at me."

"But Emily," Molly argued.

"I do get it, really I do," Emily replied in a tone just above a whisper. "I probably would have done the same thing, but I'm not seventeen."

"You've got to be more careful," Isabel warned.

"Just know that we're always here for you."

Molly nodded her understanding.

"And don't let your mother know we had this talk," Emily advised.

"Hey, what's going on here? Didn't I hear something about ice cream?" Peter asked.

~*~

After celebrating Molly's release from the hospital for an hour or so, the party broke up and those who needed to, returned to work.

Colin drove Emily home, planning to drop her off before heading back to the station.

She unfastened her seatbelt and shifted in her seat to face him. "Why don't you come by for dinner tonight?"

"I have a better idea. We haven't been on a proper date since I got back. Why don't I take you out? Someplace nice—it'll be a surprise."

"All right." She gazed at him, full of curiosity.

"I was wondering something—I mean, after Delia's confession—there's just something I want to talk to you about." He leaned over, put his arm around her, and drew her near. He studied her face, looked deeply into her eyes, then wove his fingers into her hair.

He looks so serious. I wonder what's wrong.

He brushed his lips softly against hers. "I love you, Emily Parker."

She brought her lips urgently to his and felt his passion for her.

After a long moment, he released her. "I hate to leave you, but I need to get back to the station. See you at seven?"

"Yes, I'll be looking forward to it." She flashed him a sweet smile and pushed the car door open. "I love you, too, Colin Andrews."

She glanced back at him over her shoulder, noticing he was watching her sashay up her walkway to the front porch. The smile on his face said he was appreciating the sway of her hips.

Once she was inside, he drove off.

All afternoon she wondered what he wanted to talk about. He'd looked so serious. She hoped it wasn't bad news, like his needing to return to San Francisco again. He'd said something about Delia, though. Maybe he was upset with Emily's reaction to her comments and thought she wasn't over Evan.

Emily hoped not. But if it was, she would just have to show him she was ready to move on with him.

Having fought through the last few hectic and stressful days, and wanting to keep her mind off negative thoughts where Colin was concerned, Emily decided to pamper herself for the afternoon.

With Jerry confined to the hospital, Delia under arrest, and the mysterious gun no longer in her possession, she felt safe in her home once more. She took a long bubble bath, polished her toenails, and gave herself a facial.

Then she took her time getting ready for her date, piling her loosely tousled curls in a twist on her head and carefully applying her makeup. She lightly spritzed a new perfume on her hair and both sides of her neck.

Standing before her full-length mirror, Emily slipped into a deep blue-green fitted dress that the salesgirl said played up the color of her eyes and showed off her slender figure. Checking the fit from all angles, she hoped Colin would be pleased with what he saw.

As she retrieved her cell phone from the nightstand,

she noticed Evan's little black address book sticking out from under one of the pillows on her bed. She pulled it out and flipped through the pages filled with names and codes, remembering the boxes of CIA files still in the storage unit. The sooner she got that book and the files into Isabel's hands, the better—but it would not be tonight. She tucked the little book under her pillow again, for now.

Standing before the mirror in her bathroom, putting her dangly gold earrings on, Emily recalled she still had Camille's white twinkle lights strung around the backyard garden and the gazebo. She considered the idea of flicking them on and inviting Colin out to the beautiful white gazebo that Evan had built for her. She had already taken him out to the deck, ready to show him the garden before they had been interrupted by the exploding potatoes.

Taking him all the way out to her gazebo at the edge of the garden would be a big step for her—proving to Colin she was, indeed, ready to move on. Tonight, if she led him out to it, she hoped he would realize the significance of it, that she had finally and completely closed the chapter on her life with Evan.

The doorbell rang at seven o'clock sharp, and Emily hurried to answer it, trying to fasten her necklace clasp behind her neck as she walked. She flung the door open wide.

Colin stepped across the threshold wearing a handsome black suit with a crisp, white open-collared shirt, holding a bouquet of at least two dozen red roses down at his side.

"Right on time," she said with a smile, stepping aside to let him in.

"You look gorgeous, Babe." Colin leaned forward to

kiss her, slipping his free arm around her waist. His hand splayed on her back as he pulled her toward him.

She reached up and put her hand on his cheek, then slid it to the back of his neck as he bent down. Their lips met, sending a tingling shiver feathering up her back at the pleasure of his kiss.

"Boy, you smell good," she whispered, taking in a slow, deep breath before releasing him, her head lightly dizzy from his musky scent.

"These are for you." He held out the lavish bouquet ensconced in a sheath of clear crinkling wrap.

"Oh, Colin," she gushed. "They're beautiful. Let me put them in some water." She started off to the kitchen and he followed close behind. "Can you get the vase down for me?"

Emily watched as he extended his arm to an upper cabinet to retrieve it, enjoying how GQ and sexy he looked.

She filled the crystal vase with water and carefully arranged the long-stem blossoms in it, before inhaling the scent of the fragrant blooms. After setting the roses in the center of the table, she gently took Colin by the hand. "I want to show you something."

"I don't know if we have time, Babe. We have reservations."

She pushed up on her tiptoes and kissed him softly, enjoying the feel of her body against his. "It's important, Colin, and it'll only take a minute."

"All right, lead the way."

Emily led him across the deck and onto the lush green grass. The bushes and trees were aglow with tiny white lights, as was the gazebo. He slowed to take it all in. She tugged on his hand to continue following her. When they came to a stop, they were standing in the middle of the lovely gazebo.

"Are you sure you want to be out here?" Colin lifted her hand and lightly kissed her fingers. "I know how you've avoided this place."

"That's true. I haven't wanted to come out here since Evan died."

"Why now?"

"I want you to know my life with Evan is finally in the past. I can't say I'll ever forget him, or what we shared—but I love you now, and I'm ready to move on with my life."

He drew her into his arms, pressing his cheek firmly against hers. "Emily, I love you more than I thought I could ever love anyone. You're in my thoughts constantly."

"I feel the same way."

"I want to be with you all the time—take long walks with you, snuggle with you, fight with you, make up with you, catch bad guys with you...as long as we both shall live."

She leaned her head back and smiled as she looked up into his misty, adoring eyes. She could see the reflection of the twinkle lights shimmering in them and wondered what he'd meant.

As long as we both shall live? Could it be?

Maybe she'd been worrying for nothing.

In the next moment, he released his arms from around her body and slid down on one knee, in the center of the gazebo, taking hold of her left hand.

"Colin?" Her breath caught in her throat.

He pulled a small black-velvet box out of his trouser pocket. He flipped it open with his thumb, displaying a dazzling marquis-cut diamond solitaire set in a platinum band.

"I was going to do this at the restaurant later, but this suddenly seems like a more appropriate place."

She gasped and her right hand flew up to her chest.

"Emily Bradford Parker, I love you with my whole heart. I never want to be apart from you again. Will you do me the honor of making me the happiest man in the world? Will you marry me?"

"Yes! Yes—oh, of course, you crazy wonderful man!"

Instantly, he stood to his feet and his arms were around her. His warm, moist lips on hers, and she responded to a wave of passionate kisses.

Emily felt free now—free to love him with her whole heart—and she could not get close enough to him. She laced her hands around his back and held herself against him. A warm tingling sensation started in her breast and radiated throughout her body.

For the longest time they stood together in the middle of the enchanting gazebo, clinging to each other in silence, neither seemed in a hurry to let go.

Emily was first to gently break the silence. "Colin?"

"Yes."

She grinned. "Didn't I see a diamond ring?"

"Oh, sorry." He pulled back from her embrace. "I got so excited when you said yes that I forgot to slip it on your finger." He opened the box again and pulled the ring out.

Emily offered him her hand and he slid the spectacular ring on her finger. She held it up to admire it and it sparkled in the twinkling light. "The ring is stunning, Colin. You have excellent taste."

"In rings and in women."

She smiled at him, then her gaze returned to the ring as she continued to hold it up and admire it. "Mrs. Emily Andrews. That sounds nice."

"I've never heard a more beautiful name." Colin took her left hand and tenderly kissed the back of it, then softly kissed her lips. "Mrs. Emily Andrews," he repeated, looking longingly into her eyes, "as long as we both shall live."

THE END

Thank you so much for reading my book,
The Chain of Lies.
I hope you enjoyed it very much.

Debra Burroughs

The highest compliment an author can get is to receive a great review, especially if the review is posted on Amazon.com.

DEBRA BURROUGHS

Keep Reading for a Preview of
The Scent of Lies, Book 1

The Scent of Lies - Excerpt

PROLOGUE

Life has a way of not turning out the way you had planned, of taking you down roads you had no intention of ever going. Moving in unexpected twists and turns, some bends in the road make you stronger, while others can destroy you.

***

The housekeeper gasped and split the air with a horrifying, ear-piercing scream as she burst in on the mister and misses. She discovered the wife, clothed in a creamy satin robe, with her dark wavy hair floating around her shoulders, kneeling beside her husband's almost lifeless body, which lay on the plush living room floor.

The wife stared wide-eyed at the bloody kitchen knife in her hand.

"Help me," the man whispered almost imperceptibly, terror shimmering in his eyes, trying to grab hold of her wrist.

"Ricardo," she cried, shaking her head violently. "No! This can't be happening."

"Delia..." he gasped.

"Call nine-one-one, Marcela!" the misses ordered.

"Marcela," the man hissed with his last breath.

"Oh, my God, Miss Delia!" Marcela stood paralyzed.

"For heaven's sake, Marcela, go call the police!" the wife screeched. "I think my husband is dead!"

The Scent of Lies - Excerpt

CHAPTER ONE
Friends, Husbands, and Lovers

"BABE, IT'S TIME TO GET UP," Emily Parker muttered sweetly.

She had awakened to the brilliant morning light streaming in through her bedroom window and sleepily stretched her arm out to her husband's side of the bed, searching for his warmth. At the sensation of the crisply cold sheets, her hand recoiled. Flipping back the covers, she sat up and shook her head. After all this time, she still caught herself reaching out for him.

It was late on a lazy Saturday morning. Sleeping in was so unlike her, but after tossing restlessly in the night, with imaginings of her late husband floating in and out of her mind, she hadn't drifted off to sleep until the wee hours of the morning.

Now, after a quick shower, she stood in the middle of

her overflowing walk-in closet, looking for the perfect outfit to wear for her celebratory lunch with her best friends. She surveyed the racks of clothes, unable to make up her mind. She glanced at his side of the closet. Everything was exactly as Evan had left it that final morning six months ago. Still, she had not yet been able to bring herself to get rid of his things—she had her reasons.

From time to time she would drape herself in one of his shirts or sweaters just to smell his scent and to feel him near. Today would be one of those times.

Compelled as she was by her dreams, her need to feel close to him won out over her need to hurry, and she buried her nose in a navy blue hooded sweatshirt hanging on the rack. Breathing in the lingering trace of his rugged masculinity brought him vividly to her mind. She could not help herself—she still missed his crooked smile, the warmth of his strong arms wrapped around her and how glorious he made her feel when they made sweet love.

Emily pulled it off the hanger and shrugged it on, hoping for some emotional comfort. Then she zipped it up and stuck her hands in the pockets, surprised to feel the crackling of paper in one of them. She pulled out a small folded note. Her curiosity piqued, she opened it. In blue ink, the name Delia and a phone number was scrawled in the cursive penmanship of a woman.

Who is Delia? She frowned at the note. Was she a client, an informant, a friend? A lover? As fast as the thought about this female possibly being Evan's lover popped into her head, she pushed it right out again. She'd always had complete trust in him. They had been absolutely happy, until the horrible night he was killed.

THE CHAIN OF LIES

The Scent of Lies - Excerpt

He'd never given her any reason to suspect he had ever been unfaithful to her. *I'm just being silly.*

Her cell phone beeped a reminder and she realized she had spent far too long wallowing in Evan's clothes. Now she really needed to hurry and get dressed for the lunch date with her girlfriends. They were celebrating five years from the day they all first met and began what had grown into a close circle of friends. If she was late, they'd never let her hear the end of it.

She grabbed a pair of white slacks that she knew would show off her slim figure and added a silk turquoise blouse that everyone said set off her dazzling greenish-blue eyes and her head of tousled honey-blonde curls. Emily stepped into her trendy Espadrilles, grabbed her oversized leather purse, and flew out the door.

The girls had chosen the Blue Moon Café—the current hotspot in Paradise Valley—because of the nouveau-gourmet menu and outdoor patio with a breathtaking view of the river. Emily pulled her white Volvo sedan into the crowded parking lot. As she approached the front door, she spotted her party seated under a large blue umbrella at a table on the patio. It was a good choice. They could enjoy the breezy spring air and the sound of the rushing water flowing by while they toasted their anniversary.

Emily made her way through the bustling restaurant, lively with laughter and conversation, and as she stepped out onto the sunny patio, the girls were chatting away. "Hello, ladies." She eased the empty chair out and tucked herself into the group.

"Emily, you're late," Camille Hawthorne pointed out. Camille was like a mother hen to the girls, being a bit older than the others, having a daughter in high school and a son in college. Her looks would not give her age away, though, and she wore her fiery red hair in a cropped and spiky style. But her husband, Jonathan, a sales executive for a local corporation, was the only one who could get away with calling her *Red*.

"I know, I know. I'm sorry. I got a little distracted and lost track of the time," Emily apologized as she scooted her chair closer to the table.

"We were just concerned, Em. You're never late," Isabel Martinez added, tossing her long dark curls over her shoulder. As an FBI financial analyst, Isabel was matter-of-fact and to the point. Usually dressed in a business suit, she appeared relaxed in her jeans and designer t-shirt.

"Well, all y'all know, I'm the one who's always late," Maggie Sullivan admitted in her fading Texas accent, twirling a strand of long blonde hair around her finger. Truthfully, Maggie had a bad habit of being late for almost everything, except for appointments with her clients. As a fitness trainer, she was obsessive when it came to two things—her looks and her business. Emily always thought she resembled a blonde Barbie doll.

"You said it, not me," Isabel replied to Maggie, while looking over the menu.

"Is everything all right?" Camille leaned over and asked Emily in her caring, maternal way.

"Yes, I'm fine." Emily placed her napkin in her lap. "I was standing in my closet trying to decide what to wear and—

THE CHAIN OF LIES

The Scent of Lies - Excerpt

"Yes, I've been known to stand there for half an hour trying to figure out what to put on," Camille interrupted.

"Well, it wasn't just that." Emily's gaze lowered briefly. "I couldn't make up my mind so my eyes wandered over to Evan's clothes hanging there, calling to me. I just had this overwhelming desire to be close to him."

"Oh, I see. Well, that's understandable." Camille grabbed hold of Emily's hand, giving it a light squeeze.

"It probably sounds silly," Emily turned to Camille, "but I smelled one of his sweatshirts and it brought a rush of memories back. So I put it on. The lingering scent of his clothes—it's like he's still there with me. I miss him so much, Cam." She felt herself being pulled back into the moment and her hand fluttered to her chest as her eyes gazed out over the water. "It made me remember how I felt when he held me, when he kissed me...when he made love to me."

"Oh my, Emily!" Camille giggled nervously, fanning herself with her napkin, as her face warmed to the tones in her red hair.

"The time just slipped away," Emily said apologetically. Coming back to the present, she looked down at her menu, a blush of embarrassment heating her cheeks.

"You'll never get over him if you don't start letting go. It's been six months, hon. Don't you think you should start packing up his things so you can at least begin to move on with your life?" Camille asked. "Evan was a wonderful man, Em, really he was, but he's been gone for a while now. You're still here and you deserve to be happy." Camille looked around the table for support. "Don't you agree, girls?"

"Yes, Em," Maggie agreed, "it is time you start havin' some fun again, girl."

"Maybe she's not ready." Isabel came to Emily's defense. "Six months isn't that long, really."

Emily looked over at Isabel and gave her a smile of appreciation. "What I'm ready for is food." She was also ready to change the subject. Her gaze flew around the busy patio. "Where's our waitress?"

A young woman appeared at their table just in time to rescue her, pad and pen in hand. "Hi, I'm Katie. What can I get for you ladies?"

"I'll have the sea bass." Emily jumped in first.

"That sounds good," Camille agreed, closing her menu and looking up at the young woman. "How is that prepared?"

"Uh, sautéed, I think," she replied sheepishly. "Sorry, I'm new here."

"Don't pay any attention to her," Isabel said to the waitress, frowning at her fiery-haired friend. "She's a chef. Can you tell? I'm sure however it's cooked will be fine."

"I guess you're right, Isabel," Camille conceded. "I will have the sea bass."

"Just a garden salad for me, please, Balsamic vinaigrette on the side," Maggie ordered. "I have to watch my girlish figure, y' know." She patted her flat tummy.

At thirty-six, Maggie was obviously proud that she still possessed the slender figure she'd had when she was a twenty-two-year-old starlet in Hollywood. As a young

The Scent of Lies - Excerpt

single mother, she had moved there from Texas with her little boy, trying to get her big break. Unfortunately, her big break never materialized. So, leaving her deadbeat husband behind, she and her son moved north to Idaho, where her brother and his family lived. She'd worked hard, learned all she could about fitness and training, eventually opening her own business as a personal trainer.

"Hmmm," Isabel tapped her finger against her lips. "I'll have the Kobe beef burger, and I'd like the seasoned oven fries with that."

"Isabel, that's a ton of fat and calories," Maggie pointed out.

"I know, but it tastes so good. Besides, I ordered it just to bug you," Isabel teased.

Maggie grimaced. Isabel carried a few extra pounds and often promised Maggie she'd work to take them off when she had time, but she never seemed to find the time.

"You are what you eat, Isabel," Maggie told her for the thousandth time.

"Well, maybe I should eat a skinny person, then." Isabel flashed a mischievous smile. "But I don't see that on the menu."

"There's just no point talkin' to you about it." Maggie rolled her eyes and shook her head.

"Exactly."

The waitress collected the menus. "Thank you, ladies. I'll be back shortly with your food."

Emily took a sip of her ice water. "So, what's new in your world, Camille?"

"Oh, I have the most exciting news!" Her face lit up and her hands flitted about. "You know that big candle business that's expanding and building all those new warehouses and offices down by the railroad tracks?"

"You mean Heaven Scent?" Isabel offered.

"Yes, that one. They're also expanding into a new line of bath products and they're having a big launch party. Guess who they hired to plan and cater the event?" Camille wore a smug grin.

"Hmmm, let me think." Isabel tapped her chin mockingly.

"Me, you silly." Camille patted Isabel's arm. "Oh, I'm so thrilled!"

"Wow, that's a big job. Kudos," Maggie said.

"Yes, Camille, that's fantastic," Emily chimed in. "Congratulations!"

"Thank you all. It's going to be fabulous." Camille declared, smiling broadly. "But enough about me, what's going on with the rest of you?" She glanced from face to face.

"I'm happy to report my fitness trainin' business is goin' well. Oh, and I just have to tell y'all that I have the most gorgeous, delicious new client. He's tall, dark and oh-so-handsome," Maggie gushed.

"Sounds like you'd like him to be more than a client, Maggie." Isabel raised a questioning brow.

"Maybe." She giggled.

"He's not married, is he?" Isabel asked suspiciously

"I don't think so. He doesn't wear a wedding ring and he hasn't mentioned a wife."

"It's best to make sure, Maggie, before you start getting all dreamy over him," Camille warned.

The Scent of Lies - Excerpt

"Yes, Mama," Maggie deferred sarcastically.

"Well, I'm working on a big case," Isabel said. "Do you remember the man who was arrested for killing that family in eastern Oregon, George Semanski? The FBI is building a case against him, and he'll be going to trial in a few months. I'm headed out of town in the next few weeks as part of the work I'm doing on it."

"Oh my gosh, Isabel," Maggie exclaimed.

"Why is the FBI involved?" Emily asked.

"Because after killing the family, Semanski kidnapped the neighbor's kid—or I should say he *allegedly* kidnapped the neighbor's kid—who happened to be at the house during the murders and took him across state lines, which makes it an FBI matter," Isabel explained.

"That makes sense." Maggie nodded.

"What about you, Emily?" Camille asked.

"Me? I guess my real estate business is doing *okay*." The word okay carried a hint of uncertainty.

"Not great?" Camille asked, sticking out her bottom lip sympathetically.

"More like limping along," Emily answered. "I have a young couple I'll be showing homes to later this afternoon. I'm *really* hoping they buy today, because Lord knows I could certainly use the commission right now. A couple of my deals are set to close in the next few weeks—fingers crossed—but there are not nearly as many as there use to be."

"Are you still paying the lease on Evan's old office?"

Isabel asked.

"Yes, I'm on the hook for another year, unfortunately. And because it is such an old building, subleasing is almost impossible. The building is practically vacant as it is."

"Ouch," Isabel responded.

The server returned with a plate in each hand and another server followed with the rest of the food, setting the plates down in front of each of the women.

"Mmmm, it smells delicious." Isabel took a whiff of her burger and fries.

"Yes, it does, and everything looks great too. Thank you, miss," Camille told the young waitress.

"I'll be back to check on you ladies a little later. Enjoy." Katie moved on to another table.

As soon as she left, Emily gently clinked her knife against her water glass a few times to bring her friends' attention to her.

"First, before we dig into our lunches, I want to say thank you all for picking this lovely restaurant for our celebration. I'm so enjoying the sunshine and the river view," Emily began, and all the other women nodded their agreement.

"Secondly, in honor of celebrating the five-year anniversary of the day we met and began our friendship, I would like to make a toast." Emily raised her glass. The other women picked up their glasses, as well. "I want thank each of you for being there for me when I needed you most this last year, after Evan died, and for us all being there for each other through the ups and downs of our lives. You are the best friends any woman could have, and I love you all!"

THE CHAIN OF LIES

The Scent of Lies - Excerpt

"Here's to all of us!" Camille chimed in and they all took a sip of their drinks. "Thank you, Emily. That was so sweet." She patted Emily on the leg. "Now girls, why don't we take a walk down memory lane?"

"What do you mean?" Emily asked, as she picked up her fork to dig into her fish.

"It's been a long time since the special day we're honoring today. I thought it would be fun to talk about it. Do you girls remember that day we first met?" Camille glanced around the table. "And why you were there?"

"Of course," Isabel answered, munching on one of her oven fries. "You were holding a cooking class at your catering shop and we came to learn how to cook."

"You were all such newbies," Camille chuckled, picking up a forkful of sea bass. She had just opened her catering and event-planning business in a small warehouse space and had offered a series of cooking classes to start bringing in money and to meet potential new clients. Her idea worked brilliantly and it pushed her business forward to success. Those classes also brought this circle of women together and they had grown to become best friends.

"I remember that I took the class to learn how to cook somethin' other than my mama's down-home recipes," Maggie recalled, sprinkling a little dressing on her salad. "I had hopes of impressin' and snaggin' me a successful man, but it hasn't quite worked out that way." Maggie offered a mock pout. She was still single, much to her chagrin. But her little boy was now grown and had recently enlisted in the Marines, and she was financially independent and providing for just herself.

"Evan and I were newly married," Emily recalled, "and I wanted to learn to cook for his sake. I was the worst cook ever, and you really helped me, Camille. Of course, I was so bad it wouldn't have taken much to make me better," Emily admitted, which drew laughter from the girls.

"And what about you, Isabel?" Camille asked.

Isabel set her burger down and cleared her throat while she wiped her mouth with her napkin. "Alex wanted me to take the class. He loves to cook and he's quite good at it. With him being a lawyer and me working at the FBI, we both work pretty long hours. I took the class for him, so we could have fun cooking and creating dishes together on the weekends. It's hard to believe it was five years," she patted her tummy, "and fifteen pounds ago." A nervous giggle escaped her lips.

"Hey, wasn't there another woman in that first class with us?" Maggie asked.

"Yes, Abby something?" Emily said.

"Abby Randall," Isabel replied. Her memory was sharp and clear. As a financial analyst, she had a habit of paying close attention to details.

"Yes, poor Abby," Camille said.

"What do you mean, poor Abby?" Emily and Maggie said in unison, then turned and grinned at each other.

"Oh, you haven't heard?" Camille sat up straight and leaned forward.

"Heard what?" Maggie's interest appeared to be piqued, obviously expecting a tidbit of juicy gossip.

"Now, don't tell anyone you heard it from me, but she and Bob are getting a divorce." Camille leaned back a

The Scent of Lies - Excerpt

little, as if to let the information sink in.

"Divorced? Abby and Bob always seemed so happy," Emily commented. "I ran into them a few times around town, at a restaurant or at the store. They seemed like things were going well. I wonder what happened."

"Well, I'm not one to gossip, but I ran into her one day at the mall and we chatted for a few minutes," Camille explained, picking at her sea bass. "Abby had taken classes from me several times, so I probably knew her better than any of you. She told me she thought they were blissfully happy and everything was going along beautifully. They have three children, you know, a nice home, and lots of friends—she said their life was perfect. Then one day, out of the blue, Bob told her he had fallen in love with another woman and he wanted a divorce. I'm sure it just broke that poor woman's heart."

"How can that happen?" Emily asked. "I mean, how can you think everything is perfect, and then out of the blue your husband doesn't love you anymore?" At the mention of another woman, her mind went to the note she'd found in Evan's pocket just an hour or so earlier. She shook her head to get rid of her burning desire to know who Delia could be.

"Abby said he traveled a lot for work, so he obviously did whatever he wanted to while he was away," Camille surmised, "and then pretended to be the perfect husband and father while he was home. I guess he just got tired of pretending."

She paused and her expression became sullen. "Now

that I think about it, my Jonathan travels a lot for work too. You girls don't think that could happen to us, do you?" Camille's upbeat and carefree tone turned serious and she sounded genuinely worried.

"No, Camille," Maggie replied, putting her hand over Camille's. "You need to stop talkin' like that."

"My word, you and Jonathan are perfect together. I don't believe for a moment he would do that to you, or your children," Isabel told her. "Please, Camille, just kick that horrible thought out of your head right now."

"I agree, Camille. That's just plain crazy talk," Maggie added.

Emily didn't say anything. She was caught up in her own thoughts, wondering if something like that could have happened to her and Evan. Like poor, unsuspecting Abby, Emily had thought she and Evan were blissfully happy too, but now she was having doubts. And if it could happen to her and Evan, it could also happen to Camille and Jonathan, couldn't it?

Even in the refreshing spring breeze, sitting in the open and expansive outdoors, Emily felt like she was suffocating under all the talk about unfaithful husbands, and she felt compelled to cut and run. "I'm sorry to cut this lunch short, ladies." Emily abruptly stood, pulled a twenty dollar bill out of her wallet, and laid it on the table.

"But you've hardly touched your lunch," Camille said in surprise.

"I need to meet those clients I was telling you about. I'll talk to you all soon."

Looking stunned and speechless, Maggie, Camille, and Isabel stared in silence as Emily dashed a quick glance behind her then hurried away.

The Scent of Lies - Excerpt

CHAPTER TWO
A Ring of Deception

EMILY REGRETTED HAVING TO LIE to her friends, but she simply had to get out of there. All that talk about *seemingly* happy marriages and *possibly* unfaithful men was more than she could stomach. After that conversation, she was even more driven to discover who this Delia woman was.

At least it was true that she did have an appointment to show homes later that afternoon, but since she had a couple of hours to kill before then, she'd decided to head over to Evan's old office. One way or another, for her own peace of mind, she had to find out if her late husband had been cheating on her.

Emily pushed open one of the large wooden doors and entered the lobby of the historic gray-stone building that sat on Main Street in the heart of Paradise Valley, a quaint, picturesque town situated just to the north of

Boise, Idaho. After walking down a short hallway, she stood before the door to her late husband's office. The opaque window in the door still bore the lettering Evan Parker, Private Investigator.

Fidgeting with the key in the old keyhole, it finally gave in and unlocked. She pulled in a deep breath to steady herself as she entered, standing still for a moment, surveying the room. She had not been to this office since Evan was killed in it. The murder had gone unsolved, and she had been left to wrestle with the unknown.

Heart-wrenching memories came flooding back to her, and she was momentarily paralyzed by them. Evan had been found shot to death here, in the corner by the file cabinets, a single gunshot to the back of his head. The local police had no suspects and no prospects.

There had been a fat stack of cash with a rubber band around it found in a locked drawer of his desk, totaling five thousand dollars. Since the money was still there, the authorities figured it wasn't a robbery, but it did cause them to wonder why he would have that much cash with him. Emily wondered too—on more than one occasion.

Since Evan had been shot at fairly close range, with no sign of a struggle, the police assumed the killer must have been someone he knew. They had questioned every one of his clients after finding their names when they searched his computer and the file folders in the cabinet.

The police had even investigated Emily to rule her out. Fortunately, she was having dinner with the girls at a restaurant when it happened, so she was almost in the clear. There was always the possibility, the detective

THE CHAIN OF LIES

The Scent of Lies - Excerpt

said, that she'd hired it done. Maybe her paid killer, the detective suggested, was someone posing as a new client that just hadn't made it into Evan's records yet.

In time, the police decided Emily probably had nothing to do with her husband's murder. So, with no real clues, old Joe Tolliver, the town's only detective, eventually gave up and filed it away as a cold case. The pile of cash was eventually released to Emily.

It wasn't that Paradise Valley could not afford to hire another detective, because it had grown into a largely affluent community. In the last ten years or so, it had become known for its million-dollar homes built along the Boise River, and there were an ever-increasing number of five- and ten-acre horse property subdivisions gobbling up the surrounding farmland.

The reason for having only one detective was simply that the mayor and city council members saw no need to waste the taxpayers' money. Paradise Valley hadn't had a murder in more than twenty years—until Evan was killed.

Focus, Emily ordered herself, remembering why she was there. Her mission was to find out who this woman, Delia, was.

Sitting down at Evan's old metal desk, she rummaged through it, searching for anything that had this woman's name on it. She came up with nothing. Then she went through all the folders in the file cabinet. Again nothing. She checked the calendar in his computer and even did a total search of the hard-drive for the name—still nothing.

Her eyes moistened and her throat tightened a little when she noticed the framed photo on the desk. It was a picture of her and Evan, smiling and snuggling in happier days. Picking it up, she lovingly traced his face with her finger. Her heart missed his sandy brown hair and piercing blue eyes.

Emily spied the cross-directory phone book on top of the file cabinet and gently set the picture down. She grabbed the directory and flipped it open on the desk. Digging around in her purse, she found the slip of paper that showed Delia's phone number. She laid it down next to the book.

Scanning the pages as she ran her index finger across them, she located the number in the directory and read the name Delia McCall. The name sounded vaguely familiar. "Delia McCall," she muttered several times, but she couldn't place it. So she decided to be brave and dial the number. She needed to know this woman's connection to her husband.

The phone on the desk had been disconnected long ago, so she made the call from her cell phone.

"Hello." The woman's voice was low and sultry.

"Is this Delia?" Emily asked nervously

"It is. Who is this?"

"This is Delia McCall?" Emily asked again, her heart thudding in her chest.

"Yes. Who is this?" the woman insisted.

"This is Emily Parker, Evan Parker's wife."

"Oh, Emily, yes, Evan had mentioned you." Delia's voice changed to a lighter tone.

The Scent of Lies - Excerpt

"Evan mentioned me?" Emily was stunned by her comment. She wondered why her husband would be talking to this woman about her.

"Yes, several times."

"I have to know, Ms. McCall, what was your relationship with my husband?" Emily held her breath for the answer.

Delia stuttered and stammered, obviously caught off guard. Was she hiding something?

"Well?" Emily pressed, irritated by the woman's evasiveness. If it had simply been a business relationship, why would she not just come out and say it? She decided to ask what she was really wondering. "Were you having an affair with my husband?"

We hope you enjoyed that excerpt from
The Scent of Lies, Book 1
A Paradise Valley Mystery, Book One

Available on Amazon.com
in eBook and Paperback

Turn the page for an excerpt of
The Heart of Lies, Book 2

THE CHAIN OF LIES

Excerpt from The Heart of Lies, Book 2

"Oh, what a tangled web we weave when first we practice to deceive."

~ Sir Walter Scott

PROLOGUE

Lies are deceptive little things. Whether they are innocent white lies or the evil midnight black ones, they all have a way of coming back to expose us at the most inopportune moments.

~*~

The unsuspecting young woman approached the doorway of the dimly-lit private office. She jerked to a halt, catching sight of the man sprawled on the floor next to his desk, his body motionless, his face bloody and battered. Her hand flew over her mouth. Her other seized hold of the door frame for support, feeling her knees begin to give out.

A plethora of painful emotions roiled in her chest as she stared, eyes wide, fighting to stuff down the overwhelming urge to scream. Perhaps the attacker was still within earshot.

Who did this? Who?

The list of people who might want him dead was long—that much she knew. The only question to be asked was which one actually followed through. She needn't ask why, though, she already knew that answer.

Hot tears stung her eyes. She fought against the powerful desire to run into the office, to fling herself down and put her arms around him. Under different circumstances, she would have caressed him one last time and kissed him a final good-bye—but not now.

With her heart thudding loudly in her ears, she could hardly think, she remained frozen to the safety of the door jamb. Self-preservation dictated that she could not risk running to him. Someone could discover her there and she would be found out. And if she got his blood on her, she might even be blamed for his murder.

She struggled to hold herself back and cling to the safety of the solid frame, torn between grief, terror, and rage. Nearly choking on the knot in her throat, she whispered a raspy and tearful good-bye. "I'm sorry, James, but I can't go to prison. Not even for you. Good-bye."

Her attention was pulled away as she picked up the sound of a car door slamming in the parking lot. Her thoughts flew to the police, who would certainly be coming. Images of them flashed through her mind—finding her there, digging into her background, arresting her. She couldn't have that.

Her mother always told her that men would come and go, but no matter what, her top priority had to be to look out for number one.

THE CHAIN OF LIES

The Heart of Lies - Excerpt

Her instincts to save herself won out.

THE CHAIN OF LIES

THE CHAIN OF LIES

The Heart of Lies - Excerpt

CHAPTER 1
Rocky Mountain Oysters

"WHO'S UP FOR THE ROCKY MOUNTAIN Oyster Feed?" Emily Parker asked her cluster of friends as they stood on the sun-drenched sidewalk, watching the end of the Founders Day Parade. The music from the high school marching band began to die down as the last musicians rounded the corner, drifting out of sight.

Emily loved the parade and small town festivities in Paradise Valley, but most of all she loved the interesting women that made up her close circle of friends. After recently taking over her husband's private investigation business after his murder, no one was more important to her than these three girlfriends.

They had helped her through her devastating loss, not to mention her transition from real estate agent to lady PI.

A chorus of "count me in" and "me too" rang out from the group, with the exception of one loud dissenter.

"Eeew, fried bull testicles?" Maggie's face screwed up in a look of disgust. She tucked a strand of long blonde hair behind her ear and rolled her big blue eyes like a teenager half her age.

"Oh Maggie. You're such a drama queen." Isabel shook her head. Isabel Martínez was a no-nonsense FBI financial analyst who had seen it all. She and her attorney husband, Alex, had been looking forward to the Rocky Mountain Oyster Feed for months and they clearly weren't going to let Maggie Sullivan, the Southern belle fitness queen, put a damper on their fun. "They're delicious, Maggs. You have to put it out of your head what they really are."

"But they're fried bull testicles, Isabel." Maggie frowned. "How can y'all ever get *that* out of your head?"

"They're a delicacy, Maggie," redheaded Camille Hawthorne piped in. As a caterer and event planner, sometimes the spiky-haired diva had to put an enticing spin on some of her unique specialty dishes. "Think of them simply as Rocky Mountain Oysters—that's what I keep reminding my Jonathan."

"But the thought, Camille—" Her tall, lanky husband, Jonathan, wore a wincing look on his face. "I feel for those poor bulls—ouch."

"All right, all right." Emily waved her hands and shook her head, making her honey-blonde curls dance around her neck. "Enough talk. Whoever wants to go to the Oyster Feed, follow me."

"All y'all can go on without me. I'll meet up with y'all later," Maggie called out as the group left her

THE CHAIN OF LIES

The Heart of Lies - Excerpt

standing her ground.

The small crowd of friends chatted and laughed their way to the city park, where a large open-air tent was set up to serve the Oyster Feed. People had already begun lining up at the serving station to grab a plateful of the "oysters" along with a piece of buttered corn on the cob and a juicy wedge of ripe, red watermelon.

Emily, along with her girlfriends, Camille and Isabel, and their husbands, Jonathan and Alex, descended on a long folding table, balancing their oyster-laden plates and cold drinks.

"I wish Colin could have been here," Emily remarked.

Six months after her husband, Evan, had been killed, Emily began dating the town's new police detective, Colin Andrews. Within a few short months, he had been called back to San Francisco to help his mother take care of his father, following a debilitating stroke. He wasn't sure how long he'd be gone, but had said he felt duty-bound to help out.

Ex-Marines were like that, Emily reminded herself.

She and Colin tried to keep in contact long distance by way of emails, phone calls, and Face Time on the computer, but it wasn't the same as having him there in person. She was lonely for him, especially when she saw her friends enjoying life with their men. Her only solace was that Maggie was single too and they could commiserate together.

"How is Colin doing?" Alex asked. They had been

basketball buddies, and as an attorney, Alex found himself working the opposing side of some of the cases Colin investigated.

"He misses you all." Emily's hair hung in loose tousled curls, brushing her shoulders, as she looked down at her plate, bravely cutting into an oyster.

"But he misses you the most, I'm sure." Camille patted Emily's hand.

Emily sighed. "I'm sure you're—"

"Hey, y'all." Maggie burst in and stood next to their table. "I told y'all I'd catch up sooner or later."

"Have a seat." Isabel motioned to the folding chair next to her.

"I have someone I want all y'all to meet." Maggie gestured to a young brunette standing next to her in the crowded tent. Maggie stood behind the empty chair and put an arm on the shoulder of the young woman. "Everybody, this is Fiona. She's new to Paradise Valley, and I offered to introduce her 'round."

"Hello, Fiona." Emily was first to greet her, but the others quickly followed.

Isabel's training in the FBI caused her to always be the first to question and be suspicious. "Where did you two meet?" she asked. Isabel sounded interested, but wore a far-too-analytical look for mere small talk.

"Fiona was in one of my aerobics classes at the Y," Maggie replied.

"Yes, in aerobics class." Fiona nodded. "I don't know anyone here yet, so I figured there might be people I could get to know in an exercise class."

"Why don't you two grab some food and come and eat with us?" Emily suggested.

THE CHAIN OF LIES

The Heart of Lies - Excerpt

"I already told y'all, no fried bull's testicles for me," Maggie shot back.

"What?" Fiona's eyes widened with surprise as she looked down at the half-eaten food on the plates. "What are you eating?"

"Bull's testicles," Maggie repeated, linking her arm through Fiona's and pulling her away from the tent.

The friends at the table burst out in laughter at Maggie's over-the-top disgust with their dining choice. Soon conversation began to flow again and the meal was quickly devoured.

Camille was seated across the table from Isabel and Emily, and she leaned in toward them as if she was about to say something of great importance. In response, they inclined forward as well.

"Did Maggie tell you yet about the man she met?" Camille asked, dipping her chin and raising an eyebrow for emphasis. She glanced over at the husbands, who were thick in conversation about the latest baseball scores and rankings.

"No. What man?" Emily asked.

"Yeah, what man?" Isabel repeated with typical concern.

"Well, I thought she would have spilled the beans by now, so don't tell her I told you girls, but she met a man on one of those online dating sites." Camille sat back in her chair, running her hands through her short spiky red hair, an intentional pause, as if to let that information sink in.

"I don't like the sound of that." Isabel pushed her long black waves over her shoulder. "You never know what kind of kook or pervert is lurking on those sites."

"They seem to be getting more popular," Emily remarked. "I think the reputable ones might be safe, don't you think?" She looked from Isabel to Camille.

"I don't want to sound paranoid," Isabel crossed her arms on the table, "but no site is totally safe from scam artists and perverts."

"Any details, Camille?" Emily inquired.

"All I know is," she leaned forward again, "his name is Lucas and he has money."

"Is that what Maggie said?" Emily asked.

It was well known among these close friends that Maggie had always hoped to snag a man with money. She had grown up poor in Texas, escaping that life as a young single mother with a small son, making her way to Hollywood in hopes of becoming a movie star. When her ship never came in, she left her deadbeat husband and moved north to Idaho where her brother and his family lived.

Over the years, her son, Josh, grew up into a fine young man and joined the Navy two years earlier. Her brother, Clifford "Sully" Sullivan, co-owned and ran the local golf course and had been elected Mayor of Paradise Valley a couple of years before.

When Maggie had arrived in Paradise Valley, she'd brought little more than her young son, but she learned all she could about fitness training and she'd opened her own studio, which gave her a decent living. Still, she always said it was her dream to find herself a man of means who would love her and treat her like a queen.

The Heart of Lies - Excerpt

Maybe now her dreams were coming true.

"What does she know about this man?" Isabel asked.

"All she's told me is that he lives in Colorado, his name is Lucas Wakefield, and he's an investor," Camille reported.

"Investor? What does he invest in?" Isabel questioned.

"You'll have to ask Maggie if you want any more facts," Camille said. "But, please, wait until she brings him up. Otherwise, she'll know I told you."

"Maybe I should run a background check on him," Isabel suggested, tapping her finger on her chin.

"Oh, Isabel, I don't think Maggie would like that," Emily warned. Being a private investigator made Emily as skeptical as Isabel's FBI training had made her, but Emily knew Maggie wouldn't see it that way. "Why don't you wait on that one?"

"All right—for now," Isabel agreed. "But as soon as she tells us about this Lucas character and she starts talking like they're getting serious, I'm doing a background check."

"Enough talk about Maggie, what about you, Em?" Camille asked. "Have you found out anything more about Evan's mysterious past?"

Emily's late husband, Evan Parker, had been a private investigator in Paradise Valley. He'd been murdered while working late in his office one night about a year ago. Eventually, Emily was able to start putting her tragic loss behind her. Hoping to move on to a new relationship at her friends' urging, she began to pack Evan's things away.

While going through his closet, she had come upon a slender silver key that turned out to belong to a safe deposit box at a local bank. She had been shocked that he had kept secrets from her and angry that he had lied about his past.

Gaining access to the safe deposit box, she'd examined the contents and found three passports with three different names—Alexi Krishenko, Michael Boerner, and Sean McDonough. She'd also discovered a large bundle of cash, some Euros, a mysterious brass key, a gun, and an old photo of Evan with a pretty, young, dark-haired woman. He had his arm intimately around her shoulders and they were smiling into the camera.

Of all the things she'd found in the box, the photo had packed the biggest wallop. Emily had removed the key and the photo from the metal box and left the rest at the bank for safe keeping.

"I still haven't been able to find out who the woman in the photo is or what the key unlocks," Emily replied.

Months after Evan's death, Emily had been pulled into one of his old cases and had taken over as the investigator. She'd worked the case, but it had dragged her deeper into her own puzzling mystery. The items in Evan's safe deposit box clearly spoke of another life, a life he had kept from her, leaving her to wonder who he really was and if their marriage had been one big lie.

"You know, I did offer to help you with that." Isabel had suggested that on numerous occasions, but

THE CHAIN OF LIES

The Heart of Lies - Excerpt

Emily always put her off, telling Isabel she didn't want her to get involved, that she would take care of it herself. Still, Emily hadn't been able to solve the puzzle by herself—perhaps now she should accept the offer.

"What do you have in mind?" Emily stared seriously into Isabel's eyes.

"See, I knew you'd come around. I could see it in those blue eyes—"

"They're green," Camille interrupted.

"They're both," Isabel corrected. "Anyway, I have a friend who just retired after thirty-five years with the FBI. He's living over in Boise and he may have some contacts that could identify the woman. If I can give him a copy of that photo you found, the one with Evan and the woman, he may be able to find something out about Evan's past life for you."

"Assuming Evan Parker was his real name," Emily added.

"Whatever his name was, my friend may be able to dig something up."

"What do you have to lose, Em?" Camille encouraged.

"Okay, I'll scan the photo and email it to you, Isabel. Then you can forward it to your FBI friend."

"Retired FBI friend," she corrected.

"So, what's your *retired* friend's name?" Emily questioned. "That is, if you don't mind my asking."

"No," she waved her hand. "If I told you, I'd have to kill you." Isabel said it with a straight face, but then she snickered and Emily and Camille laughed, too. "Let's just call him Jethro."

"What are you girls laughing about?" Jonathan asked from the other end of the table. He and Alex gawked suspiciously at the women.

"Just girl talk." Emily flashed a quick smile to her girlfriends. "Hey, I heard there was a pie baking contest somewhere around here." She changed the subject and rose to her feet. "And afterwards, they're selling the entries. Tell me. Who's ready for pie?"

~*~

Emily and her friends had a ritual of meeting together on Thursday nights for a potluck dinner at one of their homes—girls only. This Thursday it was Emily's turn to host the dinner and the theme was Italian. Since Emily was the worst cook of the four of them, she decided her contribution would be a big green salad and fresh sourdough bread from the local bakery.

She was setting the table for dinner when her cell phone rang. A big smile spread across her face and her heart began to beat a little faster when she saw it was Colin.

"Hello." She answered in her sweetest tone—the one she reserved for Colin.

"Hi, Emily. I've missed hearing your voice," he said.

She missed hearing his, too. It always reminded her of warm, dark chocolate—smooth, sweet, and sensual. "Me too. How's your dad?"

"He's doing better, but Mom's not able to take care

THE CHAIN OF LIES

The Heart of Lies - Excerpt

of him all on her own yet."

"Any idea when you'll be back?" Soon, she hoped.

"No, but I'm as anxious to come back to Paradise Valley as you are to have me." He chuckled.

"What's so funny?"

"Me. I can't believe I'm actually missing that small town. I never thought I'd say that."

Colin had been a San Francisco policeman, then a detective there. He loved the big city—until his fiancée was killed. He had taken the job in the small picturesque town of Paradise Valley to escape her memory. That's when he and Emily met, and when, according to him, he was captivated by her.

"I thought it was me you were anxious to return to, not this town," Emily replied, feeling a little deflated.

"Absolutely—but I do have to admit that I was becoming attached to that place and the people in it. Before you know it, I'll be back."

"You better be, mister. I'll admit it. I'm so lonely for you I can hardly stand it."

"I'm glad to hear you say that. I feel the same way."

"Oh you do, huh?"

"Yes, I do." Colin cleared his throat. "Emily, I, I—"

Emily's attention was jerked away. "Knock, knock! Where are you, Emily?"

Camille and Isabel entered the house, calling for their host.

"I'm back here!" Emily shouted from the kitchen. "I'm sorry, Colin, the girls are here for our weekly girls' night. You were saying something?"

"Well, I was but…you go have fun with the girls."

"All right, Colin. Let's talk again soon. I miss you."

"I miss you, too—love you." He quickly hung up, leaving Emily staring at her phone.

What? Did he just say he loved me?

There had always been a mutual attraction, a strong desire to be together, but neither of them had ventured into the deep waters of "I love you" yet. Before she had time to decide if she'd been hearing things or not, Camille and Isabel strolled into the kitchen.

"You look like someone just slapped you, Em." Camille set her hot pan of lasagna down on the stovetop.

Emily shook her head and put a broad smile on her face. "Uh, no. I was saying good-bye to Colin on the phone."

"How's he doing? I'll bet he misses you as much as you miss him." Camille smiled as she rifled through the utensil drawer.

"I think you're right." Emily gave her friend a hug.

"I brought homemade meatballs," Isabel proudly announced as she set her crockpot on the counter, lifting the lid to show Emily. She had been taking cooking lessons from Camille and was becoming quite accomplished. Camille was proud of her, but Maggie, the fitness queen, often gave her grief for the extra pounds she carried with her new love of cooking.

"They smell divine," Emily complimented. "I can't wait to taste them."

"*Grazie,*" Isabel replied.

"Where's Maggie?" Camille took the foil off her lasagna.

THE CHAIN OF LIES

The Heart of Lies - Excerpt

"Late, as usual." Isabel stirred her meatballs and fresh marinara sauce around with a large spoon. That was Maggie's one downfall, being notoriously late for just about everything. "She'll probably be late for her own funeral."

"Hey, I heard that!" Maggie shouted as she came through the door. All heads turned in her direction and the girls giggled. Emily hugged her and took her dinner contributions—a container of strawberry Gelato in a plastic grocery bag hanging from her arm and a bottle of red wine in each hand. "So, what did I miss?"

"Emily was on the phone with Colin when we walked in," Camille reported. "She hasn't said if there was anything new."

"Was there? Anythin' new, I mean?" Maggie asked.

Emily felt herself blush, and it did not go unnoticed. She hadn't planned on saying anything, but being put on the spot as she was, she decided to just come out with it. "Well, nothing big."

"Go on, Em, spit it out." Camille's bright blue eyes were wide with anticipation.

Emily could feel the heat of all their eyes on her. "Well, just as Colin was saying good-bye—"

"Out with it, Em!" Camille insisted.

"He said, 'Love you,' and then hung up." Emily eyed her friends, waiting for a response. "It took me by surprise."

"Did he actually say, I love you, or just a quick, love you?" Isabel questioned.

"What difference does it make, Isabel? He said the L word." Maggie gave Emily a big hug.

"It makes a big difference—at least it would to me," Isabel replied.

"I've decided I'm going to let it slide. I'm going to wait for the real, I love you, Emily, before I say it back."

"That's wise, Em," Camille agreed. "Just make sure you let us know the second he says it. I'm going to be waiting on pins and needles, my friend."

"Maybe not the second he says it," Isabel added, grinning at Camille.

"Well, y'all, speakin' of bein' in love," Maggie interjected, all eyes turning on her, "I have some news of my own."

"What news, Maggs?" Emily asked.

"I met a wonderful man online through one of those datin' services that match you up, and we've been talkin' on the phone and emailin' for a couple of months now. We've even had a few video chats on the computer with that Face Time *thang*."

"How come you never said anything before?" Isabel asked pointedly.

"I guess I wanted to see if it was goin' anywhere before I did. I didn't want to jinx it, y'know? I haven't had the best luck with men."

Maggie had had her share of relationships with men, but none of them seemed to stick. She was a force to be reckoned with, and as a single mother she held the bar high.

"Ooh, give us some details, Maggie," Camille encouraged.

"His name is Lucas Wakefield, and he's an investor

The Heart of Lies - Excerpt

and land developer. He lives in Colorado and he's been lookin' into doin' a project in this area."

"What kind of project?" Isabel questioned.

"Somethin' up in the mountains, like a resort," Maggie replied.

"That sounds exciting. Does that mean he's coming here?" Emily asked.

"As a matter of fact, he is, in the next week or so."

"Let us know and we'll throw a big party to welcome him," Camille offered.

"Oh, Cam, that would be fabulous!" Maggie beamed.

"This is all very exciting, ladies, but the food is getting cold," Isabel noted. "Why don't we serve ourselves and we can sit down and talk more while we eat?"

They happily agreed to Isabel's suggestion and spent the next hour eating, talking, and laughing. Wine flowed, dessert was relished, and conversation of Lucas Wakefield was thoroughly exhausted.

"You've been very quiet about your work, Em," Camille noted, licking the last bit of Gelato from her spoon and wagging it at Emily. "Working on any exciting cases?"

"Ever since I solved the Delia McCall murder case a few months ago, it's been pretty uneventful."

Emily had taken over the McCall case after Evan was killed, and it quickly went from tracking Ms. McCall's philandering husband to solving his murder.

Emily had exposed the murderer, almost losing her own life in the process.

"That was an excitin' case." Maggie poured herself more wine.

"Since then, it's just been a handful of suspicious wives hiring me to follow their wayward husbands. Seems like not much happens in this sleepy little town—except maybe adultery." Emily gave the girls a playful grin.

"Oh, my," Camille gasped as a little giggle escaped her. She stood and began to clear the plates from the table.

"How can y'all say that?" Maggie asked. "We had two murders in the same year."

"You're right," Camille agreed. "And if Jonathan cheated on me, there'd be another murder in this town, for sure," she quipped, winking at Emily.

We hope you enjoyed that excerpt from
The Heart of Lies, Book 2
A Paradise Valley Mystery, Book One

Available on Amazon.com
in eBook and Paperback

Turn the page for an excerpt of
The Pursuit of Lies, Book 4

Excerpt from The Pursuit of Lies, Book 4

"Oh, what a tangled web we weave when first we practice to deceive."

~ *Sir Walter Scott*

PROLOGUE

The scariest thing about both truth and lies is that they always catch up to you, no matter how hard you try to hide them.

~*~

THE YOUNG BLOND WOMAN lay waiting on the neatly made bed, smoothing out her white silk teddy before reclining against the sumptuous pillows.

"I'm ready for you," she called out, eager for what was coming. Resting a hand behind her head, she smiled to herself, pleased with the life she had fashioned. Successful, and respected in her profession, she had no time for a serious romantic relationship—she was married to her job. So, having a handsome male friend, one with benefits and no strings, suited her just fine.

The man was charming and sexy—what woman in her right mind wouldn't have been attracted to him? He was honest enough to admit to her upfront that he was committed to someone else, but she didn't mind. That may even have been what drew her to him.

Casual dating with no commitments was all she could manage at the moment as she climbed her professional ladder to success. Her emotional needs, little as they were, as well as her physical needs were being met. That's all she wanted for now.

Stripped to the waist and barefooted, her lover stood in the doorway. She admired his physique as he turned to switch the bathroom light off. The bedroom was softly lit by the dimmed lamp on one side of the bed.

She flashed him a seductive smile as he put a knee on the bed and hovered over her, with one hand held behind his back. "Why so quiet, Colin?"

"I have a surprise for you."

"Is that what you're hiding back there? She craned her neck to see. She didn't like surprises. "What is it? Let me have it."

The thrill of anticipation rippled through her

The Pursuit of Lies - Excerpt

body. She loved receiving gifts, especially expensive ones.

His hand whipped around and he gave her the surprise. Rather than a beautifully wrapped box, like she had expected, he held a long sharp knife. She thought he was playing around until she gazed into his fiery eyes. He moved so swiftly that she'd had no time to recover from the shock of his actions or force out even one scream.

The knife plunged deep into her chest and everything went black.

THE CHAIN OF LIES

The Pursuit of Lies - Excerpt

Chapter 1

AS EMILY PARKER MEANDERED through the busy Blue Moon Café, searching for her party, she thought her chest might burst open from excitement. As she wound through the noisy lunch crowd, she picked up snippets of conversations—people talking about their family, the latest football game, or the weather—but nothing as wonderful as the news she'd come to share. She caught sight of one of her girlfriends waving her over.

Her friends had snagged a coveted booth at the back of the restaurant, along a wall of windows with a breathtaking view of the river flowing by. It was early autumn and the trees along the water's edge were beginning to turn various shades of yellow, orange, and red.

Emily slid into the booth and greeted everyone.

"You're late, Em," Isabel said. "We already ordered for you—the usual."

"Sorry, I just wanted to make sure you were all here first."

"Why is that?" Maggie asked, leaning forward with her chin on her palm and her big blue eyes focused on Emily.

"Girls," Emily glanced around the table, "I have an announcement to make."

"What is it, Em?" Camille laid a perfectly manicured hand on Emily's arm. Her short and spiky red hair looked as if it was on fire with the sunlight from the window behind her lighting it up.

"Yes, what?" Maggie repeated.

"Another juicy new case, perhaps?" Isabel asked, pushing her long dark waves over one shoulder.

"No, not a new case, juicy or otherwise." Emily paused for dramatic effect, glancing from face to face. "I'm talking about a new life." A big smile spread across her face.

"What does that mean, Em?" Maggie began to sit back in her seat, as she tucked a strand of long blonde hair behind her ear. Then she bolted forward. "You aren't movin' away, are you?"

"No, nothing like that. What it means, girls, is…" Emily stuck out her hand and displayed the sparkling diamond ring Colin had given her the night before, "that I'm engaged!"

The Pursuit of Lies - Excerpt

The atmosphere at their table erupted with excitement and congratulations.

"I had a feeling," Camille said, pulling Emily's hand nearer to her for closer examination.

"Really? Because I was totally taken by surprise." Emily tossed her head back when she laughed and her loose honey-blonde curls tickled her neck.

"Give me a break." Isabel smirked. "You're a private eye and you didn't see this coming? I saw it coming from a mile away." As an FBI analyst, with great attention to detail, Isabel Martínez was the practical, analytical one in the bunch.

"Well, okay, maybe not totally." Lately, Emily's time and her thoughts had been consumed with solving crimes and apprehending criminals. She and Detective Colin Andrews had become inseparable, both personally and in work, but the subject of marriage had never come up—at least not until he proposed.

"I'm just thrilled for y'all," Maggie cooed. She was known among her friends as the southern-belle fitness queen. Lovely as she was, with her bright blue eyes, flowing blonde hair, and a body that wouldn't quit, Maggie Sullivan had the most horrendous luck with men.

"Oh, Em, you'll have to let me throw together a fabulous engagement party for you and Colin." Camille Hawthorne was a caterer and event planner, and this engagement would give her the perfect excuse to host another of her famous affairs. "Please say yes."

Emily glanced around the table at all the smiling faces. "Yes." Her answer drew an excited round of approval from the girls.

"I'm happy to have it at my house," Isabel offered. She and her attorney husband, Alex, had a spacious, upscale home in one of the nicest neighborhoods in Paradise Valley.

"Oh, Isabel, that would be wonderful," Camille replied.

Emily smiled as she gazed around the table at her friends. "You girls are the best."

"Have you set a date?" Isabel asked.

"Not yet."

"Oh, Emily, you'd better hurry," Camille advised. "All the best venues will be booked if you don't."

"There's plenty of time for that." Emily held out her left hand and admired her sparkling new ring again. "Let me just enjoy being engaged before we have to start working on all the wedding details."

The waiter brought their food and the rest of the hour was spent eating and talking about the

THE CHAIN OF LIES

The Pursuit of Lies - Excerpt

upcoming wedding. When they had finished, the girls ambled out to the parking lot to say their good-byes.

"Hey, isn't that Colin?" Maggie asked, pointing to a red Jeep Wrangler whizzing by on the main street that abutted the parking lot.

"Looked like him," Isabel replied. "Short dark hair and all."

"Maybe," Emily said, straining to catch a glimpse of the vehicle. "I'll give him a call in a little while."

"Okay, I've got to get back to work. Congratulations, again." Isabel gave Emily a quick hug. "I'll see you all Thursday night."

The four of them regularly got together each Thursday evening for a girls-only potluck dinner at one of their homes.

"Yes, at your house this week," Camille replied. "The theme is Mexican."

"Again?" Maggie asked, wrinkling her nose.

"I have a new recipe for *Chili Rellenos* that I'm dying to try," Camille said.

"Then Mexican it is." Emily opened the door of her white Volvo sedan and slid behind the wheel. "See you Thursday."

Once Emily was out on the main road, she dug

her cell phone out of her handbag and dialed Maggie's number.

"Hello."

"Hey, Maggs, it's Emily. I wanted to talk to you privately."

"What's up?"

"I have a case I'm working that I could use your help with."

"Ooh, I love helpin' out on your cases. What's it about?"

"Possible insurance fraud. I've been hired to tail a man to see if he's faking an injury. I could use your help to trap him, see if he's lying."

"Trap him? Won't that be dangerous?"

"No, don't worry. It's just a figure of speech."

"What do you want me to do?"

Emily went over the plan with Maggie. "If this guy is faking it and he gets away with his little scam, it'll cost my clients millions."

"Okay then, I'm in!"

"Meet me at my house tomorrow at four? Then we'll work out the details."

"All right. I have a few clients in the afternoon, but I should be finished by then." As a fitness instructor and personal trainer, Maggie could pretty much set her own schedule.

"Hey, looks like Colin is calling on the other line. I'd better take it."

"Tell him congratulations for me."

The Pursuit of Lies - Excerpt

"Will do." Emily clicked her phone to the other call. "Hello, Colin."

"Hey, Babe. How'd your lunch with the girls go?" Colin's deep, masculine voice was soothing and sensual, and the very sound of it warmed her.

"They were all very excited about the engagement. Camille tried to nail me down on a wedding date."

"Sounds like Camille. Hey, I can't talk long. I'm on my way to Boise to meet with ADA Laraway about a case."

"Allison Laraway? You'll have to tell her about our engagement."

"I'm sure she couldn't care less."

Emily thought back to when Colin first landed in Paradise Valley, taking a job as the new police detective, and how Assistant District Attorney Allison Laraway, a polished and sophisticated blonde, had tried to get her claws into him.

She recalled how Colin had seemed oblivious to her overtures. Emily shook her head slightly at the thought, reminding herself that she had won Colin's heart in the end, not Allison.

"By the way, Maggie thought she saw you drive by the restaurant when we were in the parking lot getting ready to leave. Isabel too."

"Wasn't me."

"Must've been some other tall, dark and handsome guy driving a red Jeep."

He chuckled. "So, will I see you for dinner tonight?"

"I have a job to do this afternoon, but I should be done by seven. Why don't you come by then?"

"Can't wait. I'd love to stay and chat, but I'd better let you go. I'm pulling into the parking structure and I'll probably lose reception."

"I love you, Colin." As she spoke his name, she remembered his soft warm lips on hers the night before, after he had proposed to her, and a light tingle spread across her body. She hoped he heard her before losing cell service.

~*~

While Colin went to meet with ADA Laraway, Emily drove across town to check on her assignment, Mr. Martin Dillingham. The overweight thirty-eight-year-old man claimed to have severely injured his back during a fall at one of the popular restaurants in the area. He now wore a back brace and walked with a cane.

The man had a report from a doctor in town stating he was truly injured, but from experience, she knew that just because something was in writing didn't make it true. The patient in question could

THE CHAIN OF LIES

The Pursuit of Lies - Excerpt

have found a doctor willing to split the sizable settlement in exchange for his testimony. That wasn't completely farfetched.

It was time for Emily to see what Mr. Dillingham was up to. If he was truly injured, the insurance company was willing to compensate him, but he had filed a three-million-dollar lawsuit against the restaurant owners and they wanted to be certain he was telling the truth.

Her clients had provided her with a photo of the man and she spotted him as soon as she pulled into the apartment complex's parking lot. He had a little pug on a leash and looked like he was attempting to take the pint-sized dog for a walk. His gait was slow and he used a cane.

The man couldn't know he was being watched, yet he hobbled along as if he was in pain. Maybe he really was hurt.

Emily followed him at a safe distance as he walked the dog around his complex, then took the animal back to his place and left it there. She watched as he went to the parking lot and carefully slid behind the wheel of his small pickup. She tailed him for a few blocks until he turned into the parking lot of a grocery store. He appeared to be in pain as he slowly climbed out of the truck, grimacing with each deliberate movement.

She followed him into the store and kept an eye on him as he went up and down the aisles, putting only a few things into his cart with one hand. He checked out, lumbered back to his truck with a single plastic bag of items, and gingerly climbed back in.

Emily remained hidden between the cars with her small video camera ready, but there was nothing to capture.

At a respectable distance, Emily tailed Mr. Dillingham back to his apartment and observed as he struggled to work himself out of the small truck with the plastic bag hanging from his right arm. Either he was a very good actor, assuming he knew he was being watched, or he really was injured.

He plodded to his main-floor apartment. Emily waited for him to go in, hoping she could get a peek inside one of his windows. There was only one window on the main level, next to the front door, and the blinds were shut. She moved to the side of the window and tried to peek in through the small gap between the blinds and the window frame, but she couldn't see anything.

She decided to try her luck again later. As she drove home, she thought of Colin's meeting with ADA Allison Laraway and wondered how that was going. Even though he had always claimed that he hadn't noticed Allison's advances toward him when

The Pursuit of Lies - Excerpt

he'd first arrived in Paradise Valley, Emily believed he only said that for her benefit.

Allison Laraway was a strong and decisive woman—all about the win. It wasn't like her to let anything, or anyone, stand in her way. Emily was sure Colin knew a confrontation between Allison and Emily would have become ugly.

Both women were beautiful and strong, but Colin had told Emily she possessed qualities Allison lacked. She remembered him saying that he was drawn to her because she was sweet and compassionate, which balanced out her strength and stubbornness. He said those were important qualities, and he loved that about her.

Raising her left hand from the steering wheel, Emily admired her diamond engagement ring as the sunlight filtering in the window danced off the facets, making it sparkle and shine. She was pleased with how things had turned out with Colin, and now she would soon be Mrs. Emily Andrews. She wondered what Miss Laraway would have to say about that.

~*~

Emily drove back to the apartments a few hours

later and found a place to park with a clear view of Mr. Dillingham's front door. After sitting in her vehicle and waiting for the next couple of hours, with no sign of the man coming or going, she gave up for the day. She had a plan to find the truth, though, which Maggie had agreed to help her play out the next day.

The sun was starting to sink over the western mountains as Emily pulled into her driveway along the side of her charming bungalow in the older part of Paradise Valley. Colin would be coming over soon, so she rushed to straighten up her place and get ready for him.

When the doorbell rang, Emily went running to answer it. Seeing it was Colin, through the small windows at the top of her Craftsman-style door, she flung it open wide.

"Hello, gorgeous." Colin stepped inside and gathered her up in his arms. "I missed you today."

"Missed you too." She tilted her head back and smiled up at him, enjoying the warmth of his embrace.

He planted a quick kiss on her lips.

She pushed the door shut with her bare foot and snuggled back in his arms. "What shall we do for dinner?"

"I ordered delivery," he said. "I hope you don't mind. The pizza should be here soon."

"I guess I should make a salad then." She

The Pursuit of Lies - Excerpt

pulled away and took his hand, leading him back to the kitchen. "Can you get the big glass bowl down from the top shelf?"

Reaching the kitchen, he pulled her into his arms again. "I love you, Emily. I've wanted to say it all day."

"You can say that any time you want. I will never tire of hearing it."

He gazed longingly into her face, his smoldering hazel eyes seeming to study her eyes and lips. He traced a finger delicately along her jaw line. She closed her eyes as he kissed her, long and slow. The heat that spread through her body was so intense she could hardly stand on her own. Her hands clung to his muscular back and she felt his embrace tighten around her.

"The door," she gasped, coming up for air.

"What?"

"The doorbell just rang." She drew in a breath. "I think our pizza is here."

"Oh, right. Pizza." Colin released her and rushed to the front door.

We hope you enjoyed that excerpt from
The Pursuit of Lies, Book 4
A Paradise Valley Mystery, Book Four

DEBRA BURROUGHS

The Pursuit of Lies, Book 4 is
Available on Amazon.com
in eBook and soon to be in Paperback

AUTHOR BIOGRAPHY

Debra Burroughs grew up in the San Francisco Bay Area before moving to the beautiful Pacific Northwest. Most days she can be found sitting in front of her computer, dreaming up interesting and exciting characters and story lines.

If you've ever read any of her books, you'll agree that Debra writes with intensity and power. Her characters are rich and the stories are full of compelling suspense and real romance. If you're looking for graphic violence and explicit sex scenes, hers are not the books for you. But if you're looking for stories with heart-fluttering real romance and "I can't put this book down" suspense that will entertain you, grab your attention, touch your heart, and leave you wanting more, then dive into one of her captivating books.

Made in the USA
Monee, IL
16 October 2020